Lisa Walker is an award-winning short story writer. Her play *Baddest Backpackers* aired on ABC Radio National in 2008. She has worked as a wilderness guide and environmental communicator. She writes, surfs and works in community relations on the far north coast of New South Wales. Her first novel, *Liar Bird*, was published in 2012. *Sex, Lies and Bonsai* is her second novel.

www.lisawalker.com.au

SEX, LIES
&
BONSAI

Lisa Walker

HarperCollins*Publishers*

HarperCollins*Publishers*

First published in Australia in 2013
by HarperCollins*Publishers* Australia Pty Limited
ABN 36 009 913 517
harpercollins.com.au

HarperCollins*Publishers*
Level 13, 201 Elizabeth Street, Sydney NSW 2000, Australia
Unit D1, 63 Apollo Drive, Rosedale, Auckland 0632, New Zealand
A 53, Sector 57, Noida, UP, India
1 London Bridge Street, London, SE1 9GF, United Kingdom
2 Bloor Street East, 20th floor, Toronto, Ontario M4W 1A8, Canada
195 Broadway, New York, NY 10007, USA

National Library of Australia Cataloguing-in-Publication entry:

Author: Walker, Lisa.
Title: Sex, lies and bonsai / Lisa Walker.
ISBN: 978 0 7322 9413 7 (pbk.)
ISBN: 978 0 7304 9679 3 (ebook : epub)
Dewey Number: A823.4

Cover design by Natalie Winter
Author photo by Tim Eddy
Typeset in Sabon 11.5/15pt by Kirby Jones
Printed and bound by CPI Group (UK) Ltd, Croydon, CR0 4YY

For Tim
My webmaster and film director extraordinaire

Chapter One

There are no accidents whatsoever in the universe.
SIGMUND FREUD

I always knew Daniel would find me out one day. That's why his text message, although it was a shock, wasn't really a surprise.

E, I can't stand it anymore, his message said. Daniel never uses abbreviations when texting. Apart from my name. I wonder why that is.

It wasn't defined. I knew what he meant though. *It* was the gap between the image of myself I'd sold him on and the reality. He'd fallen for the advertisement, but hadn't read the fine print. Now he wanted to return me like a defective product.

It was my deficiencies – my social awkwardness, lack of interest in being a domestic goddess and laziness, for starters. Then there was the way I drifted off when he explained the finer points of his job to me and how I hid in a corner at his important work functions.

It was the way I couldn't understand the effect of nitrates on river systems, how I stuck my fingers in my ears and hummed when he tried to explain this to me and how I never gave the right answer when he asked what he'd been saying.

It was me.

Another one-word text came through shortly after the first. *Sorry.*

I'd contemplated that word with all its meanings and decided to take it at face value. Daniel was nothing if not politically correct and if he said sorry, then he meant it. But if he was sorry, I was sorrier.

Daniel and I were together for twelve months and twenty days. I've spent most of my time since we broke up wondering how I can fix *it* so that Daniel will love me again.

I swerve to avoid a large fish head someone has left on the sand. Its eyes are dull and glassy, its skeleton bare. It has been six weeks since Daniel dumped me, but I still feel no less gutted than that fish. A cold wind is whipping up the waves; it's time to head home. My feet drag as I make my way back up the beach. My shoulder bag bumps against my hip and I can feel the sharp edges of my new purchase inside.

Daniel and I met at a poetry reading organised by the local writers' centre. This unlikely intersection of Daniel's interests and mine occurred in Gleebooks in Sydney. I say unlikely, because Daniel isn't into poetry. Daniel is into environmental law. Our meeting was doubly unlikely because I had never planned to read my work aloud at all. On such strange chances lives do turn ...

The night started predictably enough. A middle-aged woman with fire-engine-red hair emoted about her secret lover. She counted off the syllables with hand movements that made me dizzy. An earnest young man delivered a ringing testament to vegetarianism – 'No meat/It's sweet'. A dreadlocked student rapped about being oppressed. It was hard to see how he was – he was wearing ninety dollar Vans on his feet – but you had to keep an open mind.

I had been to open mic events before. I liked to sit in a dark corner and listen. Poets are used to people like me; they leave me alone. Though I never performed, I always brought a poem and told myself *maybe next time* as I left. I knew I never would.

On this night, the featured poet, a scary woman with asymmetrical black hair and elbow-high vinyl gloves, was launching her first collection – *Dark Hymns from the Street*. Cheap plonk flowed like the Parramatta River in flood. Alcohol contributed to the ensuing events, but it was not solely to blame. A lucky door prize was on offer – the winner would receive one hour of tattooing from the local tattoo shop. Tattoos have become so run of the mill lately. For most people that is. Not for me.

However, after three glasses of wine, it seemed possible that a tattoo might be just what I needed. After four glasses of wine, as it turned out, it was very easy to make a simple mistake regarding the correct hat in which to place your name for the lucky door prize.

I was thinking about what sort of tattoo I wanted when they called my name – perhaps a small line of poetry in a hidden location? 'The Tay Bridge Disaster' – the worst poem in history – sprang to mind. *The stronger we our houses do build/The less chance we have of being killed.* So true. I ran up to the stage; hand out, ready for the voucher. When the MC passed me the mic and asked me to read my poem, I was too bemused and terrorised to resist. Coughing, I pulled my crumpled paper from my jeans. Luckily, I'd already written an introduction.

'My poem, "Three Deer and a Sheep", is a thrilling epic in rhyming couplets about a New Zealand hunter who woos a single mother by making sausages to his special recipe ...' The mic squealed and I blinked like a spot-lit deer.

It was at this point that Daniel just happened to wander in, looking for the latest book on climate change.

I read my poem as if it were a shopping list. Later, my understated delivery was much praised; Leonard Cohen may have been mentioned. 'Three Deer and a Sheep' was a smash hit – a sensation. The poets clapped and cheered and yelled for more. The featured poet looked distinctly pissed off – no one had cheered for her. I felt like Mick Jagger. One more glass of wine and I definitely would have crowd surfed. One less, and I never would have read at all. The whims of fate ...

Soon after, when I was naked in Daniel's arms (I never have been good at playing hard to get), he told me he was entranced from the first line.

4

I have never understood what it was about *It rains a lot in Glenorchy* that captured his interest, but I'm grateful it did. Even now. When I'm feeling low, which is quite often, I think 'Three Deer and a Sheep' was almost certainly the zenith of my performance poetry career.

So here I am back in Darling Head – a place I thought I'd escaped. I'd thought I was settled in Sydney for life. A seagull squawks above me in a judgmental way. 'I know you don't blame Daniel,' I mutter. 'I don't either.' Of course he was sick of me. I was sick of myself. The bird lands on the beach in front of me and squawks again. *Worms*, it seems to say. I ignore it. The worm incident is not one I wish to dwell on. As I pass the seagull, my bare foot slips on a rubbery, rancid piece of seaweed. My stomach squirms, but not as badly as it did when I got Daniel's message.

As I walk, I recite the poem out loud from memory in the faint hope that it will help me find a way of bringing Daniel back. By the time I get to the second stanza, I have hit my stride.

Venison is a little lean.
It won't make a woman keen.
For a sausage that she'll want to keep,
You really need to add a sheep ...

There at Gleebooks, as I said the words *add a sheep*, I noticed the attractive dark-haired man in a black denim

5

jacket down the back of the room. His eyes were on me. From then on, I read for him only.

Sausages. As I climb up the path from the beach, I wonder for the first time if it was something about the sausages themselves that caught Daniel's attention. Throughout the twelve months and twenty days we were together was he perhaps waiting patiently for me to make deer sausages? I imagine him opening the door every evening, praying this might be the day. Did he yearn silently but hopelessly for the vision of the perfect sausage I created that night? Was he too shy to mention this almost illicit craving, this desire, this obsession? Had it withered within him, a secret, dark hunger?

I stop, pull my new notebook out of my bag and make a note: *Deer sausages*.

If this is what it takes to bring Daniel back, I will learn how to make them tomorrow.

Flushed with the success of my accidental poetry reading, I radiated the confidence of a different person that night. No doubt that was what attracted him. I couldn't sustain it though. Nor could I sustain my faked interest in the environmental issues plaguing him. I know this makes me a shallow person. It's not that I don't care; I do – deeply. I just find the detail excruciatingly dull.

At home, I climb into the hammock which hangs on our verandah and pull out the notebook. It is hard-covered, black and suitably serious looking. I have decided that I am going to fix myself, scientifically, as Daniel would do. Like all great scientists I will conduct research on myself, my topic – how long does it take to heal a broken heart?

Inside the front cover of the notebook I write: *Forge ahead, one step at a time. Turn a negative into a positive.* This is what Sally has instructed me to do. Since my break-up, my best friend, Sally, has been dispensing advice freely and generously from her base in Rio de Janeiro, where she is teaching English. Sally has studied psychology. She can quote Sigmund Freud and Carl Jung. Sally tells me that 'the sexual life of adult women is a dark continent'. She is the kind of friend one needs when love makes you crazy.

I chew on my pen and consider how best to proceed. My mind is blank.

Luckily my phone rings. Yay, double yay and hurrah. It is Sally. She has just got back from South America and wants to pop around for a cup of tea. Saved by the bell.

Chapter Two

One is very crazy when in love.

SIGMUND FREUD

Sally lies back on the verandah couch, her long brown legs exposed in her Mexican skirt and slides her sunglasses up over her unruly mane of blonde-tipped hair. The last time I saw her, her hair was black. She also has a new tattoo on her ankle. I think it is an Incan temple. This means she has had a South American lover.

Sally got her first tattoo as soon as she turned the legal age, eighteen. The dolphin on her hip is a memento of her First Great Love, a surfer called Marcus. A Balinese god on her lower back is a souvenir of a brief, but intense holiday romance. It is lucky that Sally is picky with which lovers she chooses to commemorate or she would be inked from head to toe. Her criteria for selection is whimsical, shifting and has nothing to do with the length of the relationship. For Sally's lovers the arrival of the tattoo is a bad sign, not a good one. Tattoos are only procured once the love affair has ended.

Sally falls in and out of love with the same frequency and lack of complication which she brings to changing her hairstyle.

Neither love nor hairstyles have ever come easily to me.

I point at her new tattoo and raise an eyebrow.

'So hot.' Sally sighs and fans her face.

Sally's lovers are always hot.

'Arsehole,' she says, when I mention Daniel's name, and, 'Don't be an idiot,' when I try to explain how I don't blame him because I am, really, a particularly annoying person.

'You're not annoying at all, you're great, you just need to get out more,' she says.

'I don't like getting out.' And this is the crux of the problem.

Sally and I have been friends since we first shared our lunch in pre-school. She had Vegemite sandwiches and I had zucchini slice – Mum was into green vegetables. We eyed each other's food and, without a word, swapped when the teacher wasn't looking – lunch-swapping was prohibited.

From then on, wherever I went, it was Sally and me, me and Sally. On finishing school we went to Sydney University together. While I stayed on to be with Daniel, she took off to see the world. We have emailed constantly while she's been away, but I've still missed her a lot. I'm not sure what it is that makes our friendship work, but it does. Like Starsky and Hutch, Turner and Hooch or Tango and Cash, we are a mismatched buddy pair.

My mate Sal doesn't have a shred of self-doubt in her body. In that way, perhaps, she is not the most useful friend for me to have.

Sally approves of my research plan. 'Recognising that you have a problem is the first step to solving it,' she says. 'What is required, I think, is a chart. Charts are scientific. People who use charts are copers not mopers.'

An ache inside my chest tells me that I am still a moper.

Sally supervises me while I draw up a chart.

On the first page I write *Pain diary*. I rule up four columns. The first column I title *Day of the week*. In this I write, *Saturday*. The second column is *Days since break-up*. In this I write 42. The third column I title *Pain level 1–10*. After some thought, I write 9. This is optimistic, but I think I've had worse days.

'What's the fourth column for?' asks Sal.

'I'm leaving that spare for any further research questions.'

Sally nods. 'Good. Very scientific.' She taps the notebook with her finger. 'You can put tips for improvement in the back. Start a list.'

A list. I decide not to tell Sally that I have already started my list with *deer sausages*.

'So, what's it like being back in Darling Head?' asks Sal.

'Fishy. The seagulls seem more obnoxious than they used to be.'

'That's progress,' says Sal. 'We're getting a more uppity class of seagull now.'

From where Sally and I sit on the couch, we can see the sea and the chequerboard of houses that make up this place we know so well. Darling Head is a surfer's town. Every day after school the break in front of the pub is packed with blonde-haired kids flexing their muscles and their attitude. And that's just the girls. The wetsuit is the look on the street and the clothes shops stock only surf wear. Sand blows into houses and coats the pavement. Brazilians, French, Japanese, Americans and English come here seeking the famed Darling Point break.

'Do you ever wonder how someone dropped in here from Mongolia would find this town?' I ask as we look towards the sea.

'Mmm, can't you just see them raising their rabbit-fur hat to the bikini girls?' replies Sal.

'I think they might feel as out of place as I do.'

'If this was Ulaanbaatar,' Sally's grasp of geography has been improved by her year abroad, 'your father would be the Mongolian champion bareback horse racer.'

My father is, in fact, a former Australian surf champion. This makes him something of a legend in Darling Head. 'They've just named a lookout after him, you know.'

'Go Dave.' Sal raises a fist.

'I can't imagine having anything named after me.' I pull my pen out of my mouth and inspect its gnawed blue end. 'I now name you, the Edie McElroy Memorial Pen.'

Sally rolls her eyes. 'Not that again.' We are venturing into well-trodden ground. 'It's hardly unique, this "I am a child failure" thing of yours, you know. Heard of Donald Bradman?'

'That hitting balls guy?'

'Excuse me? The Greatest Living Australian, you mean.'

'Now dead.'

'Beside the point. He's got a son. Did you know that?'

I shake my head.

'You see,' says Sal. 'His name's John, by the way.'

'I'd like to meet him one day. I think we'd have a lot in common.'

I'm a dreadful disappointment to my father. He had high expectations. While I was named Edie, Dad has always called me Eddie. I think he was hoping for a boy, though he never said so. But the fact that I'm named after Eddie Aikau, a legendary Hawaiian surfer who was lost at sea is a bit of a giveaway. Dad has told me how he picked me up in the hospital and dangled my legs on the bed just after I was born.

'Look at that, Jenny,' he said, seeing my right leg stuck out in front. 'She's a goofy footer.' I've never heard what my mum's response to this pronouncement was. I imagine she would have laughed and they probably would have kissed. I imagine they were terribly much in love at that stage.

Despite his bedside prediction I am not a goofy footer or even a regular; I am a no footer. Dad knows the pain of parents whose children don't inherit their talent.

'I think you have some unresolved parent issues that we should talk about,' says Sal. 'Talking always does you good.'

'I prefer thinking.'

Sally frowns. 'You think too much, Edie.'

She is probably right.

'Freud believes childhood experiences impact greatly on our adult lives,' says Sal.

I have a feeling that I may be hearing a lot about Freud in the weeks to come. Once Sally gets her teeth into something, she doesn't let go.

When Sally has gone, I climb back into the hammock and open my notebook again. I am so proud of my scientific chart that I almost ring up Daniel to tell him about it. I breathe slowly until the urge passes. They are very tricksy things, these urges to ring Daniel. Often, just when I think I've vanquished them, I find myself dialling his number.

As soon as I am sure the urge has passed, I turn to the back of the notebook and write *Tips for self-improvement*. Underneath this I write:

Don't ring Daniel.

I chew my lip and try to think of some more tips but fail. No doubt something will occur to me in time.

My father is leaning on the doorway watching me now, as I swing in the hammock with my notebook on my lap. I know he's wondering how a blond-haired, brown-skinned down-to-earth Aussie like him ended up with this pale red-haired daughter who's totally unfit for life in the surfing capital of the north coast.

His sea-washed blue eyes regard me above his drooping moustache as he leans, hands in the pockets of his baggy shorts. My father is worried about me. 'Take the surfboard out tomorrow, Eddie,' he says. 'I'll come with you.'

This is somewhat less likely than peace in the Gaza Strip. He knows this, but still he persists. Dad wants me to be happy. Surfing makes him happy; therefore surfing will make me happy, he reasons.

Surfing has never made me happy, but Dad is tenacious in his belief that I just need to give it a go and all my worries will disappear. I shake my head, smiling to soften the blow.

His face falls and he goes back inside. A gentle blues rhythm soon drifts from the house. Dad always plays guitar when he's unsettled. He's played it a lot since I came home.

Dad's glory days are in the past, but he's still a celebrity in our town. I've had people tell me surfers give him waves. They say this in the tone you'd usually reserve for kidney donors. I'm glad for my father that he commands respect in the surf and I'm sure he'd like it if I showed more interest in his passion. I try, but he knows I'm faking it.

He's astute like that, my father. Not many men realise when women are faking it.

Daniel didn't. Not at first, anyway. Not when I was really trying hard.

I look up from my notebook and push the couch with my foot to make the hammock swing. As I sway back and forth, watching the waves, I wonder if any of the men I've been with really liked me. I think maybe they liked the idea of the pale red-headed poet more than the reality. Why wouldn't you? What's to like about a bulk-order of insecurities?

Oh yes, I always did my best to hide this side of me. I don't think any of my lovers ever knew exactly what type of person they were dealing with. They might have guessed, but they didn't know. To let someone know you and then be rejected – now that would hurt.

Before Daniel, there was Peter. We got together in my first year at Sydney University. He was way too cool for me. Pete used to perform poetry wearing a top hat with a flower in it and an open waistcoat that showed off his slender, tanned torso. For the whole six months we were together I knew he would dump me. Pete had a thing for redheads, but it wasn't enough in the end. I couldn't match his erudite arguments about the meaning of poetry. Secretly, I felt that to talk about it sucked the life out of it. But maybe that's because I couldn't talk about it, or not very well. I could only write it.

Now, I don't seem to be able to write it either.

Peter didn't dump me by text; he just turned up at the Glebe Pub one night with a different redhead and acted like we'd never met. No one was surprised except me. I've always been slow on the uptake.

Looking on the positive side, which I do try to do, I have learnt something from all of my lovers. From Peter

I learnt how to sound intelligent (but never intelligent enough). From Daniel I learnt how to act confident (but never confident enough). My problem is that I can never walk away from a learning experience – even when it hurts. This is mad, bad and just plain silly and my life would be much calmer if I stopped treating my heart like a guinea pig. I wonder what my next lover will teach me and if I will enjoy the lesson. At the moment this seems far from likely.

Me and men. Men and me. I push off the couch again, sway to and fro and wish they would invent a magic potion to dissolve this achy angst of mine.

Dad and his girlfriend, Rochelle, are plotting something. I can tell by the way they stop talking when I drag myself off the hammock and enter the lounge room.

'If I was an animal I would be a dolphin,' says Rochelle as she cooks us up a stir-fry that night.

While this is not original – who doesn't want to be a dolphin – in her case it fits. She is permanently smiling and if she isn't wet, she just was or soon will be. Her surfboard is propped up against Dad's on the verandah. It looks companionable there, about one foot shorter than his board, but otherwise almost identical. This is a metaphor for Rochelle herself.

Dad and Rochelle fit together in a way he and Mum never did. They are both out the door at sunrise with their boards under their arms. They like the same music, mostly blues, and if Dad had ever had a female twin she probably would have looked a lot like Rochelle. Their eyes are the same blue, their hair the same blonde and their skin the exact same shade of suntanned brown. At the moment they are both wearing Billabong T-shirts. I am glad they are different colours or they would look like twins who have been dressed by their mother.

I understand dolphins are highly sexed and suspect Rochelle is too. I deduce this from the punch-drunk look on Dad's face most mornings. I am way too old to be observing my Dad's sex life and feel like I'm cramping his style, but what can I do?

We sit down at our triangular dining table. Twenty years ago, my mother painted it with a galaxy of planets, moons and stars. They are now fading but, despite his enthusiasm with a paint brush, this is one job Dad hasn't tackled.

'If I was an animal I would be a cuckoo,' I say.

I am a twenty-three-year-old cuckoo returned to its nest.

Chapter Three

One day, in retrospect, the years of struggle will strike you as the most beautiful.

SIGMUND FREUD

Sunday: 43 days
Pain level: 9.5

Daniel and I used to go out for breakfast on Sundays. After coffee and eggs on toast we would go to the market; or the beach if it was a nice day. Sunday afternoons we almost always ended up in bed, before rising, warm and languid, to see what the evening offered.

The markets weren't about shopping. They were more about the passing parade, exotic snacks and buskers. But eight months ago, on Daniel's birthday, I saw something I couldn't go past. I had been looking for a present for Daniel for weeks. I needed a gift that would show him I was the urbane, worldly companion he required. I'd spent hours in CD shops, bookshops and clothes shops but these all seemed too risky. Being the right sort of girlfriend for Daniel was hard work.

And then I saw it – the bonsai. Ropy vines trailed from its branches to the white pebbles below. Bulging roots crept towards the rim of its basin. It was an exact replica of a rainforest giant – exotic, striking and just right for a man with an interest in nature.

Don't touch what you can't afford, it said to me as I picked it up. And while I wasn't particularly surprised to hear it talk, its grouchy tone was rather off-putting. But it was so beautiful, so perfect, so very, very Daniel. I looked at the price tag, then checked my purse. I could do it, just, if I skimped on lunches for the next few weeks.

I bought it while Daniel was distracted at the falafel stand and presented it to him with a flourish. He fell in love with it at once. He and the bonsai were soul mates.

Thinking about the bonsai makes me sad and I know I mustn't mope, so after breakfast I decide to visit the library. I need to fill in some more tips for self-improvement in the back of my book. Sally might ask to inspect it.

Darling Head Library is a short walk from our house. It is surprisingly large for such a small town and the self-help section takes up almost half the space. Self-help is big on the north coast.

There is so much on offer and so much that I need, it is hard to prioritise. I am tempted to take out twenty books, the maximum allowed, but Sally has told me to deal with one thing at a time. As I trudge up and down the aisles it occurs to me that improving myself is a very big task and one that needs to be approached scientifically.

Should I:

Increase my self-esteem,
Manage my stress,
Take control of my moods, or
Improve my relationships?

Maybe I need to seek and find happiness, improve my time management or learn new sexual techniques? Finally, I make my selection.

The librarian, a fortyish woman with wispy blonde hair, glances at my book. She looks at me over the top of her glasses and murmurs something that I can't quite catch.

'Pardon?'

She raises her voice to a whisper. 'It's very good.'

'You've read it?'

She nods and blushes.

I'm not sure that her endorsement carries much weight, but never mind. I walk out of the library with *Conquering Shyness* under my arm and a self-satisfied glow. I am taking control of my situation.

My self-satisfied glow lasts until I stumble on the stairs up to the house, crack my shins and drop the book into the bushes below. Lying down on the wooden platform, I extract it from the jungle's clutches and continue up through the narrow tunnel overhung by vines and trees.

Our house is a hippy house. Dad's parents moved to Darling Head in 1973, when he was six. They came for the Aquarius Festival – ten days of peace, love and dope in nearby Nimbin – and stayed for the surf, cheap land and lifestyle. The pole house my grandparents built is now one of the oldest in Darling Head. It is like a ship: all angles and portholes to the sea. The sea breeze races through it and in strong winds it sways. It is built on a steep slope and surrounded by trees which grow like magic beanstalks in the subtropical climate.

My grandparents, their hippy days behind them, prefer to live in a unit on the Gold Coast these days. 'Had enough of those damn stairs,' says Pop, whenever I ask him if he misses the house. 'Miss the possums though.'

I settle in the hammock but have not got very far with *Conquering Shyness* before I am interrupted.

'Hi Edie,' a cheerful voice calls up the stairs.

Rochelle has just got back from the surf. She has white zinc smeared over her nose and her sun-bleached hair hangs in salty threads past her bare brown shoulders. The day being warm, she is wearing only a sleeveless wetsuit top and board shorts. She places her surfboard next to Dad's.

Rochelle is originally a Sydney girl. After a marriage break-up she had a brief stint finding herself in Hawaii. As far as I can figure out this required her to work on a taro farm run by a group of men who promoted ancient traditions – such as women being naked in the fields.

I'm not sure what was in this naked taro farming for Rochelle, but I can imagine what was in it for them.

On return to Australia, she moved to the north coast, as people who have found themselves often do.

I expect that I will never find myself as I am way too cynical.

'Been gettin' any?' I ask.

Darling Head has its own vernacular. When running into an acquaintance here, you don't ask 'How ya goin'?' you ask 'Been gettin' any?' You don't need to say 'waves'. It's understood.

That's not what they say to me though. When I run into boys I went to school with they usually go, 'Hi, um …'

'Edie.'

'Yeah right, yeah.' They nod eagerly like we're really getting somewhere now we've established who I am. 'Edie. I knew that.'

To move things on and put them at ease I usually ask 'Been gettin' any?' No more is needed. They'll rave on about The Point, The Right-hander, The Bank, The Sets, The Tide, The Swell, The Beach Break, The Left-hander, The Barrel, The Wipeout … All I need to do is nod. And it's not like I don't understand. I'm often tempted to tick Non-English-Speaking-Background on the types of forms that ask the question. Surfing is my first language.

'Awesome out the Point,' says Rochelle. 'It's barrelling. Going out again soon. Just had to have something to eat.' She pulls a block of board wax from the table near the door and rips off the wrapping. Lifting her board onto the railing, she starts to wax up.

'What sort of wax is that?' I ask.

'Sex Wax.'

'I thought you liked Five Daughters.'

She shrugs. 'Sex Wax is better in cool water.'

Darling Head supermarket sells board wax in three types – Mrs Palmers Five Daughters (extra sticky), Sex Wax (for your stick) and Far King (farking great wax). No one except me seems to think this is in bad taste.

A water dragon scuttles across the verandah and into the house. Wildlife makes no distinction between the inside of our house and the outside. Possums, water dragons, magpies, bats and a range of other creatures use the facilities at their leisure.

'Feel free.' I eye the dragon as it disappears into the lounge room. 'Do you ever worry that the wildlife will all gang up and drive us out?'

Rochelle gives the matter some consideration. 'If it hasn't happened yet I think we're pretty safe.' After a quick snack she is gone again, with her board under her arm. Her voice carries up from the street as she greets one of her friends – 'Been gettin' any?'

A speeded-up montage of the day would show me lying in the hammock with the pages of *Conquering Shyness* turning while surfboards appear and disappear behind me. The sun moves across the sky and finally vanishes behind the hills as I close the book.

'Rochelle's brother is coming to stay with us,' Dad announces at dinner. 'He's taking a break from Sydney for a bit.'

Rochelle works nights a few times a week, so she is not here at the moment.

I look up – a forkful of pasta halfway to my mouth. 'Why is he coming here?'

Dad waggles his head. 'Holiday.'

The way he says this makes me suspicious. 'I didn't know Rochelle had a brother.' Dad and Rochelle have been living together for almost a year and this is the first I've heard of him.

'They don't see much of each other. He's a fair bit younger.'

'How long's he staying for?' I'm not happy about the idea of a stranger in the house, but I'm a guest here too, so there's not much I can say.

Dad shrugs. 'We'll see how it goes. Time for the weather.'

This ends our conversation. The Weather is sacred. It lets Dad and Rochelle know whether they need to get up early for a surf.

I hear him talking to Rochelle later, when I've gone upstairs. '... low off the coast; reckon it'll be good ... out the Point, six-thirty.'

In bed that evening I think about Daniel. Trying not to think about Daniel is hard at any time, but especially in bed. This is not only because I miss his body next to mine, but because of the bonsai.

Daniel and I shared a unit in Glebe for six months and five days. When I left, all my belongings fitted easily into two boxes. Everything else was his. If Daniel had been there when I moved out, I wouldn't now be lying here looking at the bonsai, which I stole from him when I left.

Daniel did love that tree. He was always pruning, watering, attaching wires and otherwise tending it. He bought books on bonsai care and read them assiduously. 'Bonsai,' Daniel said, 'is about discovering the essential spirit of the plant.'

When it was Daniel's tree the bonsai was an object of precision and beauty. Six weeks later, it is like a neglected child; hair too long, dirty clothes. I took the tree to remind me of him but now it is only reminding me of myself. The tree reproaches me with its shabby limbs.

'I'm sorry. I should never have taken you away from Daniel,' I say.

The tree maintains an icy silence. I wonder how long that's going to last.

I decide to check my emails before I go to bed. Decide makes it sound more decisive than it is. In fact, I decide this in the same way that I decide to keep breathing. It just happens. Email and phone checking has become a serious addiction since Daniel and I broke up. While I try my hardest not to ring Daniel, he will never know how often I check my messages, so there is no harm done.

I hit Send/Receive. Yes, there is an email coming through. My heart accelerates as I watch the black bar inch across my screen. It will be Daniel. I am sure of it. *I miss you. Please come back.* I am smiling in anticipation as the email hits my inbox.

It is from eBay. They are offering great kitchen deals tonight. I feel like I've been stabbed through the heart with a spatula. Who was it who said that insanity is doing the same thing over and over and expecting different results? I disagree. I prefer to think of my obsessive email checking as a triumph of the human spirit. One day there will be something good there, I just know it.

Climbing into bed, I read more of *Conquering Shyness* until my eyelids start to droop. As I fall asleep I wonder, again, what it was about *It rains a lot in Glenorchy* that captured Daniel's attention. Or was it the sausages? And I wonder if, even mismatched as we were, we might have muddled through if not for the worms.

Chapter Four

Love and work ... work and love, that's all there is.

SIGMUND FREUD

Monday: 44 days
Pain level: 8.5

Breaking up with Daniel has not only been hard on my heart, it has also been hard on my pocket. In Sydney there was plenty of work for graphic artists. In Darling Head, my choices are limited. I have had to be creative.

Professor Brownlow is my new boss. For him I draw crab larvae on Mondays, Wednesdays and Fridays at the university. The job is not very well paid and I need to think of ways to supplement my income. So far I have not succeeded in this endeavour.

I have been drawing crab larvae in a haphazard way for four weeks, but Professor Brownlow doesn't seem to have noticed. He has told me to call him Ralph and I do, to his face, but I prefer to think of him as Professor Brownlow.

Professor Brownlow advertised for a research assistant with drawing skills and a scientific background. I have a degree in fine arts and some experience illustrating for the catalogue of a funky retail mob called Hotpunk whose wares are far from scientific. I did, however, live with an environmental lawyer for six months. I am also a talented liar, and on a good day possibly an exceptional one. I can only assume the field for the position was not strong.

Drawing crab larvae is not as exciting as it sounds. Crab larvae, or zoea, look like baby elephants with a pointy horn and feathery legs. At first I was concerned that they might be wriggly or slithery, but in fact they are kind of cute. However, being less than one millimetre in size, they are not at all cuddly.

In my induction, Professor Brownlow pointed out the main features I needed to draw. 'The mandibular palpus ... blah, blah, blah ... integument ... blah, blah, blah ... first maxilla ... blah ... endopodite ... blah, blah ... plumose hairs ...'

I refrained from putting my fingers in my ears and humming, but it didn't help my powers of retention.

From time to time Professor Brownlow gets very excited with the drawings I hand him. I can hear him muttering to himself, 'Single spine without secondary hairs, no trace of exopodite ...'

This worries me a little. I fear I may have set back the cause of crab research several years by omitting one or two details in my compulsive rush to get on with the next larva. There is no logic in this as I'm not paid at a piece rate. I just can't shake the feeling that the next larva will be more exciting than the last. The persistence of this idea in the face of all evidence to the contrary may say something profound about human nature. Or perhaps just about me.

Professor Brownlow wears khaki shorts, collared shirts and loafers. His suntanned, muscular legs make this outfit look sexy rather than nerdy. Sadly, Professor Brownlow is married and has two children under ten. For this reason I try not to take too much notice of his sexy legs. Lusting after married men would be bad for my karma. Not that I'm into that stuff.

Daniel had sexy legs too, but they were only revealed on the beach and in the bedroom. I know what he'd think of Professor Brownlow's shorts and loafers ensemble. Thinking about Daniel's sexy legs in the bedroom makes me sigh. Breaking up with Daniel has not only been hard on my pocket and my heart, it has been hard on other parts of my body too. I am not used to going without.

Today at work, a strange thing happens. Professor Brownlow gives me a book. 'I saw you reading at lunch yesterday. I thought you might like this one.'

I am startled. Firstly, that he has noticed me reading. He never seems to notice me at all. Secondly, that he has thought of me enough to bring in a book. Thirdly, about his taste in books. If I had imagined Professor Brownlow reading, which I hadn't, I would have imagined him reading zoology textbooks or maybe on holidays, as a break, he might plough through the odd thriller; John Grisham or Matthew Reilly.

I gaze down at the book he's given me. A downcast and vaguely sinister cat decorates the cover.

'Have you read any Murakami?'

I shake my head.

'He's a Japansese writer. Very funny. In a strange way. But also serious.' His face colours. 'You might not think so, of course.'

I smile and also blush. 'Thank you. Ralph.' As Professor Brownlow walks away I let my eyes linger on his legs for the first time. Not for long, but they do linger and I let them.

Professor Brownlow's wife works as a casual tutor in the human movement section of the university. She is also a personal trainer. She too has muscular brown legs and wears short shorts and T-shirts which hug her taut stomach. She is charming to me in an impersonal way that makes me tongue-tied. Impersonal charm is not one of my areas of expertise. My social repertoire swings between over-the-top sincerity that scares people off and mute shyness.

Professor Brownlow's wife is very attractive – much more attractive than me. I glance at the book on my desk. But maybe she won't read Murakami? I slap my thoughts down. That is no way to be thinking about a married man with two children and a wife who could easily flatten me with one swing of her well-toned arm.

I wonder though, when I see them together, what it is they have in common. The attractiveness of his wife makes me suspect it is sex. Perhaps, for him, the legs are enough. Perhaps they are for her too. But I now suspect Professor Brownlow has hidden depths. And hidden depths are one of my favourite, favourite things.

Thinking about the hidden depths of married men is also bad karma; maybe even worse than ogling muscular legs. I sigh as I draw my last zoea of the day. Going without sex is affecting my judgment. I need to do something positive to improve myself, not wallow in inappropriate feelings about people who are way off-limits.

On the way home I focus on positive thoughts about what tomorrow will bring. I have already written my goals for Tuesday in my notebook:

Think up new money-making ventures
Write poetry
Find more tips for self-improvement
Consult Sally!

The days that I'm not drawing crab larvae usually go something like this. I wake with a feeling of dread, have breakfast, go for a long walk then come back and check my emails. Usually there are none, apart from offers to transfer millions of dollars from Nigeria into my bank account.

After deleting the Nigerian emails I am filled with despair at the blankness of my mind. This is soon replaced by self-loathing. How can I make some more money? Why do I waste my time writing poetry? Does the world need more poets?

This takes until lunchtime, when I can have a break, after checking my emails and phone messages again. After lunch I have a nap. At two o'clock, in an effort to salvage something from the day, I check my messages again, then finally attempt to write poetry. My words are bland, dull and predictable. I hate them.

So why do I keep trying? It can only be the memory of moments of grace I've had in the past. Perhaps poetry for me is like surfing for my dad. There are moments that leave me euphoric, when time disappears. These rare moments may be something like heroin – they leave me uplifted, but life is just one big withdrawal in between.

Now I think about it, both surfing and heroin seem much more reliable forms of pleasure. But they don't work for me.

Chapter Five

Sexual love is undoubtedly one of the chief things in life.

SIGMUND FREUD

I dream I am nude hiking in New Zealand and wake up early, relieved to find I am not. This is particularly the case since it was raining in my dream (as it does a lot in Glenorchy) and very cold. I wonder what this dream signifies. No doubt it is linked to Daniel.

My mind drifts. If I was nude hiking with Daniel, well, we probably wouldn't be hiking; we would be finding a cosy hut and getting warm beneath the covers. A mountain hut would be very sexy – the cold air, the warm bodies, the isolation ... A long breath escapes me.

As I try to go back to sleep I have a fantastic idea, possibly related to the nude hiking. I will ditch poetry and become an erotic writer. Why haven't I thought of this before? This could be the answer to my financial difficulties. Sex sells! If I can write poetry, surely I can write erotica. How hard can it be?

I am so excited about this plan that I jump out of bed and, what is more, skip my normal morning self-loathing routine. *Live dangerously, Edie!* Instead, I get straight to work.

First, I seek guidance from the internet on how to write about sex, transcribing helpful points into my notebook.

Points to consider when writing about sex:
Never mention the penis or vagina;
Never use euphemisms for these parts of the body;
Tell it like it is, not how it is in porn movies;
Less is more – don't take the reader all the way;
Be subtle – cut to the morning after;
Choose whether to be erotic or convincing, it is impossible to be both;
Choose whether to be practical or metaphorical in your descriptions, that is, the dark waves and white horses school versus the throbbing cock and dripping cunt school;
A dash of humour can be good;
Don't cut to the chase too quickly, build the tension; and
The difference between erotica and porn is the emotion.

Several of these points seem contradictory – how do you avoid mentioning the 'p' or 'v' words, but not use euphemisms? How do you tell it like it is and still be subtle? I don't let this faze me. I am too excited by the potential of this new venture.

I pause for just a moment, seeking erotic inspiration, then, opening a new page on my computer, I plunge straight into it like a wild horse jumping a gate. My fingers race across the keyboard, leaving a trail of sweat behind them. Strangely, despite the mountain hut fantasy, I find myself in a laboratory ...

Edaline peered through the microscope, carefully tracing the mandibles of the crab larva that lay, delicately exposed, before her. Its feathery legs reminded her of the curling golden hairs on the back of Professor Brown's strong, brown hands.

Wisps of chemistry had been drifting between the Professor and Edaline for some months now. Along with the formalin and cleaning wax, the subtle aroma of attraction had established its place in the laboratory. Edaline felt it each morning as she walked in the door – a charge that made her stomach leap like a randy salmon migrating upstream through grizzly bear-infested waters.

'That's a particularly fine pair of plumose hairs,' said a melodious baritone voice behind her.

Edaline swivelled in her ergonomic chair, her heart beating a light staccato drum roll on her ribcage. She shifted her shoulders back, accentuating the cleavage she had, so daringly, exposed today in a low-cut black T-shirt.

The Professor's gaze was on her drawing. His white lab coat looked thrilling against his suntanned face and vivid blue eyes that gleamed behind his wire-rimmed glasses. He bent closer and Edaline caught a whiff of sweat. She gasped, her nipples hardening, and leaned further over the lab bench, her breasts hovering above the drawing. 'Do you like them?' Her voice was low, seductive, throaty.

The Professor nodded, still studying the drawing. 'The mandibular palpus is rather accentuated.' He thrust his hands in the pockets of his khaki shorts, rocking back on his heels.

Edaline's nostrils flared like a horse at the end of a hard gallop. His meaning couldn't be clearer. 'Professor,' she ran her tongue over her lips, leaving a glistening trail, 'would you like to take a look down the microscope?'

I lift my hands from the keyboard and stretch my fingers. Something occurs to me. I have forgotten to fill in my pain chart. I flip to the front of the notebook. *Tuesday: 45 days. Pain level …*

I consider that. My chest isn't aching. Today the pain has moved to the bottom of my throat. This is new. I wonder if it is an improvement. With a sense of satisfaction I title my spare column *Location*. It is lucky I planned for expansion.

It's strange, this broken heart thing. The Romans had it right: when Cupid fires his arrow, it can really hurt. On reflection, I decide the throat pain is an improvement. *Eight*. My best day yet. This erotic writing must be good for me.

My eyes wander back over my writing. My cheeks burn and I can hardly bear to read it, but, on the other hand, it's been so much fun. And I think it might actually be okay. Pretty sexy really. But why am I writing about Professor Brownlow? It is extremely inappropriate and rather alarming. What will people think when they find out this is what's in my head? I couldn't bear it.

My mind flashes back to my dream. Was nude hiking a portent? Will I be exposed, cold, naked and ashamed with the rain pouring down? Maybe I can publish under a pseudonym. I have one ready as it happens, having recently played that game where you give yourself a name based on your first pet and the first street you ever lived in – *Sooty Beaumont*.

The name has a certain ring to it. I imagine Sooty Beaumont is a raven-haired beauty who writes in a red satin dress with a cigarette hanging out of her mouth. She has a roster of lovers who bring her exotic and carefully selected gifts. In return, she delights them with her sexual prowess. Yes, Sooty Beaumont is a name to work magic with.

I place my fingers on the keyboard again. I am reaching the sharp edge of the sex scene. I now have some tough decisions to make. Convincing or erotic? Metaphorical or practical? Show the reader what is happening or cut to Professor Brown putting his lab coat back on and Edaline adjusting her low-cut T-shirt? Just when I am on a roll, my old enemy, self-doubt, seems about to make a reappearance.

Luckily the phone rings. It is Sally. 'How are your tips for self-improvement going?'

I scan the back of my notebook. *Deer sausages. Don't ring Daniel. How to write about sex ... Consult Sally.* 'What sort of improvements do you think I should be making?'

'You could start by getting out more. How are you ever going to meet guys if you never talk to anyone?'

I don't tell her about my new crush, Professor Brownlow. I know what she would tell me – *Get real, he's married, Edie.* And I know she'd be right. Professor Brownlow is my dirty little secret. 'You're right,' I say. 'I'm going to talk to people more.'

Sally is so shocked I have listened to her she doesn't speak. This is a first.

'I've been reading a book about conquering shyness. It says I need to speak to a stranger every day to build up my confidence.'

'Where are you going to find the strangers?'

I hadn't considered that. Sally has a good point. Darling Head is a town of five thousand people, and I am at least on nodding acquaintance with most of them. This is not to say they are friends, and, in fact, many of them don't actually nod, but I know they know who I am.

The nice part about living in Darling Head, as opposed to Sydney, is that you do know who you are dealing with. I sometimes think our town is like the 'Twelve Days of Christmas'. On the twelfth day of Christmas, Darling Head sent to me:

Twelve trained baristas,
Eleven school teachers,
Ten sporty nurses,
Nine well-dressed lawyers,
Eight pretty hairdressers,
Seven fashion retailers,
Six surfing doctors,
Five real estate agents,
Four surfboard shapers,
Three drug dealers,
Two millionaire developers,
And a milkman in a white van.

To be honest, you don't normally see that many lawyers and I think there might be more than three drug dealers, but you get the picture. In our town, no one is anonymous. 'I think I can classify anyone who is not a friend or a relative as a stranger,' I say. This leaves a field of approximately 4997.

'Okay, but you have to choose them randomly, Edie. You can't just wait for a friendly looking one.'

Sally knows me too well.

'You have to speak to the fifth stranger you see or something like that.'

I murmur assent, but there's no way I'm going to be speaking to the guy with the goatee who once accused me of pushing in, in the supermarket queue. Then there's that woman in the newsagent who suspected me of swapping the price tags on the boxes of crayons and the owner of the surf shop who never gives me a local's discount even though I was born in this town.

'Edie.' Sally's voice is stern.

'Okay, okay, the fifth stranger. So, what are you going to do with yourself now you're back in town?'

'I'm kicking around a few ideas. Something psychology-related maybe. I've got out my old uni notes. There's some really good stuff in there. You should see this essay on Freud I wrote in first year.'

'Cool. Let me know what you come up with.'

'What's your opinion on penis envy?'

'Pardon?'

'Have you ever wished you had one?'

I consider this for a few moments. 'There was one time I drank too much before getting on a train with no toilet. It would have been handy then.'

'Mmm, true, but apart from the practicality angle … I think Freud had that one wrong. Why would you want something that just …'

'Dangles?'

'Exactly. Some female psychologists thought that he suffered from womb envy.'

'So, who won the argument?'

'I'm not sure; I missed the second *Anatomy is Destiny* class – had a hot date the night before.'

'Speaking of penis envy.'

'That's not envy, it's desire. So,' Sally gives a deep and meaningful pause, 'what are you up to at the moment? Apart from crab larvae, I mean.'

This question seems particularly probing, coming as

it does on the heels of the penis topic. But I don't want to talk about my new project. The erotic writing is beyond private. Even thinking about it makes my heart beat faster. 'This and that,' I murmur.

'Mmm.' Sally must be still thinking about penis envy as she lets me get away with this.

After Sally hangs up, I try to return to my writing but the erotic moment is gone.

As I have had such a successful morning, I decide to give myself a break and open the book by Murakami which Professor Brownlow gave me.

Kafka on the Shore is described on the back cover as a 'metaphysical mind-bending mystery'. This is not a genre I am familiar with. After an hour of reading I realise my assessment of Professor Brownlow as having hidden depths was correct, but didn't go far enough. If he is into metaphysical cat mysteries his depths are not just hidden, but also uncharted, eccentric and mysterious.

This is deeply, deeply sexy. I sigh as I think about Professor Brownlow and his short shorts, his hidden depths ...

Little does Professor Brownlow know that by lending me this book he has set in train a course of events with which I am rather familiar. But then, if it hadn't been the book it would have been something else.

Strangely, my crush on Professor Brownlow does little to diminish the symptoms of my broken heart. Infatuation and love are two very different things. I still love Daniel, but Professor Brownlow is very, very sexy.

And now that he has lent me a book, there is no telling what will happen. Cupid's chemistry lab is hard at work.

Before I know it my fingers are racing across the keyboard again.

'Are you interested in metaphysics?' asked Professor Brown. As he leant down to look in the microscope, his hard shoulder brushed against Edaline's soft one.

She jumped, as though a high-voltage shock had zapped between them. 'M-m-metaphysics?' What was metaphysics? She should know, but her brain could think of nothing but the smell of Professor Brown's sweat, the touch of his crisp, clean, lab coat against her arm. She caught a glimpse of his stomach through the gap between his shirt buttons. What would it feel like to run her hand across those dark hairs? To press her lips to that sweetly hollowed navel? To slip the tip of her tongue inside? Her mouth tingled at the thought.

Professor Brown lifted his head from the microscope. Edaline felt his warm breath on her nose. It smelt like oranges and chocolate, like puppies and milk, like freshly mown grass. It smelt like ... desire.

'The nature of the soul,' he said.

'Oh.' Edaline looked into his eyes. They were the blue of an autumn sea, with specks of seaweed green.

His pearl-black pupils fixed on her and a thrill ran through Edaline. Danger lurked in those depths.

She felt he was looking into her, not at her. That he saw not just her face or body, but her spirit, her ... soul. 'Yes,' she breathed. 'I'm interested in metaphysics.' Her hand reached out and touched the side of his face; that delicious angle of smooth-shaved jaw.

His hand grasped hers, drew it to his mouth. He pressed his lips to her moist and quivering palm.

Edaline could have sworn he'd branded her, his lips were so hot. She gasped with a voluptuous pain.

'Some philosophers believe free will is an illusion,' he said.

'Do you?' She sighed, clenching her thighs.

'Right now, I do,' said Professor Brown. His thumb – an electric eel – stroked her palm.

Edaline stood, pushing away her ergonomic chair. It rolled backwards and fell to the ground, the wheels spinning like a metaphor for her heart. Then she did what she had always wanted to do, from the first moment she had seen Professor Brown. She pinched his cheek.

It was even more thrilling than she had expected. His skin was warm, pliable and had a slightly sandpapery texture. Standing on tiptoe, she pressed her hungry lips against his. Only for a moment. Professor Brown was a meal she wanted to eat slowly. 'Now I can die happy,' she whispered.

Behind Professor Brown's fogged-up glasses, his eyes glinted like the sea on a misty day.

'Sorry, you were saying?' said Edaline.

'There's nothing I can do to stop me wanting you,' said Professor Brown. His mouth pressed against hers – burning, searing. His rapacious tongue felt its way into her mouth, met its partner, exchanged gluttonous caresses ...

I fling myself back on the bed. It's exhausting stuff, this erotic writing. Exhausting and yet, I can barely admit it to myself, thrilling. Writing about sex when you haven't had any for almost two months gets rather ... overwhelming. And I haven't even got to the crux of it yet. Still, I, or rather, Sooty, is making progress – my characters are kissing.

I hear Dad coming back from work and decide to leave it there for today. I title the file *Crab sex* and save it. As I turn off my computer I imagine Sooty grinding her cigarette into her ashtray, checking her roster to see which lover to expect today. Will it be Marc, bringing gifts of French perfume, Sergei bearing vodka or Antonio, her secret favourite, who holds soft Italian cheeses to her lips? Mmm, yes, Antonio today ...

Dad looks up as I come down the stairs. He is starting a new home-renovation project. At the moment this involves pulling the lining off the lounge-room ceiling. Dad is never content unless he has a renovation project in progress. The bigger the project, the more content it makes him. In the last few years he has built a new deck outside, added a new bedroom, fixed skylights in almost every room and retiled the bathrooms. This is in addition to the usual ongoing house maintenance.

Dad pauses in his exertions, a sheet of plywood half removed, and gives me his well-known Dad-look. It is a look that a duck might give to a swan which has just hatched out underneath it – a mixture of confusion and affection. 'You're a bit flushed, Eddie. Are you okay?' he asks.

I smile. 'Busy day.'

After dinner, Rochelle and I do the washing up while Dad divides his attention between renovations and a documentary titled *Great Explorers*. Tonight it features Captain Cook. At one point the host mentions that he had five sons and one daughter, Elizabeth.

'I wouldn't mind meeting her,' I say.

'Who?' Rochelle has her back to the television, putting glasses away. She is wearing her work clothes: a white polo shirt and khaki mid-calf pants that hug her slim thighs. Rochelle is one of those nurses who care for people in their homes. I bet she knocks the socks off her male clients.

'Elizabeth Cook.'

'I've never heard of her.'

'Exactly. We might have shared interests.'

Rochelle gives me a quizzical look.

'Two of a kind.' I hang my tea towel on the rack. 'Unknown children of legends.'

'Who? Oh.' Rochelle's eyes flicker to Dad. She steps closer and gives me some extended eye contact. 'So, how are you going? Really?'

'Daniel-wise?' A geyser of sadness gushes up as I say his name.

She nods.

I shrug. 'So so. But really, it was a miracle we lasted as long as we did.'

She cocks her head. 'Why's that?'

I hardly know where to start. 'Daniel is ...' Daniel is confident, capable, organised, switched on and socially responsible. He flosses his teeth, exercises, recycles religiously and keeps up to date on current affairs. He was captain of his school and won numerous awards at university. He keeps a large range of herbs and spices in his kitchen with which he produces creative, nutritious, multicultural meals. Daniel once showed me a picture of his school formal. He looked distinguished in his three-piece suit and, I suspect, was escorting the hottest girl in the school, though he was too modest to say so.

I try again. 'I am ...' I shuffled through high school, lurching from one social gaffe to the next, then blundered my way through an undistinguished degree. I think the recipe book *4 Ingredients* may be overdoing it. Pasta with cheese on is the extent of my culinary abilities. I have destroyed all pictures of my school formal, but I can't destroy the memories. My dress, which I had chosen with

46

such high expectations, turned out to be transparent when back lit. All photos of the evening highlight the not terribly fetching flesh-coloured big knickers and sports bra I wore underneath it. If only I'd had a mother to advise me, this might not have happened.

I open and shut my mouth. 'We were different.'

'Roch, give me a hand with this, will you?' Dad gestures at a piece of wood that seems about to decapitate him.

Thus ends our intimate chat.

Later that night, my mind turns back to Sunday afternoons with Daniel. In bed, as in all things, Daniel was a high achiever. He would never, ever come before me. This was a point of honour. I appreciated this at the time, but now I wonder if he didn't desire me enough to let go. What a funny, strange, mysteriously wonderful thing sex is. I miss it. I miss having Daniel hold me tight.

My self-control is worse at night. Those tricksy urges sneak up on me while my defences are down. Before I know it, Daniel's number is on my screen and I am pressing the call button. This time he answers.

'You've got to stop calling me, Edie.'

His gentle voice only makes it worse. If he was mean I'd get over him quicker. 'Sorry. I didn't mean to.'

'Are you looking after my tree? It needs regular watering, you know.'

I look over at the bonsai. Daniel's tree is decidedly unwell. Its formerly glossy green leaves have a dull hue.

It is missing Daniel too. 'I don't have your tree.' We've had this conversation before.

'If you say so.' His tone is neutral, but I sense he is wondering how he stayed with me as long as he did.

I didn't realise how attached to his tree Daniel was until I took it. I am now too afraid to admit that I have it. He only has circumstantial evidence against me. 'I just needed to ask you something,' I say.

He sighs and I imagine his face; the way he looks when he's had a difficult day in court. 'What?'

'What was it about the rain in Glenorchy?'

'Huh?'

He has no idea what I'm talking about. I am astounded. It's as though Humphrey Bogart in *Casablanca* forgot the words to 'As Time Goes By', the song which signified his love for Ilsa. Then he never would have said *Play it again, Sam*. My whole relationship with Daniel was based on this huge romantic moment – a moment he has completely forgotten.

'Edie?' he says. 'I need to —'

'It rains a lot in Glenorchy.' I enunciate each word, hoping to jog his memory.

'I'm sorry, Edie, I've got stuff to do, a big case tomorrow ...'

'When we met, you said you were attracted to me from the moment I said, "It rains a lot in Glenorchy".'

'Did I? I must have thought you were talking about climate change.'

I nod. That makes sense. A giggle explodes out of my nose, followed by a sob.

'What?' says Daniel.

But I can't explain the sheer absurdity of a relationship based on a misconception so huge. I press *end*.

In the middle of the night I remember that I didn't ask him about the sausages.

Chapter Six

The interpretation of dreams is the royal road to … the unconscious.

SIGMUND FREUD

Wednesday: 46 days
Pain level: 8.5
Location: Chest

It is only after I fill out my diary that I remember my dream. I was nude hiking. Again. And it was still raining. This time more details were revealed. I was wearing a pack. Nude could mean sexy, but the pack spoils that. No, this is not a sexy dream. Someone appeared on the track ahead of me. They were not nude. This made me anxious and I woke up.

A recurring dream must be significant. I think my erotic writing is weighing on my mind. I am feeling exposed. It is exciting, but at the same time scary. No one must ever find out what a depraved person I am.

Thinking about last night's phone call to Daniel makes me sad. I can't believe he has forgotten 'the rain in Glenorchy'. I resolve to never call him again. In the back of my notebook, next to *Don't ring Daniel*, I write *Ever again!* This doesn't seem quite decisive enough so I add, *Or else!*

I am in the kitchen making coffee when Sally rings. It is only seven am. Days start earlier in Darling Head than in Sydney.

'This is your life coach. I want you to strike up a conversation with the fifth stranger you see today.'

'Strike up a conversation?' I squeak. 'I thought we agreed on talk to. Like, hi, nice day, isn't it? That sort of thing.'

'I've revised my requirements. Minimum five-minute conversation.'

'Am I paying you for this?'

'No,' says Sally. 'You're my test case. I'm thinking of starting a business.'

'Coaching shy people?'

'Not just shy people. Fat people, people lacking motivation, people who are having trouble achieving their goals. I might even do date coaching.'

'Date coaching?'

'Yeah, get with it, Edie. This stuff's big in America. Life coaching is the second fastest growing industry in the world.'

'What's the first?'

'I don't know. Yoga instructing probably.'

'So what does a date coach do?'

'It's sexual psychology: how to flirt, how to look for someone compatible. For an extra fee I'd tag along on a date incognito and give feedback.'

'And you're an expert on this stuff?'

'Come *on*,' Sally drawls.

I know she's right. Not only did she study psychology, but she has a natural knack for social skills. Our Grade Twelve yearbook named her the girl most likely to flirt her way to the top.

'Have you got a name for your business?'

'I'm thinking of motive eight.'

'Motivate?'

'No, it's a play on words. Motive. Eight.'

'I like the sound of it but what's the eight for?'

'I'm working on that part.'

'Maybe you offer eight types of coaching?'

'Maybe.'

'Or an eight-step process?'

'Yeah, yeah, an eight-step process. I like it.' I can almost hear Sally's brain ticking over. 'And the first part of your eight-step process is to start a conversation with a stranger.'

'Any hot tips, coach?'

'Start shallow, move deep.'

'That's it?'

'Well, in your basic five-minute conversation, you might not get to deep. Aim for medium – one step beyond weather and current affairs, but not as far as identity, beliefs and values.'

'Sal?'

'Yeah?'

'I think you've mistaken me for an advanced-level pupil. I signed up for basic conversation.'

Sally sighs. 'Okay, Edie. We'll start with small talk. Say hi, ask an open-ended question.'

'Like, been gettin' any?'

'That's not actually open-ended; they could just say yes.'

'How about, how would you rate the quality of the waves today?'

'Better. From there, try to segue into a more interesting topic. Pay attention to their non-verbal cues to see what interests them. You'll get the hang of it.'

'You lost me at segue.'

'Just fucking talk to them, Edie. I expect a full report.'

'Okay, coach.'

'Failure is not an option,' says Sal.

'Is it a requirement?'

'Ha!' She hangs up on me.

While we have been talking I have been gazing at a brochure Dad has left on the bench. It says SurfAid and has a picture of dark-skinned, curly-haired kids on a beach. *Kids on a beach without surfboards, tut, tut.* I imagine that SurfAid must be a missionary-type mob carrying, not bibles, but surfboards to poor deprived children who are yet to experience the thrill of wave riding. To my father, and most of Darling Head, surfing is no mere pastime, it is a spiritual pursuit. And I am a heathen in need of conversion.

Going outside, I settle on the couch with coffee and toast. When I finish I glance at my watch. Unfortunately, it is only seven-thirty, so I still have time to conduct my conversation before work.

As I get dressed my mind turns to Professor Brownlow. I feel like our relationship has moved on since I last saw him, but realise he, not having been writing erotic fiction about me (I assume), may not feel the same way ...

I fuss around with my wardrobe for longer than usual. Nothing is right. My entire range of clothing is absolutely useless in the following ways:

The dress I picked up at the market for ten dollars is too hippyish;
My T-shirts are too tight, too faded and make my arms look fat; and
My Sydney clothes are too hot, too black and scream wanker.

I settle on my Astro Guevara T-shirt and jeans – the best of a bad lot.

I turn on the computer so I can check my emails before I leave and glance in the mirror as it boots up. It's a good day. If I cross my eyes so the image blurs and don't move too close I look a little like Nicole Kidman when she was still a fuzzy redhead whose face moved. I know if I uncrossed my eyes and moved closer, I'd look like Mum in the photo I keep in my drawer. I move away from the mirror before that happens. Thinking about Mum is not a good way to start the day.

Unfortunately, thinking about not thinking about Mum has the opposite effect.

How did you and Mum meet, Dad?
   You know that story, Eddie Bear.
   I want to hear it again.
   It was when I won the Australian champs in Bells Beach. Your turn, Jen.
   I was sent down from Melbourne to interview him. The normal sports journalist was sick.
   Among all those suntanned surfers and hangers on your mother looked like a vision from another world.
   I was wearing my biggest hat and sunglasses.
   She had red hair down to her waist and her skin was like milk.
   Everyone was crowded around him, but I took off my sunglasses.
   She had eyes like the sea.
   It was love.
   At first sight.

Before I know it I am kneeling next to the camphorwood chest which is beside my bed and, what is worse, I am pulling out her notebook.

Mum's notebook has a hard red cover with black binding. Inside, her scrawling writing charts years of her thoughts, dreams, poems and whimsical fancies. The thing that I sometimes forget about my mother is how funny she was. How much she made me laugh. That was her gift. Our house was full of laughter when I was a child. My mother liked to play with words. Words were her toys, her tools and her passion.

'You're my little sweetiepiekins.' Mum tickles my tummy as I lie on the bed.

'And you're my great big honeybunchkins.' I know this game.

'You're delightful.'

'You're delicious.'

'You're luscious.'

'You're lovely.'

'I'm going to gobble you up for dinner.'

I squeal in mock terror.

A scribble of black ink runs across the inside front cover. I know the words by heart but they always make my chest ache. The urge to read on is almost irresistible, but I have been there before and I know Mum's notebook is a ticking bomb. My eyes follow the line just once then I close the book before I go too far.

My computer is humming now, inviting me to look her up. That famous woman I have never Googled. I know she had children – a boy and a girl. I already know one half of their story. I don't know if I am ready to find out the other half. I tap my fingers on the keyboard in a little drumbeat, type her name, then erase it. As I shut down the computer my heart is beating like I've had a lucky escape.

My mother's notebook sits in my bedroom like a junkie's fix. I am both drawn to and repelled by it. I wish

I could find a way to settle it in my heart in a way that didn't hurt. I put it back in the chest and pick up my car keys.

Driving down to the village, I park next to the shops. The fruit shop man nods at me as I climb out. That makes him a friend, rather than a stranger, so I can't count him. As I cross the road, the man I know only as unfriendly goatee man is crossing the other way, surfboard under his arm. Even though we have seen each other many times and I suspect he knows who I am (that is, my father's daughter) he stares straight past me. I make a mental note – stranger number one.

A couple I've never seen before are enjoying breakfast outside the beachfront café. They have a well-groomed look that almost invariably separates the blow-ins from the locals. Strangers two and three. My heart beats faster. I am getting dangerously close to stranger five. What if I don't like the look of them? I can move on, I tell myself. Sally will never know.

My prepared opening line will work best if I am looking at the sea, so I walk over the grass towards the railing lining the beach. As I do so, I realise I have my hands clasped behind my back. My hands become a bit of a problem when I am anxious. Clasping them behind my back is comfortable, but Sherlock Holmes-ish. Dangling by my sides feels wrong and I suspect makes me look deranged. Having them in my pockets can work, but my jeans are too tight today. Resting my elbows on the railing provides instant relief.

Darling Head turns on amazing autumn mornings. The sea is a cliché of transparent blue and even I can see the waves are good. Line after line of swell rolls in; not a single wave is left unmarked by a board rider slicing along the smooth face.

Even though I am not tempted to join the surfers I can see how it might be fun if you were so inclined. I am, of course, no stranger to the surf. I was brought up in the great Darling Head tradition. At five, I was signed up for the Darling Head Surf Nippers. Every Sunday during summer Sally and I lined up on the beach, ran races, paddled boards out through the breakers and were dumped face first into the sand on return. These days left me freckle-faced and red-nosed but fair skin was no excuse for non-participation. It wasn't until I was twelve that I dug my heels in and retreated indoors. Nothing Dad could do would tempt me into the waves again.

A self-possessed black cat stalks up the path from the beach with its tail in the air.

'Hi, puss,' I say.

Clearly a cat of discernment, it completely ignores me.

'Don't worry, the feeling's mutual,' I mutter as it strolls away.

Stranger number four, a fisherman with an ancient wiry-haired dog, goes past. For a moment I think he might be the one I've been looking for. But I think that every time I see an old fisherman heading back from the sea. This quest for The Fisherman has plagued me for years. I wish I could stop looking, but I can't. Would I know him if I saw him? If I knew him, would I know what to say? But I can't be thinking about that now. I am on a mission to overcome shyness. I have a report to make to Sally.

The next person I see will be stranger number five (as long as I don't already know them).

I have the panicky sensation I get when people are going around the room introducing themselves and my turn is coming soon. My throat is constricted and my mouth is dry. Any moment now I'm going to have to open my mouth and say something. It's impossible. I can't talk.

Down the beach, Dad and Rochelle are coasting into shore, side by side on their surfboards. As they reach the sand they stand, picking up their boards with one hand. This action is so well practised it is almost a dance. I wonder what it would be like to be so sure in your body. As I raise my hand to wave at them, a guy comes up the ramp from the beach.

Stranger number five.

I freeze, my hand half-raised, my smile half-formed, my breath half-breathed. He looks at me, obviously wondering if he knows me. It is the worst-case scenario. He is about my age, but I can already tell our auras don't align. Not that I'm into that stuff. And, here's the major surprise, he actually is a stranger. I've never seen him before in my life.

He has a panicked look on his face and a ring through his eyebrow. I've always found body piercings intimidating. It's the bold statement they make – hey, I'm hip; I've got a pierced eyebrow. I could never carry it off. It's the same with tattoos and asymmetrical hairdos. The guy is wearing a long-sleeved T-shirt with a giant tongue on it. His jeans are damp at the bottom. His bare feet are pale – too pale for Darling Head. He is holding black basketball shoes in his hand and a bag dangles next to his hip, its strap running across his chest. He might have just stepped off the streets of Kings Cross. He pauses at the top of the ramp, looking as if he is calculating the relative risks attached to running off or appeasing me.

I decide to let him go past and find a friendlier victim. But then I realise my hand is still raised in a frozen greeting. I am committed. I lower my hand. 'Hi.' My voice comes out in a squeak, but at least it comes out. Conversation has commenced.

His eyes flicker down and up again, possibly checking for weapons. 'Hi?'

The inflection in his voice confuses me. Is he saying hi or questioning me? I decide on the latter. 'Yes. I said hi.' I cough to clear my throat. I'm pretty sure Sally would be handling this better. What was I supposed to say to move the conversation on?

'Do I know you?' he asks.

'What do you think of the quality of the waves?' I ask, then registering what he has said, add, 'No.'

He frowns, lowering his eyebrow ring, shakes his head and walks off without another word.

A hot flush spreads across my face. I suspect our conversation has lasted less than five seconds. I stand, cemented to the spot with humiliation. My errant hands have moved themselves onto my hips and are projecting an aggressive image totally at odds with what is going on in my head.

'Eddie,' says my father.

He and Rochelle are standing in front of me. They look like trained seals, the water running off their black wetsuits.

'What are you doing?' Dad looks at me hard. 'What's up?'

'Nothing, just ... checking the surf.'

Dad smiles, immediately distracted. 'Beautiful, isn't it? When are you getting in?' He has been saying this for eleven years, but still sounds hopeful. Like me, he is a testament to the futile optimism of the human spirit.

I smile back, waggling my head in the indeterminate way which has served me well over this time.

'Did you meet Jay?' asks Rochelle.

'Jay?'

'My brother. I saw you talking to him. He just got off the overnight bus. I told him to look for us down the beach.'

'Oh.' I register this fact. Rochelle's brother is a stuck-up git who thinks I'm mentally deficient. And he's coming to stay with us. Great. Things couldn't be better.

Rochelle smiles, her eyes creasing into a ripple of wrinkles which only make her look happier. 'You and Jay should get on well. He's creative too. He plays in a band.'

That figures. He's a pierced, superior nob who thinks he's a rock god because he plays at pubs every now and then.

'I'd better go to work,' I say.

As I am unlocking my car, someone calls out to me.

'Hey.' A boy rides up to me on his bike. He is about thirteen and, like most kids in town, has the white-blond hair and peeling nose of a surf fiend.

I pause with my hand on the open car door. 'Yeah?'

'Do you know Dave McElroy? I saw ya talking to him.'

It is my usual practice to deny such accusations, but today I find that my bruised ego needs massaging. 'He's my father.'

His mouth drops open and he gives me a look usually reserved for minor celebrities. 'Rad. So, who are you sponsored by?'

Now is the time to nip this in the bud. I open my mouth to tell him I don't surf, but the words don't quite come out. His hero-worship is a little intoxicating and in the wake of my debacle with Jay, I need all the uplift I can get. 'Just Rip Curl,' I murmur modestly.

'Cool. I'm hopin' to get them. I'm coming top in my division. Going down to Bells for the nationals soon.'

Bells is Bells Beach in Victoria – a famous break. 'Rad,' I say.

'Yeah, thanks. I'm Tim.'

'I'm Edie.'

He fishes around in his pocket and pulls out a crumpled grease-stained paper bag. 'Can you get your dad's autograph for me?'

So that's what he wants. Dad stopped giving autographs years ago. He said his time was over. Kids

62

still approach him but he turns them down gently. Tim has found a better way. I take the bag, then wonder what I'm supposed to do with it. 'But how will I get it back to you?'

'I'll see you round.' He waves and rides off.

I look at the greasy paper bag. It's not like we don't have paper at home. But perhaps the bag is significant? I fold it up and push it into my purse. *Rip Curl*. With any luck I won't run into him again.

Chapter Seven

Flowers are restful to look at. They have neither emotions nor conflicts.

SIGMUND FREUD

The drive to the university takes half an hour. I wind through macadamia farms and patches of rainforest, slowing to let an echidna cross the road. Its worried little face pokes out between its spines as it waddles at a leisurely pace across the tar. Life in the country has its compensations – trees, flowers, fresh air …

What strikes me about the north coast, after living in Sydney, is how green it is, how slow the pace, how randomly friendly the locals. I grew up here, so I should be used to it, but after a five-year break it all seems new again. What I do miss about Sydney is the anonymity, the sense that no one is going to report you to your parents or gossip about you behind your back. Yes, I do miss that.

Along the way I pass a church. It has one of those newfangled signs out the front with changeable letters. *Failure is a success if we learn from it*, it says. This is very upbeat, very appropriate to my current situation. But is it true?

Can my encounter with Jay be called a success? What about all my failed love affairs? My failure to become a surfer girl? My social inadequacies? Can I somehow reframe these as successes?

Jesus Saves says another sign, fixed to the picket fence a little further along. Having recently watched *The Da Vinci Code* on DVD, this reminds me that Jesus supposedly had a daughter called Sarah. I don't recall her founding any new religions. *Hah.* I'm pretty sure being the water-shy daughter of a surf champ is trivial in the failure stakes compared with being the unknown granddaughter of God. Sally is right; there is no shortage of child failures out there.

This cheers me up and I tune my radio to the university radio station. While it is amateurish and often boring, it needs support. I turn up the volume as a song I haven't heard before comes on. It is a love ballad with a thumping backbeat. The production isn't the best but the singer sounds like Chris Martin from Coldplay, only not so whiny. I listen for the credit at the end, as I already know I want the album.

'Um, that was ... ' there is a shuffling sound, '... Jay Spooner with "Tangled Web".' The announcer is clearly reading from a CD cover. He is either stoned or naturally vague. 'Ah, he sent us this CD. I thought I'd play it as he is performing at the university bar on the —'

I punch the off button. *Jay.* It's him. I just know it. Maybe he actually is a rock god. So what? *Failure is success if we learn from it. Right on, church.* I have learnt that I should cancel that mental note to buy the CD.

'Hello, Edie,' says Professor Brownlow as I come in. He is seated in front of his microscope.

I blush. I feel like my microscope seduction scene is written on my forehead. How did I write such things? Imagine if he ever found out. I need to stop it immediately or at least change the character beyond recognition.

Professor Brownlow's hair is messier than usual. This gives him a rakish air that goes straight to my, er ... Damn, why aren't there any decent words for it? No wonder writing about sex is so hard. If I was a man I'd just say I got a hard on, but being a woman ... my pelvis tingles. I store the phrase away for future reference. It's not perfect, but it will have to do for now.

He waves his hand. 'Can you come over here for a second?'

My pelvic tingle is squelched. This sounds rather like a prelude to some long-overdue counselling on my work performance. I am right.

'Your drawings are very good, very aesthetically pleasing, I like them but ...' Professor Brownlow coughs and spreads out my last five drawings. He has circled various parts. 'I just double-checked the morphology of a few of these.' He sounds apologetic, although it is me who should be apologising. 'The antennules of this one should have eight aesthetascs, and its maxilliped one has nine setae, not seven.'

Unfortunately, he has lost me at morphology. I nod. 'Sorry.' I feel bad. I am patently unfit for this job, which requires minute attention to detail. I suppress an urge to put my fingers in my ears and hum as he continues.

' … maxilla … protopodite … telson … '

'I'm sorry, Ralph,' I say again when I can't stand it any longer. 'I'll concentrate harder.'

Professor Brownlow pushes the drawings towards me and smiles. 'I know you will.' He reaches into a folder behind him and pulls out another drawing. 'I like this one.'

I stare at the drawing. It was apparently done by me, but I have no memory of it. The crab larva is dressed in a military-type jacket with epaulets. A top hat rests jauntily on its head. It has an Hercule Poirot moustache. If Hotpunk, my former employer, sold crabs they would be retro-chic like this. A speech bubble comes out of its mouth with the words, *Draw it again, Sam*.

'A *Casablanca* reference?' asks Professor Brownlow.

I nod. Gulp. It is a little alarming that I could draw this without having any recollection of doing so. Is there such a thing as sleep-drawing?

He cocks his head and looks at the drawing. 'It's a little Dali-esque, isn't it? I think I might frame it. If you don't mind.'

I shake my head. I am so overcome with gratitude that he is not about to sack me I almost offer to have his baby. Luckily I don't as it would be inappropriate and, besides, he already has enough babies.

He takes off his glasses and polishes them.

I swallow. It is like a scene in one of those stupid movies where the shy, ugly secretary takes off her glasses and – *ta da* – everyone realises she is gorgeous. But it's true. Without his glasses, Professor Brownlow is beautiful. Not just sexy with hidden depths, but beautiful. If I had known that I never would have let myself develop this ridiculous crush on him.

'How are you liking the Murakami?' he asks.

I look away. It's the only way I can concentrate. When I look at him my brain loses power. I am functioning at the IQ of your below-average sea slug. 'The Murakami?' I stall for time.

I catch a glimpse of his face out of the corner of my eye. He looks disappointed, though still beautiful. I have let him down. 'The Murakami is fantastic,' I blurt.

He doesn't say anything. He is waiting for more – some deconstruction, perhaps? 'Very post-modern.' That's usually safe. 'Quite surreal, the protagonist is extremely original.' I am plucking these phrases out of the ether. I hope they fit.

Professor Brownlow replaces his glasses.

Thank goodness. My IQ rises to that of an intelligent sheep.

He smiles. 'I'm glad you like it.' He pushes the drawings towards me.

Our little session is over. I pick up the drawings and stand up. 'I'll redo these.'

He nods, turns back to his microscope and is soon lost in his world of crabs.

Before I commence work, I pull out my notebook and write: *Do not daydream when drawing zoea.*

My poor work performance has lowered my spirits, so while I'm at it, I update my pain dairy:

Wednesday (still): 46 days

Pain level: 9.0

Location: Head

I start the day with good intentions. But, as always, it is not the first zoea of the day which is the problem, or even the second. The issue is, while not unattractive, zoeas just don't do it for me. There is apparently nothing I can do to stop my mind wandering while I examine them under the microscope. And that is when mistakes happen.

Professor Brownlow's wife calls in at eleven o'clock. She looks as alarmingly fit and gorgeous as always. Her shoulder-length blonde hair bobs against her tight Nike T-shirt. I watch them out of the corner of my eye. He doesn't kiss her and there is a slight reserve in both their manners. But perhaps that is just because I am here.

'Back in a minute, Edie.' Professor Brownlow gets to his feet.

As soon as he is out the door I call my life coach.

'Edie.' Sally sounds out of breath.

'What are you doing?'

'I've been running all around town, putting out flyers for my business.'

'You move fast. You only decided you had a business this morning.'

'Hope you don't mind. I put a quote from you on the flyer.'

'What?'

'Well, you're my first client.'

'What did I say?'

'Sally is magnificent. I thoroughly recommend her coaching to anyone looking for a new direction in life.'

'Sounds like something I might have said, I suppose. Am I looking for a new direction in life?'

'Do you see a possibility to improve your personal and business relationships?'

'Is this a quiz?'

'Answer the question,' says Sal.

'Has anyone ever told you you'd make a good bondage mistress?'

'Edie.' Sally sounds like she's drawing her whip through her fingers.

'Yes,' I say quickly.

'Would you like to examine your habits and beliefs?'

'Yes.'

'Are you ready to create plans and take action to achieve your goals?' Sally's voice is rising to a crescendo.

'Yes and yes.'

'Then you are looking for a new direction in life and life coaching is for you.' She says this in the tone of someone announcing you have won a major prize.

'What if I'd said no to everything?'

'Then you are in need of some attitude adjustment and life coaching is absolutely for you.'

'I thought that might be the case. But, are you sure you want me on your advertising material? I'm not exactly a success story.'

'You will be. I have a one hundred per cent success rate.'

'But I'm your only client.'

'Exactly. And I haven't failed you yet, have I?'

'No. You're the best life coach I've ever had.'

'I'm going to email the flyer to you. Print out a few copies and stick them up around the uni, will you? How did your first conversation go?'

'Total crap. This guy basically blew me off. Then I found out later he's Rochelle's brother.'

'Rochelle?'

'Dad's girlfriend – I forgot you haven't met yet. You'll like her. But her brother ... what's worse is, he's coming to stay with us. I don't know why, but it's not like I've got any choice in the matter.'

'Step me through it.'

'Is that life coach speak?'

'You like it?'

'Yeah, give me more.'

'You're not getting out of it by distracting me,' says Sal. 'Step me through your encounter.'

I sigh. 'You're a hard woman.'

'Edie.' Sally's voice is definitely verging on Madame Lash material.

'Okay.' I tell Sally about my conversation with Jay. '... and then I say, "What do you think of the quality of the waves?" and he just looks at me like I'm something stuck to his shoe and walks off.'

Sally is silent for a while after I've spoken.

71

'Now you're wishing you didn't quote me on your flyer, aren't you?'

'No, I'm not.'

She says this so quickly I know I'm right. 'Maybe you should start off with an easier client. Donald Bradman, for example.'

'But he's dead.'

'So are my conversation skills.'

'Edie, I'm going to let you in on a little conversational secret here that is going to stand you in good stead for the rest of your life. Listen carefully.' Sally pauses for dramatic effect. 'The key to making a connection is to know what interests the other person.'

'But how do I know what interests them?'

'It's pretty simple. If you're talking to a man, chances are he's thinking about sex.'

'How do you know?'

'I've noticed it time and again. Ask a guy what he's thinking about and he'll just look guilty and say "Nothing much". Dead giveaway. You can bet your bottom dollar the topic of sex is going to be raised sometime soon.'

'I don't think that's what Jay was thinking about when I was trying to talk to him.'

'Bet you he was.'

I think of his look of disdain. 'No. Definitely not.'

'Freud said that sex is the primary motivator of humans.'

'Maybe that's only around you.'

'Well, perhaps I need to meet this Jay. In order to advise you better. I'll come around to your place tonight. Gotta go. Believe it, live it, do it, Ed.'

And before I can reply, she's hung up.

I look up and realise Professor Brownlow has come back in while I've been talking. 'My life coach.' I point at the phone. Like this is some kind of excuse. As if life coaching is the kind of urgent matter which cannot be delayed even when you're getting paid to draw crab larvae.

Professor Brownlow looks distracted. He nods and sits down. A few seconds pass before he speaks again. 'Did you say life coach?'

I look up from my maxilliped, startled. 'Yes.'

'What does that involve?'

I wish I hadn't mentioned it because now there doesn't seem to be any way to get past admitting I am the sort of failure who requires coaching just to function in the way most people find easy. Luckily the email on my computer goes *ting* at that moment. 'Here's a flyer, I'll print it out for you.'

I hand Professor Brownlow the flyer. Sally has been moving fast, she's got the whole concept mapped out.

Motive

Attitude is everything.
Eight steps to a more fulfilling life.

Career direction

Life purpose

Self-expression

Business coaching

Mentoring

Relationships

Creativity

Etiquette

*'Sally is magnificent.
I thoroughly recommend her
coaching to anyone looking for a
new direction in life.'*

Edie McElroy, client

Etiquette? I've got a feeling Sally was struggling to find eight strings to her bow.

Professor Brownlow scans the flyer and places it in his in-tray. 'Thanks.'

When it is obvious he has no further comments, I return to my desk. I try to enjoy the variety of each new zoea as I slide it into view. Sadly, like politicians and chickens, they are more alike than different. But after my counselling session with the divine Professor Brownlow I can't afford to shirk. Professor Brownlow loves zoea, so they must have something going for them; I just need to discover it. Maybe I can form a Facebook group for people who are into zoeas? Maybe my soul mate and I will bond over discussions of maxillipeds and telsons. *Oh, darling, I knew you were the one for me by the way we both loved the* Pyromaia tuberculata.

By the tenth zoea I have decided I will need Valium if I am to continue in this job.

By the eleventh I have decided I will have to seduce Professor Brownlow.

By the twelfth it is blindingly clear; only the combination of prescription drugs and sex will save me.

Chapter Eight

It is impossible to overlook the extent to which civilisation is built upon a renunciation of instinct.

SIGMUND FREUD

When I get home from work Jay is there, lounging on the sofa reading a copy of *Rolling Stone*. He doesn't hear me come in so I watch him for a moment, taking in the thick, black hair falling over his eyes, the skinny jeans and the black Converse basketball shoes. Rockstar chic.

Then Rochelle sees me. 'Edie,' she calls, and she couldn't sound any more pleased if I was an executive from Oz Lotto with a million-dollar cheque for her. She smiles her 1000 volt smile and strides out from the kitchen, spatula in hand. She has a frangipani tucked behind her ear and is wearing a T-shirt which says *Aloha* over the image of a girl on a surfboard.

I can't resist smiling back, inanely, like a stoned porpoise.

Jay looks up, catching the tail end of my smile and even though it isn't directed at him, he obviously thinks it is. His mouth twitches. 'Hey,' he says. It is a minimalist greeting. The kind a rockstar gives to a fan who is probably a stalker.

I blush.

He observes my blush, then turns back to *Rolling Stone*.

'Edie, you and Jay know each other, don't you?' asks Rochelle.

This is overstating it, but she sounds so enthusiastic I respond with eager nodding. 'We met this morning.' I sound like Paris Hilton.

Jay's eyes flicker, catching my nod and gushing response. He doesn't say anything.

I blush again. I want to ask Rochelle why he is staying with us and how long he's going to be here, but this doesn't seem like the right time. 'My friend Sally's coming over later. After dinner.'

'That's nice,' Rochelle enthuses. 'I'll look forward to meeting her.' Behind her, the crystal mobile she has hung in the kitchen tinkles in the breeze.

Rochelle is a domestic goddess. The house has been full of these gentle, cheerful touches since she moved in. She has even done amazing things to the garden. I suspect she gardens naked when I'm not around, reliving her time in the taro field. I suspect this because she doesn't have tan lines in the usual places. She and her brother don't seem related at all. He must have been adopted.

Dad comes downstairs, his hair wet from the shower. 'Good day, Eddie?'

I nod. 'The usual, drew twelve crab larvae. One of them had a particularly fine exopodite. Rather spunky really.'

'That's the way.' Dad picks up his hammer and eyes the ceiling, which has now been peeled back to bare boards. His mind is on other things.

I sit down at the table and flick through the newspaper. Dad exchanges a meaningful look with Rochelle when he thinks I'm not looking. She lifts her shoulders a fraction in reply. I don't know what that means.

Dinner is awkward. For some reason conversation is limited to 'Pass the sauce, please' (me) and 'This is delicious' (Dad). Even Rochelle's smile wilts in the chilling ambience.

Rochelle has placed a tall flower arrangement in the middle of the table in honour of Jay's arrival. I peer around the hibiscus and frangipanis, feeling like a Jane Austen heroine at a formal dinner which is going badly, and adopt a haughty air I am unable to shake. I plumb my mind for conversational topics and come up with the following questions for Jay:

Do you like tofu?
Have you considered wearing colours other than black? and,
Why are you here?

*

I clear my throat in preparation, but none of them seem quite right to drop unannounced into the strained silence.

Dad attempts to break the ice with a discussion about the forthcoming election but this falls flat.

'From politics, it was an easy step to silence,' I murmur, spearing a carrot with a chopstick. Chopsticks, like dolphins, are one of Rochelle's things. She thinks it helps you to savour your food.

Eventually Jay deigns to talk to me. 'Are you a scientist?' The way he says this makes it obvious he has no interest in my reply.

I giggle in a fetching manner. 'Oh no, drawing crabs is just a job. I need the money. I have a dreadful propensity for being poor.'

Jay, clearly not an Austen fan, gives me a blank stare then attacks his tofu surprise with renewed vigour.

In actual fact, I am not really an Austen fan either. The Brontës are more my style. Jane Austen's heroines are practical. They realise that too much romance can ruin your life, a fact I would rather ignore. Elizabeth Bennet loved Darcy as soon as she first saw 'his beautiful grounds at Pemberley'. What about his laugh? His eyes? His hidden depths? A Brontë heroine would not be so dull. Brontë heroines know that to turn your back on passion is to turn your back on life. Just look at what happened to Cathy from *Wuthering Heights* —

'Did you ever see that movie, *Attack of the Crab Monsters*?' Dad interrupts my musings on romance.

We all look at him with the level of interest that people bring to an aeroplane safety briefing.

'It's about a group of evil scientists who land on a remote island which is full of these mutated giant crabs. They can talk with human voices and they want to take over the world ...' Dad trails off.

'Hmm, no, never saw that one,' says Jay.

I shake my head.

Rochelle blinks.

'The crabs are invincible because they're, um ...'

'Mutated?' Jay's voice expresses a polite interest, but I detect an undercurrent of parody.

My dad's habit of providing long and boring movie summaries has always annoyed me, but now I come in on his side. 'It sounds fantastic. We should get it out on DVD.'

Jay gives me a long look from under his fringe.

Dad smiles. 'I'm pretty sure they've got it in the video shop.'

I wait to see if he can wring any more out of this topic, but this seems to conclude our riveting diversion into C-grade movies.

Dad taps his chopsticks on his plate to fill the silence. Now I wish we could go back to talking about crab monsters as this is his *most* annoying habit.

'If you were an animal, Jay,' Rochelle puts her hand on Dad's to stop him tapping, 'which animal would you be?'

We all turn to Jay. *What animal will he be? A drum roll, please.*

'A dolphin,' he says, deadpan.

Well, what a surprise. I was thinking more along the lines of great white shark.

Rochelle looks around the table as if this is an amazing coincidence. 'Me too. Why would you be a dolphin?'

'Because they spend about seven hours a day fucking.'

As he says this, Sally makes her entrance. She stands, silhouetted against the doorway, her dress lifting up around her legs in the sea breeze, a lock of tawny hair blowing across her face.

Jay turns and his eyes meet hers.

She smiles.

He smiles.

'I'm Sally,' she says.

'I'm Jay.'

'How are you enjoying Darling Head?'

'It's cool. Very ... sandy.'

I watch this exchange like a game of tennis. So that's how it's done, this conversation thing. I am certain that if Sally asked Jay what he was thinking about, he would say, 'Nothing much'. But I still don't think that's what he was thinking about with me.

'Hi,' says Rochelle.

Sally turns the beam of her gaze on Rochelle. 'Hi, Rochelle. Nice to meet you.'

They smile at each other and I sense an optimistic energy flowing between them – two get-up-and-go women.

Sally catches my eye and gives a quick wink as she comes to the table. 'Hi, Dave. Hope I'm not intruding. I just wanted to drop around some of my flyers. I thought you might be able to put them up at work.'

As Dad runs his own sporting photography business and has no staff, this is a fairly flimsy excuse for her visit. Dad and Rochelle take the brochures from her.

'Thanks,' says Rochelle.

'Interesting,' says Dad.

'I'm a life coach.' Sally turns to Jay.

'Is that right?' He flicks the hair out of his eyes. 'I've never met a life coach before. Why don't you drop around and give me some coaching one day. I need a bit of help.'

This is the longest speech I have heard from him.

Sally smiles – a piranha scenting flesh. 'Glad to. Are you prepared to create more balance in your life?'

Jay nods. 'Uh huh.'

'Do you see room for more fun and enjoyment?'

Jay raises his eyebrows. 'Totally.'

'Do you think you would benefit from someone to help you stay on track?'

'That's you, right?' asks Jay.

'*Oui, c'est moi.*' Sally twirls a wayward strand of her hair around one finger.

For some unaccountable reason I want to punch her in the ear.

'Then I definitely would,' says Jay.

'Check me out on Facebook.' Sal hands him a flyer and points at the address on the bottom.

Jay fingers the paper, a half-smile on his lips.

My head has been turning from one to the other throughout this exchange. I'm starting to feel awkward. They are practically undressing each other with their eyes. 'You have delighted us long enough,' I say to Sal. I smile to pretend I am joking. 'I've got some stuff I need to do.'

Sally flashes me a glance which shows she knows exactly what I mean. 'I'll call you tomorrow. Bye Dave, Rochelle ... Jay.'

'Sally,' says Jay, by way of goodbye. He says her name as if it is one he is sure to remember.

After Sally has gone we return to our interrupted boredom. Dad and Rochelle settle in front of a home improvement show on the TV, Jay pulls out his magazine and I, remembering I supposedly have stuff to do, escape to my room.

Once there, I feel ashamed of the way I rushed Sally off. Why did I do that? I send her a quick email.

Subject: Um, sorry?
Don't know what came over me. Conversational jealousy? Don't give up on me.
Your star client,
Edie

I press Send/Receive and as Sally's email departs another one comes in. How exciting. A name appears in my inbox. I can hardly believe it. It is from Daniel. Daniel has sent me an email. This hasn't happened since we broke up. Happiness bubbles up inside me.

An email.

From Daniel.

This is beyond exciting, it is fabulous.

There is no subject. My heart hammers as I click on it. There is also no message, just an attachment. I do a little jig in my chair as it loads. *What has he sent me? A love letter?* The attachment opens. It is a five-page document titled 'Care of Bonsais'. Disappointing. To say the least.

I scan it. *Caring for a bonsai requires tremendous patience and effort.* Well, stop right there.

This is a very, very disappointing email. But, still, it is an email from Daniel. It required him to remember my existence, to type in my name, to press Send. An email on bonsai care is better than no email at all. So, although I have little interest in caring for bonsais, I don't delete it. I put it in the folder with his other emails.

I can hear Sally screaming as I do this. *Delete his emails, delete his texts, delete his photos. Have no contact. Don't think about him.* I know this is the way to get over someone. But what if you don't want to get over them? What if, contrary to all logic and rational thought, you think that maybe, just *maybe* you will still get back together?

I have a lot of emails from Daniel. Communications may have been more romantic in the days before email, but I bet they weren't as prolific. There is definitely an epic poem's worth here – even a collection. *An Accidental Love Story*, I could call it. Not that I would do that. Daniel's emails are private. *For now ...*

84

I can't read his emails because they make me cry, but I will never delete them. One day perhaps, when my heart is not so raw, I will turn them into art. *Forgive me, Daniel. You will never recognise yourself.*

Daniel's tree sits on my bedside table, accusing me with its browning leaves. 'I'm sorry I took you away from him,' I say.

It's no wonder Daniel moved on, says the tree.

'Oh, talking to me now, are you?' I always knew that the bonsai thought I wasn't good enough for Daniel. It never said so while we were together, but I could sense it. Daniel and the bonsai were a pair – neat, precise and very, very good-looking. 'Why are you so spiteful?' I ask. 'Shouldn't you be all Zen? Being a Japanese bonsai and all.'

He's with a barrister now. She's a gourmet cook, fluent in five languages and a former Olympic gymnast.

'Shut up.' I drape my T-shirt over it. 'What would you know?'

And she likes earthworms. Being under a T-shirt doesn't stop the bonsai from hitting below the belt – just my luck to be stuck with a taunting bonsai.

'Mention earthworms again and you're dead.'

The bonsai is not yet ready to commit harakiri as it says no more.

Now that I think about it, it seems natural that being turned into a bonsai would make you mean spirited. All that clipping back, never having enough room to grow tall. Rather than a bonsai being the tree's essential spirit, as Daniel said, was it instead a bitter and twisted version

85

of the tree it might have been? This idea strikes me as incredibly profound. I would like to share it with Daniel but, even if he was talking to me, he would think it was silly. Daniel is a practical person.

It is strange, but as I fall asleep I find I am thinking not of Daniel, or even Professor Brownlow, but of Jay and the way he said Sally's name. He is already on the shortlist of the most annoying people I have ever met.

Chapter Nine

A certain degree of neurosis is of inestimable value.
SIGMUND FREUD

I wake to a raised voice: Rochelle's. I can't resist opening my door and eavesdropping; it is so unusual to hear her angry.

Rochelle is still in her pyjamas – a thin singlet and silky shorts. Her fists are clenched. 'You need to move on, Jay.' Her voice is a fierce hiss. 'You're stuck. You're not even trying.'

'How would you know?' Jay's hands hang by his side. He is wearing faded grey track pants, like a rockstar trying to be incognito. 'Miss *glass is always half-full.* What if I've already smashed it and there's nothing left at all?' He sounds bored, like this is a conversation they have had many times.

'Don't be ridiculous. Snap out of it. Look, you've got a chance here. You just won't take it.'

'It's not that I don't want to, Roch. I can't.' Jay turns at that moment and, for some inexplicable reason, looks up and sees me. He smiles, pushing his hands into his pockets.

I pull my head back inside my room. The memory of his smile makes me blush. It was so knowing, so ... ironic. What if he thinks I am stalking him?

Thursday: 47 days
Pain level: 7.5
Location: Abdomen. What next, foot?

As I dress, the anxiety I always get on my non-crab-larvae days grows stronger. I can feel the erotic writing calling me, but what will happen when I sit down at the computer? Will anything come out? I wonder if it is like this for other writers or does brilliance always gush from their fingertips?

I open my door, listen. All is quiet so I pad downstairs for breakfast. As my toast pops up, Sally calls.

'No need to apologise, Ed,' she says as soon as I answer.

Sally is the only person who calls me Ed, so it is our little thing.

'But he *is* seriously hot,' she says.

'Is he?' I am often surprised when told that someone is hot. My taste is contrary. The strangest things spark my interest – with Professor Brownlow it was the book. But now that Sally says it, I realise she is right. Jay has the tortured artist persona down to a T. He is more Nick Cave than Nick Cave ever was. He makes Daniel Johns look like Kylie, Michael Hutchence like Britney.

'Fuck, Ed, open your eyes.'

'You never used to swear this much before you went to South America.'

'Fell in with a fucking bad crowd in Rio.'

'So ... we're good?'

'We're good. But, if you're not making any moves ...'

I'm not sure how to respond to this. I don't like the idea of Sally with Jay. Why? I'm not sure, but I can't be a dog in the manger. 'No. He's not my type. You know, the pierced eyebrow ... the black clothes.'

'Okaay,' drawls Sally. She sounds doubtful. 'Well, I've been working on the next stage of your program.'

'Oh, right. You know, I'm not sure if I need to take it any further. I can live with this shyness thing, it doesn't inhibit me much, it's not such a —'

'Stop right there,' says Sally. 'Do you think I'm letting my first client get away with that? You ... are ... going ... to ... overcome ... this ... phobia.'

'Phobia? I haven't got a phobia. I just don't like social situations all that much.'

'Ah ha,' says Sally, as if a spy she is interrogating has let slip some vital piece of information. 'You just admitted it yourself. You have social phobia. Did you know almost six per cent of Australian women suffer from social phobia?'

'Maybe we should all get together sometime.'

'Only no one would turn up.' Sally catches the ball. 'I've been looking into this. You need to rebuild the pathways in your brain and stop negative thoughts about social situations. And I know just who you can practise on.'

'Huh?' Unfortunately it is already dawning on me what she means.

'Jay. It's good that you don't fancy him; that'll make it easier for you. You're building up this silly "He thinks I'm stupid" scenario in your head, aren't you?'

'It's not a scenario. He does think I'm stupid.'

'Of course he doesn't think you're stupid. Why would he think you're stupid?'

'Gee, I don't know. Maybe because I act like a half-wit every time I see him.'

'Ant,' says Sally.

'Pardon?'

'ANT. Automatic negative thoughts. You need to notice, catch and stop your negative thoughts and replace them with positive, rational statements.'

'Such as?'

'I am an intelligent, interesting woman whose opinions are valued.'

'I'm not so sure about that one.'

'Say it.'

I think she might be on the verge of swearing at me again. 'Hang on, you're not valuing my intelligent, interesting opinion.'

'Edie.' Sally sighs.

'Okay. I am an intelligent, interesting woman whose opinions are valued.'

'Good. Say that to yourself every time you get an ANT. Today you have to have a conversation with Jay which goes beyond small talk. Make some personal disclosures about yourself and he will follow.'

'How do you mean personal disclosures?'

'You tell him you like curry. He tells you he's into Indian music. You tell him you read books. He tells you he likes Dan Brown.'

'Dan Brown? What about Dostoevski?'

'All right, Dostoi-effing-evski if you want to be all cerebral and high-minded. That was just an example. The point is, it's tit for tat.'

'Am I titty or tatty?'

Sally sighs. 'I'm about to lose patience here, Ed.'

'So that's how it works, huh?'

'That's how it fucking works, mate.' Sally laughs.

It's good to have Sally back. I've missed our verbal jousting. After Sally hangs up I finish my toast and write in my notebook. *I am an intelligent, interesting woman whose opinions are valued.*

I then retire to my room to check my emails. I often wish I lived in a time before email. Every time I click on Outlook and there is no message there from Daniel it feels like a rejection. In a seven-hour working day, this can happen about fifty times, more if my self-control is particularly bad.

Sometimes I try to set myself limits – *if I don't check my emails before twelve, there will be a message there from Daniel.* I usually manage to negotiate myself down – *okay, eleven. Twist my arm, ten then.* Predictably, however, I can never wait even that long and, also predictably, there is no message.

And it is not only Daniel. There are a whole lot of other people who also reject me fifty times a day, but if I dwelt too much on them, I'd never leave my room.

If I was Emily Brontë I imagine the mail would be delivered, at most, daily. A horse might thunder up to the house and she would run out, hoping to hear from her sweetheart. What bliss, what joy to be rejected merely once a day. The only light in this dark tunnel of rejection is that I don't have an iPhone. This means on the days I work at the university I can't check my personal emails until the evening.

Today I have the pleasure of a long email from someone in Nigeria called Philip. I skip over the more wordy bits.

Dear Beloved,
This letter may come to you as a surprise due to the fact we have not yet met ...
Right now, I have only about a few months to live ....

Philip shows a fine eye for melodrama – the evil relatives, the death-bed epiphany ... But really he is appealing to the worst in me – the gullible but greedy me, who would take his hard-earnt dollars and pocket them. If I sought to rob poor, dying, Philip, he would, in turn, no doubt, rob me. I resist the temptation to enter into correspondence with him and delete the email.

Now it is time to write.

I read back over my erotic scene between Edaline and Professor Brown. Should I change the characters so they are less recognisable? I know this is a good idea, but I am worried it will inhibit me. Let's face it, Professor Brownlow is my current lust object and inspiration and there's nothing I can do to change that. I decide to press on and alter the details later. I brace myself for some steamy sex.

Just as I am about to begin, the door bangs downstairs. Jay is back from wherever he went. Removing my fingers from the keyboard, I sigh. I may as well get it over with. There is no point in trying to fob Sally off on this one.

The door to Jay's room is ajar when I creep downstairs. I'm not sure why I am creeping, but I can't help it. Ants are crawling through my brain. They are all familiar to me and I squash them with determination. I pause outside his room. My hands are sweaty, my pulse is sprinting and my mouth is dry. *He thinks I'm an idiot.* Squash. *Why would he want to talk to me?* Squash. *I should just go back to my room.* Squash. I can almost smell the formic acid. I take a deep breath, as Sally instructed and knock on the door.

As I do this, I realise he is playing the guitar. *He'll be annoyed I interrupted him.* Squash. The guitar stops.

'Yo,' he says.

Yo? How can I talk to someone who says yo? What could we possibly have in common? 'Yo,' I hear myself say as I step forward.

Jay is perched on the edge of his bed, guitar on his lap and a notebook beside him.

Not only guitar playing, but songwriting. This is a very bad time. Squash.

He is wearing a long-sleeved black T-shirt. His hair is damp. He doesn't smile when he sees me.

Why doesn't he smile? He thinks I'm an idiot. Squash. My mind is a blank. I stare at him.

He stares back.

Why is he just staring at me? I had a conversation starter prepared, but now it's vanished. I am frozen to the spot, unable to retreat, unable to go forward. I can't just say *I like curry.* Not out of the blue. Even I can see that isn't going to work.

Jay looks down at his guitar, plucks a string, then looks back up at me. He plays a few chords then scribbles a word down on his notebook.

Reading it upside down it looks like 'kismet'. I have encountered this word before but I can't now recall its meaning. *Perhaps it is a code for dickhead.* Squash.

He seems perfectly relaxed; as if this is a normal way to behave. As if I always come into his room and stand there, speechless.

I back out, shutting the door behind me. My legs are trembling like I've run a marathon. I sink to the ground outside his room, pressing my forehead to my knees. Tears seep into my eyes. I hate being like this.

'Edie?'

I don't lift my head. I wish he'd go away and stop looking at me.

He doesn't. I hear his back slide down the wall until he is sitting next to me. He strums a chord. It sounds ironic.

Strum.

So here we are sitting on the floor in the corridor. The scout ant goes out.

Strum.

This is what I always do. It finds the pack and rounds them up.

Strum.

Why am I such a social incompetent? Led by the scout, the ant pack returns. They swarm uninterrupted through my brain. There are way too many of them to squash.

But I can't sit here like this anymore. I lift my head.

Jay meets my eyes but he doesn't smile. He plays a few more chords, segues into a rocky number and back to a ballad. He's good. He makes Mick Jagger look like Nikki Webster. 'Kismet,' he says as his fingers dance over the strings.

That word again. I wonder if he's speaking a different language. I nod in an ambiguous way, hoping this fills the gap.

I watch him for a while. It seems to be okay to be sitting here not talking. He plays some more. My pulse settles. Eventually I get to my feet and walk away without another word. His music follows me and, I don't know why, by the time I get back to my room I am smiling.

Can saying 'yo' be called a conversation?

Chapter Ten

In the important decisions of personal life, we should be governed … by the deep inner needs of our nature.

SIGMUND FREUD

Professor Brown lifted Edaline onto the laboratory bench. His hands slid under her skirt, caressing her quivering thighs. Edaline barely registered the cold metal beneath the globes of her milky bottom. She wrapped her legs around his waist as she undid the buttons on his lab coat.

Professor Brown lowered his head, pressing his burning lips to her slender neck. Her hair brushed over his face.

'So fine. Like plumose hairs of the megalopae of the zuwai crab,' Professor Brown murmured, blowing out her hair with his orange-scented breath.

But Edaline didn't know whether he was talking about the hairs on her head because his hand was now entwined in the forest elsewhere. She unwound her legs from around his waist long enough for Professor Brown to pull her cotton-stretch panties off. He held them to his face and breathed deeply.

Professor Brown's long slender scientist's fingers explored the ridges and crevices of her secret place. 'So wet.' His voice was husky.

Edaline's breath caught in her throat as he knelt.

'Like the brine from the Sea of Japan,' he murmured, tasting with his dexterous tongue, 'where I found my first <u>Artemia salina</u>.'

Edaline was aware only of his rough, muscular tongue. 'Take me now,' she cried, 'you sexy fiddler crab.' She pulled Professor Brown up and drew him towards her.

Professor Brown gasped, 'So soft, like the folds of a clam.' Then he spoke no more ...

I print out my scene, well satisfied with what I have achieved. My sex scene is humming, it's even turning me on, but what can happen next? Have I got to the sex too fast? Maybe I should have delayed them more?

I rework the scene many times, printing it out, making corrections and stowing the rejects in my recycled paper pile. I am in an editing frenzy, a delirium of re-writing. I have the hopeful, drained, satisfied glow I get when my poetry is working. I know Professor Brown and Edaline aren't great literature, but writing about sex is more fun than I'd expected. There is only one problem. I can never show this work to anyone. My erotic writing is a secret love child. It will never see the light of day.

Does it matter that I can never show this to anyone? I was, after all, hoping to make some money out of it. And it seems a little sad that no one will ever read about Edaline and Professor Brown. I am becoming rather fond of them both. Maybe I should try a more decent form of writing, one that I am not afraid to own? This seems like a good idea, but it just doesn't interest me. A writer must write what she feels and it seems I am, for now, an erotic writer.

My alter ego, Sooty Beaumont, taps her cigarette on her Japanese ceramic ashtray and adjusts her silk kimono. She winds her long dark hair into a topknot and secures it with a chopstick. Today she will entertain Takuya. Her nipples harden at the thought of his hot wasabi.

In the afternoon I walk down to the boat channel. Swimmers are enjoying the sea, despite the cool air. A little girl kicks water at her mother, squealing with mischief. I stand well back on the soft sand, where the waves can't touch me.

A little further down the beach a fisherman casts a line. He flicks his rod and his hook sails over the waves. I inspect him although I already know he is not the one I want. He is too young for a start, not much older than me, but it is a habit as ingrained as breathing.

My stomach knots as a larger wave rushes towards me. I jump backwards, a jolt of fear making my spine tingle.

I haven't always been like this.

'Look, we both have red goggles and black swimsuits, Mum.'
'We both have red hair and white skin too.'
'And we both like to swim.'
'You are my mini-me, Edie.'

I press my toes into the sand, trying to ignore the craving I get when I look at the water. I want to but I can't. My heart accelerates at the mere thought of diving in. It's the same when I see someone I'd like to talk to. I want to but I can't.

Further down the beach I see a man – a young man. He has rolled up his jeans and is poking at some seaweed with his foot. He is doing this in a way that says his head is miles away. His dark hair is flopping over his eyes. I peer harder and see it is Jay. A gust of wind catches his hair and blows it backwards. He looks like Heathcliff on the moor, a doomed wild child.

Heathcliff from *Wuthering Heights* has been a shared passion for Sally and me since we were fifteen. Our English teacher Mrs Endicott, a large-busted elderly woman, used to go pink whenever she talked about him. The original Heathcliff, who was not a very nice person at all, has vanished in the mists of time. Only his essence remains. For Sally and me, Essence of Heathcliff stands in as a symbol of a passionate, romantic, manly man.

I don't know why Cathy married Heathcliff's nemesis, the weak, prissy Edgar Linton. Silly Cathy. People who don't follow their passions deserve to end up wandering the moors for eternity.

Jay looks as if he is trying to work something out. I get the sense that he is going about this the same way I would. He is not weighing up the pros and cons; he is waiting for the answer to reveal itself, for inspiration to strike. This is what we romantics do. We favour intuition over logic.

Daniel is not a romantic. If Daniel was standing on the shore he would be thinking about rising sea levels and depleted fish stocks.

'You're kind of a primitive, aren't you, Edie?' he said to me early on in our relationship. 'You just *feel* things, you don't *think* about them.'

'But I do think about things,' I said. 'I think about things constantly.'

'But not logically. You think about them emotionally.'

I hadn't realised until then that this was a problem. I'd thought everyone was like me. Yet another problem; I already had so many.

'You don't work problems out, do you?' asked Daniel.

'No, I wait for the solution to strike me. It just happens. You mean you weigh up the pros and cons and then go with the majority?'

'That's how everyone does it, Edie.'

I found it hard to believe. Everyone except me was running their life as if it was an accounts book? Surely not.

I watch Jay poking the seaweed. I like the way he does that. He is concentrating. It is just him and the seaweed. What is he thinking? Should I go and talk to him?

But what would we talk about? I can't just go up to him without a plan. Although we have now shared a strange and intimate hall floor moment I am far from at ease with him. His spiky aura and pierced eyebrow daunt me. I wish Sally was here to coach me.

Then it comes to me – his music. I can tell him I heard him on the radio, how much I liked his song. As I take a step towards him a line from the song runs through my head: *You looked at me, as if I was the answer, though you didn't know the question.* And this strikes me as being so true, so honest and so deep it stops me in my tracks. Can I really talk to him about that? Don't I have to move through shallow and medium before I get to deep? Weather, then curry, then meaning of life?

But I am not good at shallow or even medium. I am an all or nothing girl, either frozen on the edge or plunging straight over the precipice into beliefs and values. I am, perhaps, the Evel Knievel of the conversation world.

'Kismet'. I have looked the word up. It means luck, fate or fortune. Perhaps I can talk to him about that? Ask him if he is writing a song about it.

As I stand there, working on an opening line, a girl runs down the track to the beach. She is wearing jogging shorts and a singlet. Her hair is pulled back from her head in a ponytail which bounces in a joyful way behind her. It is Sally. She runs straight towards Jay and punches him on the shoulder.

I would never have thought of doing that. Not even if I'd had a day to prepare for this encounter. Not even if I'd had a week. But Sally just does it. Spontaneously.

He perks up. I can see this even from a distance. His shoulders straighten.

She touches his arm, tosses her ponytail.

Watching Sally flirt is like watching Olympic gymnastics. I could no more do that than execute a triple back-flip off the mat. I swish my hair experimentally and imagine the judges holding up their score cards. *Zero, zero, zero for Australia.*

He touches her arm back. I bet they're not talking about kismet.

I visualise myself as Sally, that flirtatious charge running from Jay to me. My heart accelerates. *I want to but I can't.*

They laugh. Could they be laughing about me? I turn and walk in the other direction before they can see me.

A voice accosts me as I pass the skate park. I am deep in thought and don't register who it is at first.

'Hey, Edie.' Tim, the surfer boy, slides down the ramp towards me. Stopping just centimetres away, he flicks his skateboard up with his toe. 'How's the surf?'

I drag my mind back from thoughts of Heathcliff and windy moors. 'Blown out.'

'Thought so.'

'Might be good tomorrow morning. Bit of southerly swell pushing in. There's a low off Fiji.' I might not be sponsored by Rip Curl, but my years with Dad have left a legacy – I could surf chat at an elite level.

'Reckon the Point'll be working?' he asks.

'Worth a shot if it glasses off. The banks are pretty good.'

'What sort of board have you got?' Tim looks at me as an acolyte would at a guru.

This adulation goes to my head. 'Six three, thruster for when it's big.' This is what Rochelle rides. 'Got a fish for the not so solid days and a mini-mal for the small days. Sometimes ride a seven four, when it's in between.'

Tim nods. 'Yeah. I need a few more boards; that's why I want the sponsorship. What length do you reckon is best for Bells? I'm on a five nine here.'

'Best to go a bit longer.' I am not making this up. Name any well-known break in Australia and I could tell you the optimum board length given the prevailing swell direction and size. This knowledge has seeped into me by osmosis. Who knows how far I could have gone with this if I'd actually had any interest in it?

'I told my dad I needed a new board.'

This reminds me … 'I got Dad's autograph for you, but I haven't got it with me.'

'That's okay. I'll see you round.'

I am starting to suspect this is more than likely.

'See you out there tomorrow,' Tim calls after me as I leave.

Chapter Eleven

Everywhere I go I find a poet has been there before me.
SIGMUND FREUD

I am nude hiking. Again! The figure I saw last time approaches. It is a man. He is wearing old-fashioned clothing – a black wool coat and battered felt hat – and has a gun slung over his shoulder. He is either too polite or too shy to mention my nakedness.

'Seen any deer?' he asks. Rain drips off the brim of his hat.

I am too perturbed at being naked to answer.

Friday: 48 days
Pain level: 8.5
Location: Upper intestine

I can tell Friday is going to be a bad day as soon as I wake up. There is the lingering unease from my dream for one thing. Nude hiking makes me uncomfortable. I don't like it. *Stop dreaming about nude hiking*, I write in my *Tips for Self-improvement* section.

Rain is thundering on the tin roof and the trees outside my window are bowed over with the southerly squall. The surf is roaring. Mum always liked it when the surf was big. She would bodysurf on the breakers, arms stretched in front of her, gliding towards the shore like a dolphin. She danced with the danger, the wildness, returning invigorated like a warrior. Sometimes she scared me.

I am paddling in the shallows when I see Mum stand up on the sand bank. The tide is low, so inside the reef the beach is sheltered, safe. Outside, the waves roll like sea monsters, smash on the sand bank, suck and roar.

Mum waves to me. I wave back and continue to bob and splash, confident she is now on her way back. The water is warm and clear. The fish are swimming in silver shoals. I chase them across the rocky reef, trying, always trying, to touch them, but never succeeding. Only when the sun turns orange do I realise it has been a long time.

I lift my head, looking seaward, expecting to see Mum, my beautiful Mum, pop out from beneath me. She isn't there. I swim some more. Eventually I haul myself from the water, shivering. I know when I stand up on the sand I will see her.

And there she is, her long arms slicing through the water. Back to me.

*

I listen to the waves crash on the sand. No doubt Dad and Rochelle are out there somewhere, undeterred by the minor inconvenience of wind and rain.

You should be doing that, says Daniel's bonsai. *What's wrong with you? Your father is a surf champion.*

I glare at it. 'Shut up. I wish I'd never stolen you. I wouldn't have, if I'd known you were so mean. You didn't talk much in Sydney.'

Daniel's bonsai maintains a huffy silence; its ever-browning leaves indicate an unspoken accusation.

'Do you think Daniel would have liked it if I'd made sausages?' I ask.

You wouldn't have been any good at it, says the bonsai. *Did I mention his new girlfriend's a gourmet cook?*

Oh, a critical bonsai is the last thing I need in my life. I would send it back to Daniel, but that would mean admitting I'd taken it in the first place. And I can't just throw it away. The bonsai and I are stuck together until death us do part. A leaf falls from a branch into the pot.

'I'm sorry,' I say.

You should be, says the bonsai.

Pulling the blanket over my head, I contemplate the day ahead. Twelve zoea to draw. The good part, of course, is I get to see Professor Brownlow. And even though he is out of bounds, I can't stop the little pulse of excitement this gives me. I suspect my crush is counterproductive, even harmful, but I am powerless in the face of his sexy hidden depths.

Nature has a lot to answer for. Your body brews a

potent cocktail to put you in a state of erotic obsession. I know this, but I am still a hopeless addict. You can't buy opiates this strong, but you can make them at home with nothing more than a conveniently available male. Regardless of his marital status.

Last night I finished the Murakami and I am ready to dazzle Professor Brownlow with my insights.

What insights? asks the tree. This is a very insightful question.

To be honest, I have borrowed most of my insights into Murakami from Google. But intellectual appropriation is the new black as far as I'm concerned. *Idiosyncratic humour, poignant nostalgia, alienation and loneliness*. I jot these down in my notebook so I won't forget them.

The other interesting thing I read about Murakami is that he likes to run. This is an understatement. Murakami likes to run in the way a fish likes to swim. He runs ten kilometres every day, more if he is training for a marathon. He has said that everything he knows about writing he has learnt from running. I find this hard to fathom. What would you learn about writing from running?

I wonder if I should take up running. I have tried it once or twice before, but the trouble is – it hurts my legs. Perhaps *that* is the point: it hurts, but you keep going. *Take up running*, I write in my notebook. I will start tomorrow. It is too late today.

I get out of bed and, in keeping with my mood and the weather, I wear brown.

Sally calls at seven o'clock as I am munching Vegemite toast in the hammock. 'Hustle, hit and never quit,' she says by way of hello.

Sometimes I think Sally is from a different planet. On Sally's planet everyone is upbeat and rah rah all the time. They believe that anything is possible, you just need to live the dream and that life is not a dress rehearsal.

Personally, I am hopeful that my life *is* a dress rehearsal. In that case, I might be able to get it right next time. 'I'm not in the mood for life coaching. Go on without me in your quest to bring fulfilment to the masses,' I say.

'ANT.'

'I get depressed when I can't think negative thoughts. I'm getting withdrawal symptoms. Too much optimism gets me down.'

'You're cross with me, aren't you?'

'No.'

'I saw you on the beach last night.'

'So what?'

'You are such a liar sometimes, Edie.'

'What did I say?'

'That you don't fancy Jay.'

'I don't. I don't like his aura.'

'Okay, just checking. Thought you might have been cross with me for flirting. Since when were you into auras, anyway?'

'Hey, I grew up on the north coast. It goes with the territory. His is spiky. Mine is soft and fuzzy. I feel like I might get stuck on his spikes if I get too close.'

Sally laughs. 'Jesus, Ed, you make things hard for yourself. Okay, let's do the coaching. Do you believe that within yourself there is the potential to make real and positive change?'

'Um ...'

'Yes, is the correct answer,' says Sal.

'Yes.' *Herr commandant.*

'Do you want to clarify your personal values and live your purpose in life?' Sally's voice has the ringing beat of a television evangelist.

'Yes.' I click my heels. I would stand to attention, but it's hard in a hammock.

'Your task for today is to do something you would normally never do. Something fun and exciting.' Her voice rises. 'Something ... spontaneous.'

'Hallelujah, sister.' I throw my spare hand in the air. 'Like what?'

Sally sighs. I have disappointed her. 'It's spontaneous, Edie. I can't tell you or it wouldn't be spontaneous, would it?'

'You could give me some tips.'

'Spontaneity just happens. You follow your instincts, you take yourself by surprise. You do something on a whim. That is the objective of the exercise.'

'That sort of thing doesn't usually work out very well for me. I'm better at planned stuff. Give me a few days and I'll think of something spontaneous to do.'

'Ha ha,' says Sal. 'It had better be good, Ed, or I'm going to use you as a case study of what happens to people who don't take their life coach's advice.'

'What if I don't want to do it? Can I terminate our contract?'

'No, you can't. You're my only client and I'm hanging on to you.'

'Sieg heil, mein führer.' *Me and Sal. Sal and me.* Sometimes I think my relationship with the bonsai might be more functional.

Be spontaneous, I write in my notebook.

Inside, Rochelle is lying on the lounge-room floor lifting a barbell. Her iPod and speakers are blaring out Michael Jackson. She is wearing flimsy nylon shorts and a singlet that shows off her toned arms. 'Training.' She puffs. 'For the All Girls.'

The All Girls is the only all-female surf competition in Australia, held here in Darling Head. Practically every year of my life, Dad has asked me if I am going to enter. He has left the brochures lying around and dropped not-too-subtle hints. The chances of me entering the All Girls are rather less than that of resurrecting the dodo. I change the subject before Rochelle asks me if I'm going to enter. 'You like Michael Jackson?' I ask.

Rochelle puts down her barbell and sits up. 'Good rhythm for weight training.'

'Thriller' starts. I have to admit it's pretty catchy. Poor old Michael Jackson. Poor old Michael Jackson's children. 'What do you think about Blanket as a name for a child?' I ask.

Rochelle laughs. 'It's not as bad as Moon Unit or Dweezil.'

I have no idea what she's talking about.

'Frank Zappa's kids.'

I decide I have much to be grateful for. I could have been called Sex Wax or Wipeout.

The church on my way to work is telling me that forbidden fruit creates many jams. I frown, thinking of Professor Brownlow. This is rather close to the bone. A balding man in a pressed blue shirt stands next to the sign. He has the freshly scrubbed look I associate with Christians. He catches my eye and I accelerate away. I have a creepy feeling that he can see the evil Sooty Beaumont lurking beneath my mild-mannered Edie exterior.

At work, the beautiful and mysterious Professor Brownlow also seems to be in a sombre mood but he smiles as I slide the Murakami towards him.

'Thank you for that, Ralph. Very idiosyncratic humour, isn't it?' I try not to think of him lifting me up onto the laboratory bench and having his way with me, but, of course, this is the only thing I can think of. My mind is not the humble servant I wish it would be.

'It was interesting the way he fell in love with that girl, just for her ears.' His eyes flicker to the side of my head as he says this.

I don't recall the ears part, but a warm glow spreads through me anyway. This is a man who understands desire. How many men would recognise that even the ears of the beloved have special powers? I am jelly, custard, trifle in his hands. He can have me any way he wants me. Bugger the karma. I am just about to agree with him when he frowns.

111

'No, that was a different Murakami book.'

'It sounds like a good one.'

'Do you like Japanese authors?' he asks.

My mind flickers to Sooty Beaumont and her Japanese lover. I rein it in. 'Oh, yes,' I coo. 'They have such poignant nostalgia, such alienation and loneliness.' It is lucky I prepared for this conversation. In fact, although I love to read, Japanese authors have never been my thing. All that contemplation of cherry blossoms and mountains left me cold. But after reading the Murakami I am having second thoughts.

Professor Brownlow's eyes meet mine and he smiles a smile of such beauty, such purpose and intent it illuminates me from inside. And even though he doesn't say any more, I am sure we have connected in a very, very meaningful way.

I drift off to my microscope and the first three zoeas of the day are drawn in a haze of sexual fantasy. It is the way to go; from a job satisfaction, if not work quality, point of view.

Then, just when I thought zoeas held no surprises for me I encounter The Evil Zoea. Unlike its cute relatives this one has a sinister face. The pointy horn on top of its head is longer and sharper-looking than the others. Its eyes are bulgier, protruding from its face like high-wattage searchlights.

Last night Dad brought the *Attack of the Crab Monsters* DVD home. As sappy as it was to see crabs being wheeled around a sinking island, my subconscious thinks otherwise. *Crabs are evil.* Slow drumbeats start up as I adjust the focus. *From the depths of the sea – a tidal wave of terror.* I avoid the zoea's eye as I draw it, lest it turn me into a crazed zombie who would strangle Professor Brownlow with my super-strong zombie hands.

Zoea number five is as innocuous and dull as its predecessors. *Thank goodness.* I make a mental note to avoid crustacean-themed horror in the future.

At lunchtime I remember I am supposed to do something spontaneous and fun. I sigh. I am not in the mood, but I pick up my backpack and stand up. Professor Brownlow is on the phone, but he smiles at me as I wave to show I am going out. I take this smile as proof that he is harbouring fantasies about me too. I sigh again. Such a shame he is married.

I almost bump into Professor Brownlow's wife on the way out.

'Hello, Edie.' Today she is wearing lycra bicycle shorts and holding a helmet. Her cheeks are a healthy shade of pink. She has obviously been cycling hard.

I blush hotly and resolve to stop fantasising about Professor Brownlow at once. Or at least as soon as possible. 'Hello.'

She runs her hand through her thick blonde hair and studies my face. 'You look like you've had a bit of sun.'

Considering the weather, I am unsure how to take this remark. 'Mmm, went to the beach yesterday,' I mumble.

She smiles and continues into the lab.

Usually I sit under a tree and read a book while I eat my sandwich but today it is raining, so I couldn't do this, even if I was allowed to. In search of something spontaneous and fun I trudge through the rain towards the refectory, holding my backpack over my head. I can hear music as I get nearer. This is good. I will see a band. It will be spontaneous! And fun! I am a diligent student, Sally will be proud of me.

Swinging my dripping backpack, I push through the heavy doors. The student refectory is a huge expanse of plastic tables and chairs. Only about a quarter of the tables are filled with students eating salad rolls and drinking Coke. The room has terrible acoustics. The chatter of the students and the pounding rain almost drown out the music.

At the front of the room is a low stage covered in grey carpet. A lone figure stands on this carpet with an electric guitar. He is dressed in black and is more Nick Cave than Nick Cave, more Chris Martin than Chris Martin. He is, of course, Jay.

I slink into a chair near the back of the room as he finishes his song. I don't want him to see me – he might think I'm stalking him.

'This song is one I wrote myself.' The microphone squeals and Jay bends to adjust a knob. 'It's called "Tangled Web".'

And then he sings the song I'd heard on the radio.

You left me here
Thinking I was part of you,
Thinking we were two halves of the whole.
You looked at me

As if I was the answer
Though you didn't know the question.

But now he said, she said, they said,
You're moving on
And I was just a rest stop
Not a destination.
He said, she said, they said,
You're a spider in a web
A tangled web.

The way he sings it is so beautiful it almost makes me cry, but when I look around I realise I am the only one watching. Everyone else is chatting, texting, eating hot chips and laughing at stupid jokes.

And it is almost unbearable to me. That he should expose his heart like that and no one cares.

I get to my feet and leave before he sees me.

On my way out I almost fall over a black cat that is sitting in the doorway watching Jay intently. It gives me a supercilious look before turning back to Jay. I feel uncouth – rather as if my phone had gone off during a chamber music recital.

'Sorry,' I mutter and push open the door.

Dad is mending the stairs when I come home. Our house has a lot of wooden stairs and Dad has been mending them my entire life. I can't remember a time when I could come up to our house without having to skip at least one stair.

Dad pauses in his hammering as I step past him. 'Nice little waves today,' he says.

Why does he always say this sort of thing to me? It is like he thinks I am someone else. How can my father and I have spent the best part of twenty-three years in each other's company without him realising that I am not that surf-crazy kid he has in his head.

Darling Head is full of sun-bleached, wiry bundles of energy who live for nothing but the next take-off. The streets are packed with them, my classrooms were packed with them, but I am not one of them.

I wonder if Donald Bradman was as persistent as my father. *Sorry, Dad, I'm just not that into balls*, I can imagine John saying.

At what age did Mary Magdalene realise that young Sarah wasn't a chip off the old block? *Here's a glass of water, Sarah. No, don't drink it, have a go at turning it into wine.*

At what stage does the parent of the child failure face up to reality? If my father is to be taken as the example – never. One would think the fact I haven't been in the water since I was twelve would be a clue, but no, there is a part of his brain that seems unable to believe that I might not enjoy surfing.

'Good waves, huh? Great.' I smile at Dad and continue up the stairs.

Chapter Twelve

The paranoid is never entirely mistaken.

SIGMUND FREUD

Saturday: 49 days
Pain level: 7.8
Location: Shifting between chest and upper intestine
Tips for self-improvement: Start running tomorrow

Sally comes over on Saturday morning. I haven't started my Murakami running program yet as I slept in. I will start tomorrow. We sit on the hammock and swing together, hips and shoulders touching. It is child-like, fun.

'So what spontaneous thing did you do yesterday?' she asks on the down-swing.

I don't want to tell her about Jay. It would feel like a betrayal. 'Look, there's a whale.' I point to the horizon.

'Where?'

'There.'

'I can't see it.'

'Look harder.'

By the time Sally has given up looking for the whale, I have my answer. 'I started a Facebook group for people who are into crustaceans.'

'Is that, like, a sexual thing?' asks Sally as we swing up.

I hadn't got that far, but now I decide it's definitely the way to go. 'Yeah, it's a type of fetish. Quite rare. In fact, no one else has joined yet. I'm sure they're out there, though. Crustaceans are terribly sexy. Did you know if human sperm was proportional to a shrimp's it would be the size of a semi-trailer?'

Sally screws up her nose. 'How does that work?'

I flap my hand. 'Where there's a will there's a way.'

We swing to and fro again. As I lean back, I catch a glimpse of a small tattoo on Sally's lower back above her cut-off jeans. This is an old one, a deer with spreading antlers. 'Remember that holiday we had in New Zealand after we finished school?'

Sally and I had planned to walk the Milford Track. I'd imagined us strolling across alpine meadows as rainbows danced across the valleys. We hadn't realised you needed to book the track about nine months in advance.

'What was the name of that place we ended up in?' asks Sal.

'Glenorchy.'

'Rains a lot there, doesn't it?'

'Yep.'

'How was that cabin?'

'You mean the dog kennel. I felt like I was in Guantanamo Bay.'

'No wonder we spent so much time in the pub.'

'That guy you hooked up with ...' I eye her tattoo.

'Travis.'

'That's right. Travis the deer hunter.'

'He hunted possums too,' says Sal.

'Do you think he was really a deer hunter?'

'Oh yeah. When I went to his room he showed me his gun and his camo gear.' She gives me a suggestive look. 'Why?'

'He seemed a bit pseudo to me.'

'You've never said that before.'

'No, but I thought it. His hands were too soft. I reckon he was an accountant,' I tease. 'From Auckland. Or Wellington.'

'No way.' Sally screws up her face. 'No way would I shag an accountant from Auckland.'

'Exactly. That's why he was pretending to be a Fiordland deer hunter. Much sexier.' I lean back to get a better look at her tattoo. 'You could get a calculator tattooed over the top of it if you wanted.'

Sally squeals and pushes me.

I fall backwards off the hammock and land on the deck with a thump. 'Ow, that was reckless, Sally; you could have —'

'Don't you ever say that again, Edie McElroy. Travis was a he-man. He hunted deer from helicopters. He wore big lace-up boots. He was macho and sweaty and strong and ... You think I don't know the difference between an

119

accountant and a deer hunter? He was totally essence of Heathcliff.'

'Edgar Linton.' I say this as if I am sneezing, but Sally gets it.

She leaps off the hammock and pins me to the ground. 'He was not Edgar Linton. Travis was more Heathcliff than Heathcliff. He was sexy as. You remember that scene in *Wuthering Heights* where he undoes his buttons really slowly.'

'I don't think that happened, Sal.'

'Yes, it did and that's what Travis was like. Do you want me to tickle you?'

'Okay, he was Heathcliff.' I start to laugh. 'I give up. Don't tickle me.'

Sally smiles and gets off me. 'That's what I thought.'

Sometimes Sally and I seem more like competitive siblings than best friends. I guess that's what happens when you've known someone most of your life.

We get back in the hammock again and push off.

'You can hold your meetings in the Big Prawn.' Sal changes topics with breathtaking speed.

'Huh?' The Big Prawn is a ghastly monstrosity that decorates the highway not far from Darling Head, but I haven't got a clue what she is talking about.

'Your crab fetish meetings.'

'Yeah. If we ever have a get-together that would totally be the place to do it.'

'Oh my God,' says Sal. 'Imagine the size of the sperm the Big Prawn would produce.'

'Sally, there are some things in life you're better off not thinking about.'

We swing back and forth in silence for a few minutes. I, at least, lose the fight not to think about giant sperm.

'I think Professor Brownlow might be interested in my Facebook group if I introduce it to him in the right way,' I say.

'Ralph Brownlow? Is he your boss?'

'Yeah, do you know him?'

'He's a client.'

'Get outta here.' I push off the wall. 'No way.'

'Yes way, babe. My first paying client. He called me yesterday. Guess I've got you to thank for that.'

'So ...' I raise my eyebrows. 'Which of the eight steps is he interested in?'

'Can't say. Client confidentiality.'

'Piss off.'

'No, really.'

Sally sounds serious, so I back off. 'Have you met him?'

'We're meeting downtown this afternoon. Anything I should know?'

'Yes, but I can't say. Workplace confidentiality.'

Sally tickles me. 'Come on, tell me. Is he gay?' She looks at me. 'Not gay, then, sleazy?'

I squirm away from her probing fingers. 'No, he's ... hot.' This comes out a lot louder than I meant it to as I am laughing at the time.

Jay steps out on the verandah as I say this. He takes in Sally and I on the hammock. 'Who's hot?'

I blush. Does he think I was talking about him? 'No one.'

'Hey.' Sally cleverly steers the conversation away from hotness. 'It's fancy-dress night down the surf club tonight. Why don't we all go?'

'No way,' I say.

'Okay,' says Jay at the same time.

Sally gives me a meaningful look and rustles one of her flyers in her hands. She is reminding me I am her star client.

'I hate fancy dress,' I say.

Jay collapses on the couch in the sun and closes his eyes. As usual, he is dressed in black: a tattered long-sleeved shirt and skinny jeans. 'Fancy dress is so much fun,' he says.

I suspect he is being ironic, but I can't be sure.

'What will you go as, Jay?' asks Sally.

'I'm tossing up between a fairy and a dolphin.' His eyes are still shut. 'Maybe a fairy dolphin.'

I giggle, but he doesn't smile. I bite my lip.

Sally raises her eyebrows at me. 'I knew you were a hippy at heart,' she says to Jay.

'Yeah.' Jay opens one eye, squinting into the sun. 'I'd go as a hippy if I had longer hair.' He opens his other eye and fixes his gaze on me. 'You should go as a hippy.'

As always with Jay, it is hard to know if there is a hidden meaning to his comment.

Sally, however, latches on to this as if it is the greatest suggestion ever. 'That would be perfect for you, Edie.'

I can't see how being a dope-smoking remnant of the sixties is perfect for me, but I can't resist the combined tide of Sally and Jay's will. 'Okay. I'll go as a hippy.' I feel sick already.

Sally climbs out of the hammock. 'Let's print out a few more of my flyers and stick them in some letterboxes, Edie. I'm on a roll now, I can feel it. Do you want to help, Jay?'

'Love to, but I'm flat out.' Jay closes his eyes again.

We go upstairs and I print out about one hundred flyers on my computer and fold them into neat packages. Sally does the odd one, but mainly she is occupied taking a phone call. She wanders over to the window and coos, clucks and chirps. It is obviously a man.

She rolls her eyes as she slides the phone in her pocket. 'Francisco calling from Rio. Wants to come out here. I managed to fob him off, I think.'

Francisco doesn't realise that once Sally has the tat, the relationship is dead meat.

'All done, Ed?' She picks up the bundle of flyers.

We spend the morning posting them all around Darling Head. As it turns out, I do most of the posting too as Sally is waylaid in conversations with passers-by every five minutes or so. When she is not chatting she is sending and receiving texts.

'Who are you texting?' I ask her at one point.

She winks at me. 'Not texting, sexting.'

'You didn't tell me you had a new guy.'

'Nah, I don't really – just playing. You should get into this, Ed; it's so much fun.'

'Who am I going to sext with? Where do you meet these people?'

'All over the place. Fifty per cent of the population is male, you know. I met this guy at the supermarket yesterday. He's really hot. You remember how Heathcliff used to tell Cathy that he was burning up for her?'

'I don't remember that part.'

'You need to reread it, Ed. That's what this guy's like.'

Sexting a guy I met at the shop yesterday seems about as achievable to me as flying to Jupiter on my own steam. Sally and I are definitely living in parallel universes.

'I'm working up a new coaching module,' says Sal. 'Opportunistic flirting.'

'Oh yeah?' Why am I getting an uneasy feeling that this is not good news? 'You're the woman for the job, Sal. I'm sure you'll be good at it.'

'My theory is that most people go through life totally blind to the flirting prospects that arise every day.'

'You're probably —'

'I'm talking about people like you.'

I knew it. She's lining something up for me. How can I head her off at the pass? 'I flirt all the time. Why only yesterday ...' And now I wish that Sally would interrupt me as I have no idea where I am going with this.

Sally cocks her head to one side. She is wearing her mock-alert look, as if she can't wait to hear what I say next.

'Only yesterday ...' I rack my brain, trying to think of a man I have interacted with. 'There was this guy, standing outside a building as I drove past and ...' *What would Sooty do?* 'I winked at him.'

'Winked?' Sally smiles like a trashy investigative journalist who knows her subject is lying. 'Like this?' She gives me a slow, cheeky, adorable wink. Sally's wink could double as a résumé. Sally's wink tells me that she is a fun-loving girl with a lively intelligence and a positive attitude towards casual sex. 'Show me how you winked.'

She has backed me into a blind alley and she knows it. I am unable to wink without scrunching up half my face like a Benny Hill impersonator. My wink could also double as a résumé, but it is one best kept in the bottom drawer. My wink says I am a strange, sad person who should be avoided if possible.

'Who was this man you winked at?' Sally pushes her advantage.

I can see no more point in pretending. 'A priest.'

Sally bursts out laughing. Tears run down her face. Eventually she brings herself under control. 'You're the sweetest person I know, Ed, but you desperately need taking in hand.' She gives me a one-armed hug. 'Stick with me, babe. I'll find you someone better than a priest.'

At twelve o'clock Sally leaves for her meeting with Professor Brownlow. 'I'll come and get you at seven,' she calls as we wave goodbye across the street. 'I'm expecting groovy things, man.'

My route home takes me past the beachside café strip. I am pondering my hippy outfit when someone calls my name.

'Edie?'

I swivel. A woman with glossy, asymmetrical black hair and enormous black sunglasses is sitting in the café. She has an iPad in front of her and is wearing one of those earpieces people use to talk on mobile phones without getting irradiated. Colourful drawings are spread out on the table in front of her coffee cup.

'Djennifer?'

The woman slides her sunglasses up to the top of her head and stands up. Soon I am enveloped in a soft, warm hug. Djennifer is wearing a floaty black top over black tights. Each of her plump, white arms support about twenty chunky bracelets, and rings adorn her black-nail-polished pedicured toes. Among the suntanned surf-label-wearing denizens of Darling Head, she stands out like a penguin in a desert.

'What are you doing here?' I ask.

'What are *you* doing here?'

'I live here.'

'You live here? *HERE?*' Djennifer squeals. 'This is paradise.'

I look around. It has never occurred to me to think of Darling Head as paradise. It is just the place I grew up in. The place I couldn't wait to leave. 'It's okay. So what are you doing here?'

'Holiday, darling. What else? I'm staying at the Sands Resort in Lighthouse Bay.' Djennifer waves her hand vaguely northwards. 'I'm working on a new range.' She sighs and gestures at the table. 'I needed some creative space.'

Djennifer is the owner of Hotpunk, my former boss.

126

She never took much notice of me while I was there. In a cutting-edge design outlet, catalogue illustrators are barely one step above mail boys. I always found it hard to explain to people what Hotpunk actually sold. Cool stuff, I'd say. *You should see their teapots.* This sounded ridiculous, but Hotpunk's teapots were as much about making tea as a Van Gogh is about hiding a damp patch on the wall. Hotpunk's teapots had attitude.

'How's the latest range going?'

'It's crap, darling. That's why I'm here. I need to reconnect with my inner muse. Something just came into my consciousness and I thought ... Lighthouse Bay, that's the place.' Djennifer's phone plays a techno beat. 'Mwah, mwah.' She purses her lips. 'Lovely to see you, Edie.' She picks up her phone. 'What is it now?' She waggles her fingers at me and rolls her eyes as I go.

At home, I wish with a vengeance I had not agreed to go to the fancy-dress party. Why do people like fancy dress so much? I think girls like it because they get to dress up as tarts without being taken for one. Halloween party means sexy witch, seventies means minidress and a celebrity theme is always Paris Hilton in a bikini.

For guys, it's different. Guys can never resist an opportunity to dress up as a woman. It shows how jealous they are of the primping and preening that is a woman's right. False eyelashes? Yes please! Lipstick? Of course! Fishnet stockings? Bring it on!

In some cultures it is the men who get all the gewgaws and make-up. I've read about an African tribe where the men court the ladies with the aid of lipstick, face powder and feathers in their hair. I wonder if the women of this tribe harbour a secret desire to snatch the powder and feathers off their men. Perhaps they do.

Being a hippy offers none of the satisfaction of dressing up as a tart. I look in the mirror and wonder where to start. If I mess my hair up a bit it looks long and shaggy, like Janis Joplin's, but I'm not sure about any of the rest of it.

I go downstairs. Dad and Rochelle have been surfing all morning and are now stretched out on the couch, flicking through ski brochures. This is another shared passion of theirs. When they are not surfing, they are thinking about skiing. They look like salt-streaked bookends, Dad with his feet on Rochelle's lap and Rochelle with her feet on Dad's.

I wasn't here when Dad and Rochelle met but I imagine it as being like two oppositely charged magnets coming together. While I am cynical about the concept of The One, it was obvious when I met Rochelle that there was no other way of describing the way they are together.

I am happy for Dad, how could I not be, but it also makes me feel strange. As if, in a parallel universe where we all meet our soul mates at exactly the right time, Dad and Rochelle are breeding a tribe of surfing champions. In this parallel universe there is, clearly, no place for me. I am my mother's daughter. As Rochelle is only thirty-six to Dad's forty-five, I suppose the option of a troupe, if not a tribe of surfing champions is still out there.

'Hey,' I say.

They both look up. 'Hey Eddie,' they say, simultaneously. It's a little spooky.

'I'm going to a fancy dress tonight as a hippy. Have you got anything I could wear?'

Dad and Rochelle look at each other, then back at me and I already wish I hadn't said anything. The sparkle in their eyes suggests they are latching onto this project with way too much enthusiasm. They jump to their feet. 'Let's have a look,' says Rochelle.

Dad and Rochelle's room is upstairs, like mine. Rochelle has two built-in cupboards and Dad has one. They pull open their cupboard doors in a *ta-da* way, as if they expect to see a hippy costume hanging there, waiting.

Rochelle's cupboard displays Quiksilver T-shirts, Roxy shorts, Billabong bikinis and Volcom jeans.

Dad's cupboard reveals Rip Curl T-shirts, Mambo shorts and Quiksilver jeans. There is, also, an embroidered waistcoat of unknown ethnic origin. 'Ah ha.' He pulls this from its hanger. 'That's what you need.'

Rochelle presses a pair of white flared pants and a long silky scarf on me. 'You'll look great, Edie. Fancy dress is so much fun.' Unlike her brother, there is no hint of irony.

I go upstairs, put on the pants and waistcoat and knot the scarf around my head so that the ends trail down my back. If I cross my eyes, put my head on its side and don't go too close to the mirror, I look like Janis Joplin might if she was halfway through transforming into Jimmy Page. 'Far out, man.' I hold my fingers up in a peace sign. I suspect it's not going to get any better, so I take the outfit off and put it in a pile on the bed.

I now have five hours before Sally will pick me up. Five hours to think of reasons why I can't go to the fancy dress anymore. I pull my notebook towards me. These will have to be good reasons; Sally is not easily deterred. I start a list.

1. I am sick

I chew on my pen. This will only work if I have evidence, for example, a temperature. Still, there are ways ...

2. I have nothing to wear.

I suspect Sally will not take any notice of this one. She will be expecting it, and will already have an answer prepared, maybe even a spare outfit.

3. I am too busy.

I am already scraping the bottom of the barrel and I am only up to number three. What can I be busy doing? Could there be a crab larvae emergency of some kind?

This brings me back to Professor Brownlow. I wonder how Sally is going. I am keen to hear her opinion of Professor Brownlow's hotness. Now, why would he be having life coaching? One of Sally's flyers is on my desk. I pick it up and glance through the eight steps.

Career direction, life purpose, self-expression, business coaching, mentoring, relationships ... I stop there, remembering Professor Brownlow and his wife the other day. Is he having relationship problems? Maybe there is an opening for me to comfort him? *No, Edie. Bad karma.*

I fling the flyer back on the bed. It falls face down. I stare at the back. There is some typing on it. A sentence jumps out at me, *'Take me now,' she cried, 'you sexy fiddler crab.'* I don't understand why there is pornography on the back of Sally's flyer.

Then I realise; it is my pornography. My mind flashes back to Sally and I printing and folding the flyers. I see one of her hands taking the paper from my recycled paper pile and putting it in the printer while the other holds the phone to her ear.

No, it can't be.

But I already know what has happened. We have printed off the flyers on my recycled paper. My erotic story has been strewn all around town. I feel like I am falling off a high-rise building. I am about to vomit.

I do vomit.

Chapter Thirteen

No mortal can keep a secret.

SIGMUND FREUD

I run out into the street. I have tucked my hair up into a baseball cap and put on my biggest sunglasses. I am incognito. I am not Edie McElroy the pornographic writer, I am … Anonymous.

Feverishly panting, I trace the route Sally and I covered this morning. Flicking my eyes sideways, I slide my hand in through the slot of the first letterbox. I feel around. It is dusty. Something scuttles away from under my fingers. But otherwise …

It is empty.

It is empty.

It is empty!

Our flyer has been taken inside. My sinful words have entered the bosom of an innocent Darling Head family. I am tempted to rend my T-shirt and wail, but I must press on.

The next letterbox is empty and the next and the

next. Now I do wail momentarily and claw at my chest in a deranged way, before pulling myself together. On the fourth letterbox I score. Slipping the flyer back out through the opening, I offer up a silent prayer to God, Allah and Gaia as I unfold it and turn to the back. *Please let the flyer at home be a black sheep and the rest as pure as mountain dew.*

'*Like the brine from the Sea of Japan,*' *he murmured, tasting with his dexterous tongue.* The words jump out at me like a psycho killer in a horror movie. I clutch my heaving chest. My mouth opens in a silent howl. I probably look like that painting *The Scream* by Munch. A seagull flies overhead, depositing a shit on the letterbox. It is clearly a metaphor.

Summoning reserves of emotional strength I didn't know I possessed, I stuff the flyer in my pocket and stagger to the next letterbox.

It is empty. As is the next. Then ... '*That's a particularly fine pair of plumose hairs,*' *said a melodious baritone voice behind her.* I crumple the paper in my sweaty hands and run on. My crab-fetish pornography has spread like a plague through Darling Head. I am tainted, tainted ... a scarlet woman, doomed to be shunned by all upright citizens. Damage limitation is all I can hope for.

I slip my hand into the next letterbox and touch the sharp edges of the flyer. A horrible black dog barks at me as I pull the flyer out through the opening.

'Hey,' says a woman's voice behind me. 'What are you doing in my letterbox?'

I don't turn. I hold the flyer scrunched in my hand.

'What's that?' A hand reaches out for the flyer. 'That's my mail.' She grasps it.

There is a short tussle before I pull away, stuff the flyer in my mouth and chew rapidly.

The woman watches me. She has a suntanned face, bottle-blonde hair and a freckled chest exposed in a V-neck T-shirt. Her eyes meet mine. She is the mother of a girl I went to school with. Her indignation turns to pity as she recognises me. 'Are you all right, Edie?'

I nod. 'Yes thanks, Mrs Mathews.' Small pieces of flyer spit from my mouth, decorating her red shirt.

'Do you want me to call your father?'

I shake my head and stroll off, swallowing hard, aiming for an air of nonchalance. Eating paper is not as easy as they make it look in the Bond movies. I don't dare search any other letterboxes in that street.

As I drag my weary feet around Darling Head, a reprised version of my 'Twelve Days of Christmas' keeps running through my head. On the twelfth day of Christmas, my true love sent to me …

Three drug dealers,
Two millionaire developers,
And a writer of porn-o-graphy.

Is this to be my fate? To be pointed at in the street? To have mothers pulling their children away from me? To be a figure of derision in my own town? Looking on the positive side, the drug dealers might still hang out with me and one of them is kind of cute.

By the time I get home I have only collected twenty of the one hundred flyers Sally and I dispersed. I plod up the stairs, considering my options:

Leave the country;
Have an identity change; or
Commit suicide.

What would Sooty Beaumont do? She would raise one elegant eyebrow, paint her toenails scarlet and laugh about it with Sven, her Swedish lover. But, alas, I am not Sooty and I cannot live in a town where I am known as a pornographic writer. I feel as naked and embarrassed as a snail with its shell removed.

It is just my luck Jay is sitting on the verandah strumming his guitar. Doesn't he have anything better to do?

He looks up as I climb the last stair. 'Hey.' He says this with no irony, no satire. He even smiles.

I am so grateful I find myself blinking back tears. I run upstairs before he can see.

In my bedroom, I pull out my notebook and upgrade my daily pain rating.

Saturday (still): 49 days

Pain level: 10

Location: All over, but especially stomach

Tips for self-improvement: Leave country and start again with a new identity.

The bonsai gives me a disdainful look.

'One word and you're woodchips.'

It could hardly get much worse, says the bonsai. Another leaf falls from a branch. *I knew that erotic writing was a bad idea. Who do you think you are? Anaïs Nin? Wait until Daniel finds out about it.*

I sink down on the bed and emit the tortured moan of a seal in pain.

You have no one but yourself to blame, says the bonsai.

'But the erotic writing never would have happened if I hadn't been badly affected by lack of sex. It's all Daniel's fault.'

Sex? The bonsai sneers. *Who needs sex? I'm perfectly fine without it.*

I eye its wilting leaves, its dried-out branches, and somehow I don't feel reassured at all.

I am Googling flights to Tokyo when Sally arrives at seven. I've heard it's pretty easy to get a job teaching English there. Maybe I can line something up before I go. A strange Japanese influence is taking over my life. First the bonsai, then the Murakami, and now –

'Peace, love and dope, Edie,' Sally calls up the stairs.

I have no idea what she is talking about. Then it all comes back to me. She thinks I am still going to the fancy dress. This is out of the question. I have flights to book, jobs to apply for. Japanese to practise, bags to pack ...

'Edie, what are you doing?' Sally opens my door.

'Wow. Big hair.'

Sally's hair is teased to puffy perfection. She is wearing a white T-shirt and white shorts with a polka-dotted scarf tied around her neck. White Dunlop Volleys complete her outfit. She looks both cute and trendy.

'Jessica Simpson?'

She shakes her head.

'Marie Antoinette?'

She frowns. 'Do you see me wearing a crinoline?'

'I know, I know,' I snap my fingers. 'Farrah Fawcett-Majors.'

'Good evening, Charlie,' she drawls, pulling a toy gun from her shorts. She twirls her gun and replaces it in her holster. 'So, what's the story, man? Where's the outfit?' Her eyes scan the room, alighting on my forgotten pile. 'Ah ha.' She picks up the waistcoat and pants. 'Time to get funky.'

Chapter Fourteen

The mind is like an iceberg, it floats
with one-seventh of its bulk above
water.

SIGMUND FREUD

The surf club is packed with superheroes, Paris Hiltons, men dressed as women and the odd Dracula. A four-piece cover band called Cod Play is playing 'Yellow'. The singer is nowhere near as good as Jay. I'd like to tell him this, but it seems too hard. We fight our way onto the verandah. A salty breeze blows in off the sea.

Jay hasn't come as a fairy dolphin at all. He is Elvis – the young and sexy version, not the debauched, fat one. He has big hair too, swept back from his face. He has abandoned black for a white suit with a black collared shirt underneath. He manages to make this look both ironic and cool.

My hippy outfit has none of the sex appeal of Farrah Fawcett-Majors and none of the cool irony of Elvis. I am both sexless and nerdy. I suspect Sally and Jay would prefer I wasn't here, so they could get on with what is obviously on their minds. They are bantering and flirting like two doves in heat. I am extraneous to their needs. It is nice of them to pretend they like me though. I wonder if Jay will rate a tattoo and, if so, what sort. A guitar, perhaps.

Sally keeps giving me looks when Jay's head is turned away. I am familiar with most of Sally's looks. The 'slight eyebrow raise with widened eyes' look falls into the 'pay attention' category. This look was useful in school for a whole range of things; generally to indicate couples whose actions suggested they had started to go out.

Now, however, I am unsure what I am supposed to be paying attention to. Sally touches Jay's arm and gives me 'the look'. She runs her tongue over her lips; again, 'the look'. She tosses her hair and giggles. At last I get it. She is teaching me how to flirt.

'Got all that?' she asks, as Jay leaves on a mission to buy drinks.

'Yep.' As Elvis's hairdo recedes into the crowd, I try to think of a way to distract Sally from enrolling me in flirt school.

'Right, let's get you —'

'Lisa-Marie wasn't exactly a big success, was she?'

'Lisa-Marie who?'

'Presley.' I incline my chin towards Jay. 'Imagine being the daughter of the king. Almost as bad as having Jesus for a father.'

'That's pretty random, Ed. Now, about flirt—'

'What do you know about Lisa-Marie?'

'She was married to Michael Jackson.'

'Exactly. She's put out a couple of albums but all anyone is ever going to remember is that she was married to Michael Jackson.'

'Tragic.' Sally's eyes roam around the bar.

'Hey, there's Djennifer.' Down on the beach in front of the surf club, a plump figure in a black unitard is spotlighted in the moonlight. She holds her hands up, as if worshipping, then bends forward into a yoga pose. 'I used to work for her in Sydney.'

Sally rolls her eyes. 'I've never seen the point of yoga. Sex is way better for you. Speaking of which, we need to find someone for you to practise your flirting on.'

'I think I need another demonstration first. And a drink, definitely a drink.'

'Okay, watch this.'

Along from us on the verandah a guy and a girl are leaning out over the railing. The guy is blandly handsome: swept-back brown hair, athletic. As the girl turns away to talk to her friend, Sally catches his eye. She doesn't look away, holding his gaze. His eyes widen slightly. Sally gives him her résumé wink. He smiles, his eyes give a guilty flicker sideways, then he winks back. I'm almost convinced he's about to abandon his girlfriend until she possessively takes his arm.

Sally looks back at me. 'Easy, huh?'

'Sally. That was very naughty.'

'Harmless fun. He got a kick out of it.'

The guy keeps looking over at Sally. He is hoping for another wink but she has lost interest.

Sally watches Jay's back as he somehow glides to the front of the pack at the bar. 'He's cool, isn't he?'

'He seems cool.'

Sally cocks her head. 'What do you mean?'

I shrug. I don't know what I mean. Partly it was just something to say and partly it is a feeling I have about Jay. I can't put this into words. It is intangible, just out of reach, a vibration too low to hear. 'He has hidden depths.'

Sally snorts. 'What is it with you and hidden depths? Why do you think things are better, just because they're hidden? I mean, if something's hidden, it's usually for a good reason.'

'Oh, Sally,' I sigh. 'Hidden depths are the most wonderful, wonderful thing. Don't you think that having someone served up to you on a plate is boring?'

'Uh uh.' Sally shakes her head. 'I like people to be upfront.'

'God, you don't know what you're missing out on. Men with hidden depths are just … divine.' I open and shut my mouth. I am, frankly, astonished. Doesn't everyone love hidden depths? 'It's the thrill of peeling off layers, like an onion. You think someone's one thing, then they let you get a little deeper and you find another thing. It's like being an explorer, navigating your boat deeper and deeper into the uncharted jungles of the human mind.'

Sally has a very strange expression on her face. She looks like Farrah Fawcett-Majors might if she had just encountered an escaped lunatic. Her fingers toy with her gun in a way that makes me glad it's not real.

But I don't care; I am alight with my passion. 'I would die for hidden depths. I would throw myself under a truck in defence of the right to have hidden depths.'

Sally adjusts her neck scarf. 'That would be kind of pointless, Ed.'

'But they're so exciting, like when the geeky guy turns out to be brave or a ditzy girl is actually a brain surgeon ... You've gotta love that, don't you?'

'That's only in the movies. Peel off the outer layer of most people and you just get ... ' Sally waves her hand in a circle, 'marshmallow'. She drills me with her eyes. 'If you're so big on hidden depths, what are yours?'

I think of my erotic writing, but that is somewhere I definitely don't want to go. 'You can't just tell people to reveal their hidden depths like that, Sal.' I snap my fingers. 'They have to be discovered. It's like an archaeological dig. That's what makes it fun.' Sally is making me anxious. What if I don't have any hidden depths? What if the layers of my onion reveal nothing more than Sooty Beaumont and a vague universal angst? And everyone has that. Don't they? 'Do you ever feel that everything is threatening and uncertain?' I ask Sal.

'No.' She screws up her nose. 'Why? Do you?'

'No. Never.' I shake my head. 'Absolutely not.' *Oh God, don't tell me I'm the only one.* 'I need a drink.'

I have managed to put off thinking about the flyer for the time it has taken me to get dressed and walk down to the surf club. In the end, doing what I was told was the easiest course. It was either that or tell Sally that Motive 8 is now closely linked to a pornographic crab fetish. I'd send her an email from Tokyo. My guts churn with anxiety at the thought.

'So ... Ralph,' says Sally.

'Huh?'

'Ralph. Ralph Brownlow. Your boss. You think he's hot.'

'God, yes. Don't you?'

Sally puts her head on one side. 'Short shorts and loafers?'

'You really don't think he's hot?'

Sally shakes her head.

'Really? He totally does it for me.' They should write a book – *Sally is from Earth and Edie is from Jupiter.* 'You should see him when he takes his glasses off.'

Sally frowns. 'I worry about you sometimes, Edie. You have such strange tastes.'

Sally has no idea just how strange my tastes are.

'That guy over there.' Sally inclines her head in the direction of a guy in a Batman cape.

'What?'

'Wink.'

I shake my head.

'Wink,' Sally commands. She narrows her eyes.

I eye the guy in my peripheral vision. He has a kind, roundish face. He looks relatively friendly.

Sally nudges me sharply in the ribs.

I wink, pulling up the side of my mouth, so that my eye closes.

Batman looks alarmed; he glances over his shoulder like Catwoman might have crept up behind him.

'Sexy wink.' Jay hands me a drink. He is biting his lip, trying to keep a straight face.

'That wasn't a wink. I was just ...'

'Bug in your eye?' Jay offers.

I nod. Down on the beach, Djennifer is now doing a headstand in the moonlight. I wonder if she has found her inner muse yet.

'What's this?' Sally holds up her drink. It is the same as mine, a green concoction with an umbrella poking out the side.

'Thought we'd kick off with some cocktails. They're pretty inventive with the names here. These ones are plumose hairs. Don't know where that comes from, but it sounds cool. Cheers.'

I am halfway through my first sip as he says this. I splutter. The drink sprays from my mouth across Jay's white jacket.

Jay's eyes flicker from the green splatter back to me. 'Mmm, very abstract technique, the mouth painting. Do you want to do the other side too? Even things up. Maybe I should have got you a *mandibular palpus* instead.'

I drain my drink in one gulp and shake my head. 'Sorry.' I leave Jay and Sally standing on the verandah and push my way towards the bar.

'What's in the Electric Eels, mate?' says the blond-haired surfie dressed as a Spartan standing next to me.

'Vodka, orange, Galliano.' The barman is a weatherbeaten fiftyish man. A blackboard menu behind his head is titled *Crab Cocktails to Make You Hot*. He turns to me. 'What'll it be?'

I open my mouth but only a croak comes out.

'Can't hear you, darling.'

'Fiddler crab. Three of them.' Only then do I see the bar is littered with the flyers. Someone has been photocopying them. I snatch up as many as I can. Standing at the bar, I drain my fiddler crabs one by one. They are pretty good. I am about to order three more when someone takes my arm.

I don't know how it happens, but I find myself sitting on a couch on the verandah next to Elvis. He gazes out to sea like he is thinking maybe he shouldn't have wiggled his pelvis so much in his last concert.

I follow his gaze, expecting to see Djennifer in warrior pose, but she has gone.

Elvis is looking pensive. I decide to cheer him up with some of his own music. Unfortunately my memory is a bit rusty. 'A little less da da da da, a little more traction please, all this dum de dum dum ain't satisfactioning me,' I sing, but he doesn't join in, so I stop.

'What's up?' he asks. A lick of hair has escaped his bouffant and is sliding over his eyebrow ring.

'What's up with you?' I wish he would sing for me. 'You ain't nothing but a ground hog,' I try, gesturing with my hand for him to join in. He doesn't appear to be in a singing mood, which is a shame. Perhaps he doesn't recognise the song the way I sing it. I adjust my head scarf. Perhaps he doesn't like hippies.

And then it occurs to me that there is a reason I am sitting on the couch with Elvis. I am supposed to be practising flirting. Sally must be watching me. I look around but it makes my head spin so I stop. There is a large pot plant a few metres away. She is probably hiding behind that.

I try to remember what Sally did earlier. I lick my lips and toss my hair a little. The verandah tilts in an alarming way. I stop tossing. *What next? Oh yes.* I pull the side of my face up into a wink. It seems harder than usual. I try again and think I succeed this time. I look at Elvis, waiting for him to wink back.

Elvis chews his lip. He has a very strange look on his face. Perhaps he is shy. I am not shy at all. I think I am getting quite good at this flirting. I smile in the general direction of the pot plant. *Look at me, Sally. See me flirt.*

Elvis eyes the crumpled flyers in my hand. 'Can I?' He reaches for one.

I open my hand. 'Sure. Why not? Everyone else has one. Have several.' I lick my lips and fiddle with my hair in a seductive way. *Much safer than tossing.*

I watch him as he reads. The fiddler crabs have done the job nicely. I don't feel embarrassed at all. 'You ain't never bought a carrot and you ain't no friend of mine,' I croon.

Elvis laughs.

I haven't heard him laugh before. I stop singing and inspect his face. It is crinkled up with amusement.

I can't believe he is laughing at me. I try to snatch the flyer back, but he holds on to it. He is still laughing.

'Did you write this?'

I wonder if it is too late to deny it.

'You did, didn't you?'

I shake my head, which is a bad idea. *It was Sooty.*

'It's fantastic,' he says.

Chapter Fifteen

Dreams are often most profound when
they seem the most crazy.

SIGMUND FREUD

*I am nude hiking again, but this time it is not raining.
The clouds have lifted to the tops of the mountains.
Rainbows dance along the hill tops.*

*The same man walks towards me. He still doesn't
seem to notice my nakedness. 'Seen any poss'ms?' he
asks in a New Zealand accent.*

'No. Why do you want possums?'

'You git one hundred dollars a kilo for poss'm fur.'

*'How many possums does it take to make a kilo?'
I ask.*

'Fifteen.'

I wake up. In Jay's bed. Wearing only a T-shirt, the
embroidered waistcoat and knickers – at least I am not
naked with a possum hunter. The nude hiking dream is
getting stranger and stranger. I wonder what will happen

next. My head hurts. I turn it, being sure not to rattle my brain any more than necessary.

Beside me, under the same sheet, is a sleeping Jay. He is still wearing his black Elvis shirt and – I peek under the sheet – boxer shorts. These are silky and have a red pattern. His Elvis hair has flattened into a squashed bird's nest. He doesn't look cool or ironic now; he looks vulnerable. I gaze at his face, feeling a strange desire to stroke the top of his nose.

I have no memory of how this set of circumstances came about. I'd definitely remember if we'd had sex.

Well, I think I'd remember ... Actually, I'm not at all sure about anything that happened after my second fiddler crab cocktail. I prop myself up on one elbow and examine my bed mate.

Jay's cuffs are undone and as he rolls over one sleeve slips up, exposing his wrist and a little of his forearm. I realise then that I have never seen his arms before. His wrist is white, soft-looking and marked with five angry red scars. These run lengthwise and are too straight, too purposeful to be random. I can't take my eyes off them.

Jay moans, like a puppy dreaming, and something tugs inside my chest. But then his eyes flicker open and I look away. The first thing he does is pull his sleeves down. The second thing he does is search my face. His look is calculating; he is wondering if I've seen.

'Why, fancy meeting you here.' He looks up at me. 'How serendipitous, to find ourselves in the same bed.'

Serendipity. Kismet. Jay, clearly, is someone who takes an interest in words. 'Oh, I come here often. Never run into you before though.'

We both smile at the same time. I have an urge to smooth his bird's nest hairdo into place.

'We didn't …' He pauses with great delicacy.

'Have sex?'

'In case you're wondering.'

'I *was* wondering.' And while I am relieved, this is soon replaced by something else. 'Why didn't we have sex?' This comes out all wrong – like I'm complaining.

'Sorry.' Jay shrugs and smiles. 'Most remiss of me.'

'No, I didn't mean …'

'You were smashed.'

It all comes back to me: the flyers, the cocktails, Jay and me on the couch at the surf club. I think about his answer and I'd like to deconstruct it further – if I'd been less smashed, would we have had sex? I don't think my communication skills are up to it though. In fact, I am sure they're not. And I don't mean that I wish we had, I'd just like to think he'd want to. Teasing out the nuances of this situation would be something best done in writing. Via a lawyer.

I roll onto my back and stare at the ceiling. I bite my tongue to stop myself asking if he finds me attractive. I bite it hard so it gets the message. While Jay and I are not touching, there is not much space between us. The air in that space seems to vibrate with an urgent hum. I think about the scars on his arm. His hidden depths entice me like a lost city to an explorer. If only I could find a way in.

'I liked your story,' he says.

'Did you try to kill yourself?' I say at the same time. As soon as the words are out I wish I could pull them back. Damn, where did they come from? They sneaked out while I was busy trying not to ask if he finds me attractive. Evel Knievel strikes again. Why does everything in my head have to push itself out through my mouth? *Just get out the sledgehammer, Edie.*

Jay is silent for so long I start to think I only imagined saying those words. What a relief. It would have been a totally inappropriate and insensitive thing to say. If he wanted to talk about the scars on his arms he wouldn't go around in long-sleeved shirts all the time, would he? Just when I've convinced myself I didn't say it, he speaks.

'Don't hold back, will you, Edie?'

My stomach contracts. 'Sorry. It's none of my business.'

'No. It's not.' He has closed up like a clam.

'Sorry.'

He doesn't reply. The air between us is now as dull and stagnant as a dirty pond.

I slide out of bed, find Rochelle's flared pants on the floor, put them on and shuffle out. Climbing the stairs is like ascending Everest with no oxygen. I catch sight of myself in the mirror as I come into my room. The scarf is still tied around my head but it has slipped to a rakish angle, almost covering one eye. I don't look like a hippy anymore; I look like a crazed pirate. I collapse into bed and lie there, half asleep and half awake. I feel like a pirate who has burnt her boat on the eve of an expedition.

I still don't know why or how I ended up in bed with Jay. Was there a romantic moment? Or was it just a practical arrangement? Maybe I couldn't climb the stairs.

And what happened to Sally? I'd thought that she and Jay were going to get it on. I probably ruined her night. And has she found out about the erotica on the back of her flyers yet? She might have a contract out on me for ruining her business with my sleazy crab sex.

This is just so typical of you, says the bonsai. *I had a bad feeling about you from the moment you picked me up. This girl has no concept of refined elegance, I said to myself. This is not someone who should be put in charge of a bonsai.*

I am starting to hate that tree but I am too weak to respond. I pull out my notebook.

Sunday: Day 50
Pain level: 9.5 (optimistically)
Location: Chest, throat and abdomen
Tips for self-improvement: Don't drink cocktails

My notebook reminds me that I am supposed to start my Murakami running program. I consider it briefly. No, today does not feel like a good day for new endeavours. Particularly those involving physical effort. Tomorrow will have to do. *Definitely start running tomorrow*, I write.

When I get up, I Google flights to Tokyo again. Unfortunately, it is school holidays and the first flight within my price range is two weeks away. I book it. Once I have done that, I feel better. After all, what's two weeks? I can lie low, wear dark glasses when I go out, wear a false nose if necessary ...

As always, when in doubt, I check my emails. This takes longer than usual. The Send/Receive bar inches across the screen at a tantalisingly slow rate. This makes me think I have lots of emails coming in. I get excited.

Five minutes later the bar seems to have stopped all progress. Ten minutes later it reports a Send/Receive error. I re-boot and start the process again. Eventually a thrilling *ting* announces the arrival of the post. Emily Brontë didn't know what she was missing out on. I rush to check.

My inbox is empty, apart from a new message from my Nigerian friend, Philip. I am pathetically grateful to hear from him. His father, the cocoa merchant, has now been poisoned to death by his business associates.

Philip's life seems even more tumultuous than mine. Again, I feel drawn to the idea of starting an email friendship with him. I wonder how much of his story is true. Is he really Nigerian? Is his name actually Philip? Did he ever have a cocoa-merchant father? Maybe I could introduce him to Sooty Beaumont. *My mother was a cabaret dancer and my father a lion tamer. I grew up in the slums of Paris.* What a lot of fun we could have inventing outrageous stories for our alter egos.

Don't be ridiculous, says the bonsai.

'Oh, all right.' I press Delete. I look at the bonsai. It is just a shadow of its former glory. I feel sorry for it. It is quite correct – I am not the sort of person who should be left in charge of a bonsai. 'Thanks,' I say. 'That was good advice.'

Yet another leaf falls simply and elegantly from its branch to the pot, but it doesn't respond.

I get dressed and go downstairs for something to eat. Jay's door is open, but he is not inside. I eye his bed, remembering his bird's nest hair, his puppy whimper. I'd like to go and curl up in there again, but even I know that would be a very strange thing to do.

The Sally thing is hanging over my head. I can't work out what happened to her last night. Maybe she isn't talking to me. I ring her mobile. It is engaged.

While I make toast I am thinking of Jay and those scars on his arms. I am thinking about the woman whose daughter I am too scared to Google because I already know what happened to her son. And, even though I don't want to, I am thinking about Mum.

It is late in the evening. The sun is low, so it won't burn our skin.

Mum and I are digging holes in the sand. We are building a trap for Dad. He is out in the waves, dancing on his board in the golden light. That's the way I always think of it – dancing.

Mum keeps forgetting to dig. She stares out at the sea and I have to remind her that I can't do it all by myself. The trick is to dig a tunnel and then cover up the entrances so it looks like the sand is undisturbed. I place Dad's towel on the other side of the tunnel, so he will have to cross it. Once the trap is set I wait in suspense, trying to look innocent.

As the sun sets he catches a wave in to shore, lying on his board.

I bite my lip, trying not to laugh as he heads for our trap.

Dad reaches for his towel, falls in the hole with a scream and collapses onto the sand. 'You got me good that time, Eddie,' he says.

My chest swells with pride – a job well done.

Mum laughs and laughs. She flicks her hair back from her face and laughs some more.

She is radiant.

Chapter Sixteen

Out of your vulnerabilities will come your strength.

SIGMUND FREUD

Sally rings that evening. 'Can I come over?'

Her tone is hard to read. She doesn't sound like her usual self, but neither does she sound angry.

'Sure.' I don't know if I should be worried or not. 'What happened to you last night?'

'Hmm,' says Sal in a mysterious way. 'What happened to *you* is more to the point, I think.'

This sounds vaguely ominous. 'Not much. Had a few drinks, chilled —'

'Ha.' Sal interrupts. 'Ha and double ha.'

'I have no idea what you mean.'

Sally laughs. 'See you soon.' She hangs up.

I am worried. Sally and I haven't fought in a long time, but when we did in the past, it was nasty. In primary school she took offence at some imagined slight about her new school shoes and didn't speak to me for a week. Not only did she not speak to me, she didn't even see me. I'd sit next to her at lunchtime and she'd pretend I didn't exist. We still swapped sandwiches, but she acted like my sandwich arrived in her lunchbox and hers in mine by an odd arrangement unconnected to ourselves. After seven days her pique wore off and we became inseparable again. I don't like fighting with Sally and hope I'm not about to.

Chocolate is needed to calm my nerves. I pick up ten dollars and head down to the shops. I am halfway there when I hear someone calling.

'Hey, Edz.'

Edz? No one calls me Edz. It is Tim. He waves to me from a nearby verandah.

'Been gettin' any?' he asks.

This is the first time anyone has ever asked me that; an historic moment. I smile. 'Yeah, the odd one.'

'Been pretty shit, huh?'

'Wasn't too bad at Darling Lefts on Friday.' I am playing the traditional Darling Head 'Should have been there yesterday' game.

'I was at Lefts. Didn't see ya.'

'I slept in.' I take a punt that he is out of the water in time for school. 'Waited for the tide to come in.'

'Thought it might get better.'

His mother appears behind him and I decide I'd better take off in case she knows my non-surfing history. 'I'll get that autograph to you soon,' I call.

Back home, I sit up in bed and eat my chocolate. If our house is a ship, my bedroom is the crow's nest. I climb up steep steps to reach it and, like the rest of the house, it is triangular. From my bed I can look out across the sea to the horizon. After a little while music drifts through my window. Jay is on the verandah, playing his guitar.

It is pleasant looking at the sea and hearing Jay play. I'd like to go down and listen to him more closely, but we haven't spoken since the awkward bedroom incident. He draws me to him like a moth to light but I don't know how to talk to him.

We have had several moments that felt intimate. There was the hall floor, the surf club verandah, the waking up in bed together and probably the getting into bed together part, which I don't remember. One would expect these moments to add up to something. Yet they don't. Every time I see him, we have to start again. He is still a stranger. But then most people feel like that to me.

This intimacy thing is so elusive, so divinely inviting, but it seems to recede as I approach. I wonder what it means to really know someone? I think it means you can let them see all of you – even the embarrassing bits you've never shown anyone else. And when they've seen all those scary, messy and just wrong parts they still accept you, even like you.

I know I never had that with Daniel. I was always trying to be more polished, more assured, more socially gifted than I am. I've never had that with anyone really; except for Mum.

You are my peapod buddy, Edie.
There's no you and no me.
Only us.

I wonder if Jay would understand what I meant about 'the rain in Glenorchy'. That it wasn't just about rain and it certainly had nothing to do with climate change. It was about the way you get when the cloud descends in your mind.

My seven days in Glenorchy with Sal left a big impression on me. While Sally was off shagging Travis, the deer-hunting accountant, I spent a lot of time walking in the rain. In Glenorchy, clouds drift down the mountains like floating sheep. While the rain can be depressing, it is uplifting when it stops. Waterfalls stream off the hills. They spray up around you, blown backwards in the updraft. Without the cloudy days, when would we know it was sunny?

Jay's music makes me think he would understand this and, to be honest, the scars on his arms also suggest that he has had his share of cloudy days. What would it be like to go through life with that reminder of death; to have people judge you because of them?

I think Jay is a 'deeper meaning' person. He is someone who understands that life is complex; that we don't always get what we want and when the cloud descends all you can do is keep going and hope it's going to lift sometime.

I think I know why he is staying with us. Rochelle wants to keep an eye on him. A few other things are becoming clearer too. Dad and Rochelle's conspiratorial glances, for instance. Were they hoping for something by throwing Jay and me together? Were they hoping we'd be friends?

I flick through a magazine as I wait for Sally. Even though Jay doesn't know I am here, it is like he is playing for me. And while I am not musical, I sense this would be a wonderful thing to do, to communicate this way. If you were a good enough musician, you might never have to talk at all. Or a good enough writer ...

This brings my mind back to the thing it has been avoiding – the crab sex story. And I suddenly remember something that has escaped me until now – Jay liked it.

As I listen to his music, a small, warm glow spreads through me. He likes my writing. And even though I am as embarrassed as all hell that he knows this stuff about me, it is still a nice feeling. He has seen my dirty mind and he likes it. No one has ever known that part of me before. I have shed an onion layer. It is liberating. This feels as if it could be strangely addictive.

I can hear Sally coming up the stairs. She stops on the verandah and talks to Jay. Their voices rise and fall in an easy rhythm. They laugh. Jay sounds different to how he is with me. With me, there are more silences than words. I think I have been kidding myself that we have any kind of understanding at all. I have turned three strange and awkward moments into a relationship which exists only in my mind. If I hadn't got pissed and needed rescuing, I am certain that Sally and Jay would be an item.

That is just so typical of you, says the bonsai.

'Shut up. Or I'll chop your branches off.'

I hear Sally open the front door. 'Ed-ie,' she calls.

'I'm hee-ya.' I get up and walk downstairs.

She comes in and spots me. 'Hi, babe.'

This sounds promising. She wouldn't call me babe if she was mad at me, would she? 'Hi babe.' I sit down in the leather armchair.

Sally prowls around the room like a cat, before lowering herself onto a couch and curling her legs beneath her. She seems to be containing a lot of energy. Her red-painted toenails wiggle like she wants to scratch the velour cushions. 'What's up?' she asks.

I wonder if she is toying with me. I feel like a mouse about to be mauled. 'Not much. Had a slow day.'

For no apparent reason, this makes her laugh. 'I bet you had a fucking slow day, Ed. You were smashed, mate.' She inclines her head towards the verandah and raises her eyebrows. 'Essence of Heathcliff?' she murmurs.

I play dumb. I raise my eyebrows back in a neutral way.

She frowns and gives me a double eyebrow flash and a chin lift.

She wants to know if he's still available, but I'm not going to make it easy for her. I give her a triple eyebrow flash back.

'You two look like the Marx Brothers,' says a voice from the verandah. 'We didn't make lurve, if that's what the eyebrows are about.'

161

'Hey, this is a private eyebrow flashing session,' says Sal.

Jay comes into the room, his guitar under his arm. 'Not anymore.' He gives an amazingly athletic quadruple eyebrow flash then collapses onto the floor.

Sally giggles. 'So, Ed. Why didn't you tell us you had this thing for crabs?'

'This extremely hot thing,' says Jay. It is the first thing he has said to me since the bedroom incident. His voice is teasing. It sounds like forgiveness.

'This outstandingly erotic and steamy thing,' says Sal.

'Oh, fuck off,' I say.

Sally and Jay raise their eyebrows in unison. They obviously have a strong connection going on.

'And she hasn't even been to Rio,' says Sal to Jay. She leans over and strokes my leg. 'It's okay, Ed, I'm not mad. You wouldn't believe what's been happening.'

'What?'

'Oh my God. My phone has been running hot.'

'What do you mean?'

'The crab sex thing. Just after you went to the bar last night my phone started ringing and it hasn't stopped since. I've been taking calls all day. You wouldn't think it's a Sunday. People just can't wait.'

'Huh?' She's lost me.

'The flyer drop. It's weird, people put together the crab sex with the life coaching and, well, I've now added a new string to my bow ...' Sally trails off.

I still have no idea what she's talking about.

'Well, it's not a new string or I would have to change the name to Motive 9, which doesn't work at all. I've decided it's an offshoot of relationship advice.'

The penny drops. 'You're moving into sex counselling?'

Sally nods.

'Are you qualified to do that?'

'Hey, I'm a psychologist. Anyway, it's not serious stuff; it's just, you know, spice up your love life with some steamy fantasies. You wouldn't believe it. I've signed up ten couples already. Just wait until I get my website up.'

'Anyone I know?'

Sally rolls her eyes. 'Yes, but I'm not saying.'

'Give me a clue.'

'People in long-term relationships which have become predictable.'

I immediately think of Professor Brownlow. I feel slightly nauseous. 'Have you ... Started distributing. This ... literature? Already?'

'God yes,' says Sally. 'I've been flat out all day.'

'But Sally, did I say you c—'

'So, this is where you come in. I've got a fantastic proposition for you. You're going to love it.'

I always feel suspicious when Sally tells me I'm going to love something.

'The fantasies – I need more of them. The crab sex is great, but for an ongoing relationship to keep the zest it needs more than just one fantasy.'

'You want me to write erotic fantasies for you?'

'I'll pay you. And credit you as the author, if you want.'

I shake my head vigorously. 'You haven't told anyone?'

'No, darl, I haven't told anyone. But if they were mine, I'd be shouting it from the rooftops. The men would come flocking.'

'Really?' I blush as my eyes flicker to Jay.

'Totally,' he says.

The air between us vibrates again.

Chapter Seventeen

Where id was, there ego shall be.

SIGMUND FREUD

Monday: 51 days
Pain level: 6 (a record low)
Location: Throat
Tips for self-improvement: Write more erotica

Professor Brown flicked noislily through
Edaline's drawings. Today he seemed to be
channelling some deeply repressed emotions.
His usually sanguine air had been disturbed
by something darker. Edaline sensed a build-up
of tension, like a volcano on the brink.

She worked at her illustration, her nerves on
edge. What could have provoked the normally
calm, good-natured Professor Brown?

'Two plumose hairs?'

Edaline jumped, her heart pounding.
Professor Brown had materialised beside her.

He held out a drawing. 'Are you sure there are two plumose hairs here?'

Edaline nodded, although she was not sure at all.

Professor Brown gave a sharp intake of breath. He had a light in his eyes she had never seen before. A burning ember.

Edaline felt a warm wind touch her cheek as he breathed out. An image flashed through her mind: she was climbing Vesuvius, the ground was shaking beneath her.

And then Vesuvius erupted. Professor Brown grasped her by the shoulders. 'You little minx,' he said.

She had never imagined he would use a word like minx, but this new Professor Brown seemed capable of anything.

'You make it up as you go along, don't you?'

Edaline nodded. He had found her out. She'd always known he would.

I ease my fingers off the keyboard and reread what I have written. I've had to get up early this morning to work on my erotica as it is a crab larvae day and Sally is breathing down my neck for a new instalment. When am I going to start running? Not now, anyway. Perhaps running will be an evening thing for me.

Hah, says the bonsai. *I bet you never run.*

'Of course I'm going to run. I'm just very busy. You wouldn't know what that's like. All you do is sit there and criticise. Why don't you say something nice for once?'

Did I tell you that Daniel's new girlfriend is an Olympic gymnast?

'*Former* Olympic gymnast, you said.'

I imagine she's pretty fit, says the bonsai.

'Well, I'd probably be pretty fit too if I only had to be a barrister and cook gourmet meals. She should try writing erotic fiction while holding down a job drawing crab larvae.'

The bonsai laughs snidely.

'Shut up. Who asked you anyway?' I throw a rug over it. 'And I'm going to run very soon.'

I'll believe it when I see it. The bonsai manages to exude smugness, even from under the rug.

I glare at it. 'Well, I bet I run before you do.' It is a cheap shot, but the best I can do. 'And please, be quiet will you? One of us has work to do here.'

Work? the bonsai scoffs. *Since when does writing pornography count as work?*

I ignore it and turn back to the keyboard. I'm not satisfied with the way this piece is panning out. How does one describe sex using the metaphor of the volcano? No doubt Professor Brown will at some stage erupt, but is Edaline a languid pool into which his lava flows? It's tacky, but it could work. I press on.

... Edaline felt herself to be a pool. Not a cool mountain pool, but a simmering hot pool such

as those she had seen once on a trip to Rotorua.
And in her pool, was a ...

A what? My fingers freeze on the keyboard. A volcanic
plug? A thrusting, demanding volcanic plug? No. It's no
good. It just doesn't work. I'm going to have to change
metaphors.

... Edaline felt her flower opening as Professor
Brown's mouth met hers. His touch was like a
bee collecting pollen, delicate, yet purposeful.
Her petals closed around his ...

Trunk?
    Branch?
    Woody vine?
The phone rings. It is Sally. 'Have you finished?'
I gnaw at my fingernail. 'I'm having a bit of trouble.'
'What with? It's just sex. You know how to do it;
what's the problem?'
Sally has no understanding of the artist's tortured
soul. 'It's not that easy. Doing it is one thing, writing
about it is another.'
'I've got clients lined up for this, Edie.'
'They're just going to have to wait.'
Sally's silence tells me I am sounding shrill. 'It's okay,
Ed.' If she was here, I'm pretty sure she would be backing
away with her hands in the air. 'Tomorrow will do.'
'I've got to go to work now,' I squeal.
'Edie, this is a bit of a personal question, but as your

life coach I think I need to ask – have you been getting any?'

I know that Sally doesn't mean waves. 'No, not lately. Not since Daniel. Why?'

'Freud said that the suppression of sexual desire could lead to hysteria in women. It was pretty radical at the time; no one had considered that women had sexual desires.'

'Are you calling me hysterical?'

'Hmm.' The sound of paper-shuffling comes over the phone. 'Do you have a tendency towards trouble-making, irritability, loss of appetite, insomnia or —'

A sudden dread strikes me. 'Sally, you're not doing this line of coaching for Professor Brownlow, are you?'

'Nervousness.' Sally completes her sentence. 'You know I can't tell you that, Ed.'

'But you have to. How am I supposed to face him if he's been reading this stuff?'

'People never recognise themselves in fiction.'

I am so eager to be convinced, I buy this ridiculous line.

'Tomorrow?' asks Sal.

'Tomorrow,' I confirm. This is far enough away not to bother me. I am sure the perfect metaphor will arrive by then.

'You know, Edie, I've been a bit deficient as your life coach.' Sally sounds apologetic.

I don't like the sound of this. 'No, you haven't; you've been great. I'm making real progr—'

'Your task for today is to smile at ten strangers.'

169

I sigh with relief. That sounds relatively painless. 'Okay.'

'And you still haven't mastered that talking to a stranger exercise,' says Sal.

I can already see where this is heading and I'm not going there. 'Did so. I spoke to Jay. Like you told me to.'

Sally coughs. It sounds a bit like *did not*.

'I did.'

'And was it successful, would you say?' Her voice is gentle, but she's not fooling me.

Humiliation. Terror. Nausea. Some people pay big money for that sort of thing. 'Depends on what you're trying to achieve.'

'Was it a mutually rewarding social interchange?'

'Well, no, but —'

'No buts, Ed. I'll help. I'll be coaching you all the way. What you need are cue cards. I'll see you tomorrow morning. And I'll expect a report on the smiling thing too.'

'But —'

'Byee.' Sally hangs up.

Apprehension clutches my stomach as I wind up the road towards the university. Surely I will know at once if Professor Brownlow has been reading my writing? In that case, I can resign immediately.

I tense as I approach the church. What will the all-seeing, all-knowing sign say today?

'Erotic writing takes Darling Head by storm.'

My heart leaps. Who said that?

'We are now talking to Sally Harris, who can fill us in on Saturday's startling letterbox drop,' the radio announcer continues.

'Sally, what are you doing?' I shriek.

'... it was just a fun way of generating interest in my business, Motive 8 life coaching ...'

I wind down the window and stick my head out, a squeal like that of a newborn piglet escaping my lips. 'That's *me*, you're talking about, Sally. Did I say you could?'

The balding man is standing in the church entrance. *A clean conscience makes a soft pillow* say the black letters in the sign today. Damn that man and his holier-than-thou platitudes. Of course a clean conscience makes a soft pillow. It would, wouldn't it? But how does that help when your conscience is dirtier than a dog that's rolled in cow shit?

'... so tell us, can we expect more of these stories?'

'Oh yes,' says Sal. 'Anyone who's interested in more hot stories from the Crab Sex Institute can give me a call. A good sex life is essential for mental health; after all, we're not living in the Victorian age anymore, are we?'

The church man raises his hand at me like we are friends. He has no idea he is waving to a veritable Medusa.

I smile at him through clenched teeth (smile number one) as Sally laughs gaily on the radio. 'No, I can't tell you who wrote it. Let's just call her Anonymous.'

'Well, I think there's going to be a bit of speculation about that,' says the announcer. 'Call in now folks if you think you know who the mysterious Anonymous is.'

171

I punch the *off* button as I drive into the car park. I feel an urge to pull my hat down low and drape a scarf around my face, but that will only draw attention to myself. Plastic surgery is starting to seem like a good option.

Professor Brownlow looks up as I come in. His expression is mild, good-humoured, no seething volcano, no underground rumblings. 'Good morning, Edie.'

I run these words through my paranoia meter. They pass. 'Good morning, Ralph.'

'The specimens are at your desk.'

My paranoia meter flashes orange at the mention of specimens and desk but I know this is ridiculous. I realise there is now no way we can discuss my job without everything sounding like sexual innuendo.

'Something different today.'

'Different?' I perk up at the prospect of excitement.

'Yes, I've started on the genus *Libnia*. I'm giving a conference paper on them.'

'Great.' *Yay, new genus.* I retreat to my desk, where the specimens are – indeed – waiting. Extracting the first one from the beaker with a pipette, I squeeze it onto a slide, place it under the microscope and start to draw. *Libnia* fails to excite me.

All is quiet for half an hour or so, until Professor Brownlow gets up and strolls past my desk. He pauses, examining my drawing over my shoulder. 'I like the way you've drawn those plumose hairs.' A whiff of citrus on his breath wafts towards me.

Plumose hairs – red light, red light. My heart beats faster. I slide my eyes towards him. There is nothing in

172

his expression to suggest anything except a scientist's interest in crustacean appendages. 'Thank you.' I still have my suspicions.

'Ralph?' I wonder why I have never asked this before. 'Why are we researching crab larvae?'

'Hmm.' Professor Brownlow looks puzzled, like he has never asked himself this question before either. 'There are a lot of gaps in knowledge. Some species, we don't actually know what all their larval stages look like. They moult through several metamorphs before becoming adults. It wasn't until the 1870s that the first complete set of larval forms of a ... '

I zone out. This is why I never asked. It is not interesting. I doodle a crab larva as superhero, complete with cape and thigh-high boots. *Metamorph*, I write beneath it.

Professor Brownlow concludes his mini-lecture on the history of crab larvae research.

The silence alerts me that a response is required. 'Fascinating.' I slide my drawing beneath the others on my desk.

'It is, isn't it?' He smiles and moves on.

At lunchtime his wife calls in. Professor Brownlow stands and kisses her. I pretend I am not watching and see his hand slide onto her Adidas-clad bottom. She giggles and presses against him. A stab of jealousy makes me grind my teeth. I have allowed myself to believe Professor Brownlow is suffering in a loveless marriage. Clearly this is not the case. I look up as they go past, decide that she qualifies as a stranger and smile brightly (number two). She gives me a gracious lady of the manor smile in return. I scrunch up my nose behind her back, mentally thumbing my forehead. *I'll just get back to my crab drawing then, Ma'am.*

They wander out, hands touching each other's waists. Irrationally, I feel betrayed. And then a certainty strikes me. It is my hot sex which is saving their marriage. They are having the sex *I* should have been having. I am hoisted by my own crab-erotica-themed petard.

Chapter Eighteen

Time spent with cats is never wasted.

SIGMUND FREUD

A shiny, red, open-topped sports car with leather seats is sitting on the street outside our house when I get home. They must be visiting one of the other houses as we don't know anyone with a car like that.

But as I reach the house, a voice I don't recognise is booming down the stairs. Opening the door, I see a strange tableau. It is almost like a nativity scene. Taking the place of Jesus is a crop-haired, tattooed, middle-aged man in a tight black T-shirt. Arrayed in front of him, like the three wise men and hanging on his every word, are Dad, Rochelle and Jay. In the absence of sheep and cows a solitary black cat sits at his feet, gazing at him with lemon eyes.

The man looks familiar, although I don't think we have met before.

Dad turns as I come in. He has an expression on his face I've seen before on only a few occasions – his hero-worship gaze. 'Eddie, this is Rochelle and Jay's dad.' He pauses. 'Gary Jaworski.' He pronounces this name as if it is preceded by a drum roll.

The man turns and I have that weird sensation you get when you meet a celebrity, like they are taking up more space than a normal person. The feeling comes before the recognition, which hits a fraction of a second later. 'Gary and the Grafters?'

The man sticks out his hand and takes mine. 'Just Gary now. The Grafters and I have gone our own ways.' The face that has decorated many copies of *Rolling Stone* creases into a million wrinkles.

I smile (number three) and turn my gaze back to the nativity scene. 'How come you never told me Gary Jaworski was your father?' I say to Jay and Rochelle.

'You never told her?' Jay turns to Rochelle, then swings back to me, 'I figured you knew.' His voice is softer than usual, the hard-edged sarcasm vanished for now.

Gary Jaworski – the name brings back memories. I was too young for the first, or even the second, wave of Gary and the Grafters but their music was among Mum's favourites.

'Come on, Edie, let's shake it.' Mum, jumps to her feet as 'Love Receiver' comes on the radio.

I am five years old and dancing with Mum is one of my favourite things.

'Oo, baby, can't you feeeeel it?' Mum jumps up and down to the raging beat, her red hair flying, her light summer dress floating up around her.

Dad strolls in, his hair wet from surf training. He smiles at his two redheads and joins in, holding us in his suntanned arms, jigging up and down.

A salty sea breeze blows through the house and the surf crashes. In my childhood it is always sunny.

'Dad's doing a gig at Lighthouse Bay tonight.' Rochelle brings me back to earth.

I blink and lower myself onto a chair.

'You're going to come along, aren't you?' Gary directs this question mainly to Jay.

'You're not going to play that crap Grafters stuff, are you?' asks Jay.

His father smiles; this is obviously a well-worn routine. 'No mate, it's all new. Why don't you join me for a few numbers?'

Jay shakes his head, his hair falling over his eyebrow. 'You know I don't do that shit.'

Rochelle looks at him. 'Why not, Jay? You never know who could be watching.'

Jay doesn't bother to reply.

And then I remember one of Gary's older songs. 'Jaybird'. *You are laughter, you are tears …*

'You'll come though?' asks Gary.

Jay lifts his shoulders, then glances at me. 'You want to go, Edie?'

I am so surprised I don't have time to think about my answer. 'God, yes.'

Jay's mouth twitches.

177

My voice replays in my ears. I sound like a starstruck twelve-year-old.

'Okay, Edie. It's a date,' he says.

After Gary has roared away in his red sports car, I look at Rochelle and Jay again. 'I can't believe I never knew he was your father.'

Rochelle looks embarrassed. 'Who wants to be known as Gary Jaworski's daughter all the time? I had enough of that in Sydney.'

'You knew?' I ask Dad.

He inclines his head. 'Rochelle asked me to keep it quiet.'

Jay doesn't say anything, but there is an expression on his face I haven't seen before.

The nativity scene dissolves. Rochelle retreats to the kitchen and Dad to his shed. He is now doing something to the boards that used to be the lounge-room ceiling. The ways of the home renovator are mysterious to me.

Jay and I are left alone in the lounge room. The cat jumps up on the chair where Gary was sitting. It curls itself into a ball and licks the cushion. Its air of self-possession reminds me of the despondent cat on the cover of the book Professor Brownlow lent me, *Kafka on the Shore*.

'Why didn't Gary take his cat?' I ask.

'It's not his cat. It just turned up here. Haven't you seen it before?'

Now that I think about it, the cat does look familiar. 'I think it lives around here, it's never come in before, though.' I click my tongue at it. 'Hey, Kafka.' The cat coughs, then makes a vomiting noise and expels a furball onto the cushion. This done, it leaps from the chair and slinks from the room with its tail in the air. 'Guess it just came to see Gary,' I say.

'He has that effect on people; maybe it works on animals too. You know its name?'

'It just seemed to fit.'

Jay nods. 'Good name.' He eyes the bare beams above us. 'I like this look. It's minimalist; very New York warehouse; very hip.'

I ignore the small talk. I am awkward with our changed dynamic; unsure why he has asked me out; suspicious of his motives. 'I still can't believe I didn't know Gary Jaworski is your father. That's so weird.'

'I can't believe you didn't know either. I thought that was what it was all about ...' he trails off.

'What what was all about?'

'You know, the stalking.' The side of his mouth pulls up in a half-smile.

'No way. You thought I was stalking you because you're Gary Jaworski's son? That is so ...'

'Stranger things have happened.'

'Why would I do that? Why wouldn't I stalk Rochelle? Anyway, how was I stalking you?'

Jay smiles, like he's enjoying this. 'You just kept popping up all over the place, at the beach, here —'

'But I live here. I was here f—'

Jay talks over the top of me, '... the university.'

'But I work there,' I squeal. 'You, you're such an arrogant ... Why would I stalk you? Like you're something special.'

Jay laughs. 'Okay, I was wrong, you weren't stalking me. Sorry.' He holds up his hands, palms out. 'It's happened before, that's all. You wouldn't believe how many crazed Gary Jaworski fans are out there.'

'Really?'

'Yeah, really. Some people are just weird.'

'I'm flattered you thought I was one of them.'

'I don't know what I was thinking.' He gives me a mock-rueful puppy-dog look.

'Jaybird. That's you, right?'

Jay grimaces. 'Can we not talk about that?'

'But, isn't that nice? Having a song —'

Jay's eyebrows lower.

I stop, perhaps I am getting into Evel Knievel territory. 'Why isn't your name Jaworski?'

'Well, old Gary didn't hang around. He left soon after I turned two. Got famous and started shagging models. Why would I want to use his name? Rochelle feels the same.'

'Wouldn't it help, you know, with ...'

'I don't want to be announced as Gary Jaworski's son all my life. If that's what it takes, I don't want it.'

'Yeah, I don't want to be announced as the daughter of a former Australian surf champion every time I go in surf comps either.'

'Your father?'

'You didn't know? I thought that's why you were stalking me.'

Jay laughs. 'Touché. Australian champ, huh?'

'Former Junior Champion, former Australian Champion, World Number Two.'

'Try top of the charts in Australia, top 40 in America, top 10 in the UK, ARIA Hall of Fame.'

I smile. 'You win. Your father is way more famous, so I guess I was stalking you.'

'Correct me if I'm wrong,' says Jay, 'but you don't actually surf, do you?'

'Correct. I don't surf. I am what is known in breeding circles as a runt.'

Jay smiles. 'Never underestimate the runt, I say. So, you're coming to the show tonight?'

Our eyes meet. I feel that vibration again.

'Okay.' I glance at my watch. 'I'd better write some erotica first.'

'Tough life.'

'You have no idea.'

Jay smiles and my chest hums. I want to touch his cheek. I want to run my fingers down those scars and ask him why he did that. I want to open his mind like a clam and see inside.

Chapter Nineteen

Sometimes a cigar is just a cigar.
SIGMUND FREUD

Rain thundered down outside the laboratory. It had been like this for days now. Mould was growing on Edaline's clothes. This morning she had noticed a small pink fungus sprouting on her windowsill. It was silky and damp to touch, emitting a rich, sexual odour.

Even here in the laboratory the air was thick with moisture. Edaline could hardly remember a time when she had not been wet ... This thought led her by association to Professor Brown.

A cloudburst lashed the windows, like a metaphor for her craving. Edaline's internal humidity rocketed. She felt like a sponge – drenched, sodden, saturated. She clenched her thighs tightly under her floral print Laura Ashley dress. If only a pair of strong hands would wring her out.

Professor Brown worked calmly on his spanner crab dissection as if she was not in the room. He hummed as he worked, a picture of contentment.

Edaline added an extra maxilliped to her drawing out of spite. Professor Brown would pay for his negligence. She eyed the clock on the wall. Five minutes to twelve. Edaline tapped her high-heeled black boots on the rung of her ergonomic chair.

The hands on the clock met at the top. She waited, five seconds, ten seconds ... before lifting her gaze.

Professor Brown's blue eyes glinted behind his steel-rimmed glasses. 'It's a good day for Monopoly.' His voice was deep, mellifluous, layered with meaning.

Edaline practically swooned. How could he know? She had been fantasising about playing Monopoly for weeks. Every night she had woken from dreams of landing, fatefully, on his hotel.

'Oh, but I haven't got any money, Professor ...'

'I'm sure we can come to some arrangement ...'

These dreams had been vivid, sensuous – the rolling dice, the red tower of the hotel thrusting skywards ...

Professor Brown pulled out a box from beneath his lab bench. He opened the lid, displaying the contents as if they were an assortment of luxury chocolates.

Edaline eyed the pieces. 'You choose yours first.' What would he be? The naughty puppy? The leaping horse and rider?

Professor Brown's hand reached out and picked up ... the racing car. 'And you?' His nostrils flared.

He had sent out a challenge. Edaline arched an eyebrow, touched first the shoe ...

Professor Brown sighed as Edaline lifted her hand.

Her fingers rested on the top hat.

Professor Brown's eyes lit up, but no ...

Edaline's hand drifted over the wheelbarrow, the cannon and the battleship. At last she came to it. Picking up the thimble, she slid it on her forefinger and tapped loudly on the bench. Looking up, she exposed her teeth. 'I'll roll first.'

When Professor Brown spoke, his voice was husky. 'Yes, Edaline. Anything you say.'

So far so good, but now I come to the hard part – the actual sex. I press on, hoping that the right metaphor will land, moth-like, on my computer screen. The game of Monopoly heats up in a very satisfactory way ...

A surging wave of desire washed through Edaline's rock pool. Sea foam crashed against her pink anemone. Professor Brown's sea cucumber inched its way towards the anemone. It was a large cucumber, strong and manly —

The phone interrupts me. It is Sal. 'Got something for me?'

'Nearly.'

'Let's hear what you've got.'

I read it out.

She is silent for some time after I finish.

'Sexy, huh?' I ask.

'The Monopoly is okay. Strange, but okay. Do you really feel like that about Monopoly?'

'Doesn't everyone?'

'No, it's just you, Ed.'

'Oh.'

'I'm not sure about the sea cucumber though. The anemone's okay, but the cucumber is kind of icky.'

'Icky? This is literature you're talking about. It's a phallic symbol.'

'Can't you have a different phallic symbol? Anything long and thin would do; a cigar for instance.'

'What would a cigar be doing in a rock pool? The cucumber is a metaphor encapsulating the essence of manhood. It's very D.H. Lawrence.' I can't believe she's criticising my writing.

'I don't remember a sea cucumber in *Lady Chatterley's Lover*.'

'That's only because he didn't think of it. What would you know? Have you studied literature? Huh? I didn't think so.' I slam the phone down, grinding my teeth.

There is a knock on the door.

'What?' I yell.

Jay's head peers around the corner. 'Are you ready to go?'

I resist the urge to squeal with frustration. 'I can't. I've got to do this thing for Sally.' I pull at my hair. 'I'm having trouble; we're just not on the same wavelength. She has no idea. You'd better go on without me. I'll see you there. I was going to go for a run too, but I haven't got time now.' I am pleased with the way I throw this in, casually, as if it is the type of thing I always do.

'Do you run?' Jay sounds surprised.

'Yeah. Of course I run. Running and writing are two sides of a coin. Everything I know about writing I have learnt from running.' Sadly, that could be true. I probably know very little about writing.

Jay looks doubtful.

'Why, don't I look like a runner?'

Jay's eyes flicker to my legs. As I am wearing jeans, this can't be very enlightening. 'I didn't say that. Yeah, you do look like a runner now you mention it. Can I have a look?'

It is a strange request, but I slide up one of my jeans legs a bit.

'No, I mean your writing. Although that was nice. Thanks.'

I blush, lower my jeans leg and give him a wary look. I'm not sure if I'm ready to show him my writing.

'Please.' He sticks out his lower lip. 'You know I'm a big fan.'

I am not aware of having come to a decision, but I find myself saying, 'Well ... as long as you realise that I am very sensitive about this. Is that understood?'

Jay steps closer. 'I understand totally.'

I doubt that he does. How could he possibly know what a big thing this is for me? I push my chair back from the computer screen to let him see. I can hardly believe I am doing this. Do I really want him to read my writing? I feel daring, anxious and slightly risqué. I breathe, try to rise above it, channel Sooty Beaumont.

Daniel never read my poetry. I offered it to him a few times, but he was always too busy. After that, I gave up. I never acknowledged, even to myself, how much this felt like rejection.

As I watch Jay read my work I realise that, even though I would quite like to place the blame on Sooty, my erotic writing is a part of me. I am putting my strange and intimate thoughts out there for him to accept or discard. I want to reach out and turn off the screen. Oh God, why did I let him see it? What if he hates it?

Jay's eyes run down the screen. He bites his lip.

I want to ask him what he thinks of it, but I am too shy.

Jay's mouth puckers and his shoulders shake. A laugh explodes out of him. He stifles it with a choking sound. 'I'm sorry, Edie.' He turns to me, his eyes watering.

'What?' I stare at him, pressing the power button so the screen goes blank. I feel a little sick.

'It was the manly cucumber.' He snorts with suppressed laughter.

'I am never letting you read my work again.'

'No, no. I loved it. Please, don't get me wrong. It was very, very ... sexy.' His eyes are sparkling and he

187

is looking at me in a way I haven't seen before; like he is seeing something new. 'The cucumber,' he presses his lips together, 'inching towards the anem—' he gives up and laughs out loud.

I try to hold my stern expression, but it is impossible in the face of his mischievous look.

'You're funny,' he says.

I'm not sure whether to be pleased with this comment or not. 'I don't mean to be.'

'I'm not laughing at you. You're just so ... different. You're not like anyone I've met before.' He pushes his hands into his pockets. 'I like you.' These last words seem pulled from him with reluctance.

I like you. Has a man ever said that to me before? I think I would remember it. I've had *I love you,* mainly after sex, but *I like you,* that's something different altogether. I am struck dumb. I gaze into his brown eyes and wonder what it is he sees when he sees me, what he likes. The impossibility of ever bridging this gap in understanding wraps my tongue in knots.

Jay looks at the floor, his hair falling over his eyes and I realise I have been staring at him for too long. He is waiting for an answer.

'I like you too.' My heart jumps at my daring. I blush with a mixture of terror and pleasure. Have I said too much? Too little? I want to reach out and touch his chest – that gesture of certain tribes which says more than words can say. *I see you. I recognise you.*

Jay flicks his hair out of his eyes and smiles. He seems very cool. As if he does this kind of thing all the time. Tells girls he likes them. Maybe he does. Maybe everyone does except me.

'So, you can't come to the gig yet?' His voice is low.

I shake my head, although more than anything that is what I want to do. 'I'll be there as soon as I can finish this.'

'Okay. Make sure you come.' He pauses at the door and gives a wicked grin. 'Actually, I think the cucumber's the best bit. Poetic, really. Rather D.H. Lawrence.'

I look at him in surprise. 'Have you read him?'

'Of course. *Lady Chatterley's Cucumber. Sons and Anemones. Sea Hares in Love.* Sexy as.'

A giggle explodes out of my nose.

Jay winks then, like the Cheshire cat, he is gone and the room is much emptier.

I turn back to my screen, delete everything I have written and start again.

Edaline felt herself to be a ghost, as
transparent as glass. But in Jason's arms she
became suddenly visible, whole and beautiful.
He painted her in colours she had never
imagined she possessed – a rainbow followed
his hands, swept out from the place where his
chest rested against hers. And when, at last,
they united, she felt herself forged, burnished
and gilded into a thing so rare and beautiful it
lit up the room with its glory.

'I like you,' he whispered, holding her as if he
would never let her go.

I email my piece to Sally, stand up and stretch. I feel
calm. Jay likes me. I like him. It seems very simple. Can
it really be that simple?

And what is more, he likes my writing. It made him
laugh. I have a ridiculous idea. Perhaps he will fall in
love with me by reading my writing – through words on
the page alone. I am not the first person to think of this.
Just look at the romantic poets. Writing is powerful.

On paper, I am all the things I am not in the flesh.
I am eloquent, witty, funny, worldly, cool. I am Sooty
Beaumont. I have many lovers and they never break my
heart. Yes, he likes my writing. I will write for him. I
will peel off my onion layers one by one and show him
who I am. The idea draws me forward.

I open my wardrobe, looking for the right thing to
wear to a Gary Jaworski gig in Lighthouse Bay. Usually
this would be a task taking many changes of clothes,
much hair pulling and often proving so difficult I would
give up and stay home.

Tonight my hand alights on the perfect outfit straight
away. I pull on the miniskirt, black tights and T-shirt
and glance in the mirror. I look different. I am pale, but
my skin is shining. My wayward hair is wayward in a
cheeky, not ratty way and, for once, I don't feel the need
to cross my eyes to blur my outline.

I see my notebook lying on the bed – now is a good
moment to update my pain dairy. This morning was a

record low, but I am optimistic that I can do even better. While I am not cured yet, I am definitely on the up and up.

Monday (still): 51 days
Pain level: 3 (a new record low!)
Location: Indistinct

The bonsai is quiet tonight. I pick off its browning leaves one by one like plucking a daisy. *I like you. I like you too. I like you. I like you too. I like you.*

Tossing my car keys in the air, I catch them and float from the room.

Have fun.

I turn in the doorway. 'Did you say something?'

But the bonsai speaks no more.

Chapter Twenty

A man should not strive to eliminate
his complexes but to get into
accord with them.

SIGMUND FREUD

The Top Pub in Lighthouse Bay is pumping. A naive over-confidence has carried me from the house to the car to the pub, but it wilts as I gaze at the crowd. Everyone here looks cool, with-it and dauntingly extroverted. Those ants in my brain, which I thought I had vanquished, turn out to have been taking a light nap.

You're dressed all wrong, says the scout ant.

It's weird coming here by yourself, says its friend.

What if Jay isn't here? asks the next one. *You're going to look pretty stupid then, aren't you?*

He likes me, I retort. I take a deep breath, flick the ants aside and give my name at the door as Jay told me to. The doorman doesn't know what I'm talking about. I shell out twenty dollars to enter. I am two metres past before I remember that I am supposed to smile. I turn around and smile, but he must be looking at someone else as he doesn't smile back. I count it anyway (number four).

Cool smile, says the first ant sarcastically.

Jay's forgotten all about you, says the next.

Name at the door, says the sarcastic one. *As if.*

As I push my way towards the bar I find myself face to face with a guy I went to school with. He is blond, broad-shouldered and good-looking in a generic surfie way.

'Hi, umm ...' he says.

'Edie.' I smile (number five). These smiles are starting to seem like very hard work.

'That's right.' He looks over my shoulder. 'Good to see you.'

'You too, um ...' I know his name, but why would I let him know that?

He frowns. 'Josh.'

The main thing I remember about Josh is that his girlfriend, Candy, was six months pregnant at the end of Year Twelve. 'How's the baby? Was it a girl or a boy?'

Josh looks panic-stricken. I have over-stepped the boundaries of small talk. 'Gotta go.' He wends his way past me into the crowd.

I am used to it, but it is still deflating. The evening hasn't started well. People jostle me and I wonder what I am doing here. *This is not what I do. I am not a going-to-bars kind of person.*

I make it to the bar, order a drink and smile at the barman (number six). He is too cool to smile back.

Sipping my drink, I search the medley of faces. *Where is he? Why didn't he leave my name at the door? Is he busy telling some other girl he likes her?* Hordes of people, most of them rockstar chic, mingle with no effort at all.

I thought when I was getting dressed that maybe I would fit in for once. I thought I'd find Jay and feel at home. Instead, I feel the way I always do when surrounded by people – like I want to escape. At times like these I often think it would be nice to have a box to climb into. If I could erect an Instant Shy Shelter and get inside I'd be happy to stay here all night.

Then I see a tattered blue denim jacket. My stomach takes a high dive.

Jay is up near the stage. Unlike me, he looks relaxed. His hair is falling over one eye and he is smiling in a way he never smiles at me: broadly, flirtatiously. A pale hand with long, black fingernails is draped over his shoulder. The owner of this hand has dark hair which hangs halfway down her back and long legs that emerge from a leopard-print miniskirt and pour themselves into stiletto boots.

Now that's the kind of girl Jay would really like, says the chief ant.

As I register this, she leans over and plants a long kiss on his lips.

I drain my drink, fight my way to the door and leave my glass in a pot plant on the way out. *He likes me not.*

The streets are teeming with the usual mixture of backpackers, surfers and middle-aged hipsters. I am empty from the sudden loss of joy. The ants have gone, their job is done. No one looks at me. I am almost convinced I am invisible until I hear someone call my name.

I look around, but can't see anyone.

'Edie.'

The voice is coming from the other side of the road. I peer through the cars. A man is waving at me from the other side of the street.

It is Professor Brownlow. How extraordinary. He makes his way between the cars towards me. He isn't wearing his glasses. As he approaches I am caught like a rabbit in the headlights of his astonishing blue eyes.

His legs are hidden in a pair of faded jeans and an untucked Hawaiian-print number has replaced his usual business shirt. Thongs instead of loafers complete this startling costume change. His hair is sticking up from his head in salty wisps and a towel hangs over his shoulder.

'Hello. What brings you here?' He stops as he reaches me.

'Oh, I was going to a band, Gary Jaworski, but I changed my mind.'

'Gary Jaworski?' Professor Brownlow lifts his eyebrows. 'I love his music. What was that one, "I'm Your Love Receiver, Baby?" Great stuff, but you'd be too young to remember.'

'No, I know that one. My mum was into him.' I eye his towel. 'Have you been swimming in the dark?'

'Yes.' Professor Brownlow smiles. 'I don't get to the beach often enough, so, while I can ...'

This night swimming hints at a reckless streak I hadn't suspected. 'You came down here just to swim?'

'No. There's a crustacean symposium at the Sands Resort; starting tomorrow. I'm giving my *Libnia* paper. You remember.'

'Oh yes, the *Libnia*.' It rings vague bells. 'So, a crab symposium, huh?' I visualise an excitable group of crabs seated around a table. 'Sounds, um, fun.'

'Not as much fun as you might think.'

'Are you dissing the crab symposium?'

Professor Brownlow laughs. He looks much younger and ... naughtier than he does in the lab. 'No, you know I've got a thing for crabs.'

His voice is neutral, but I am pretty sure I'm catching a whiff of sexual innuendo. No, I mustn't be paranoid. Sally wouldn't give him my writing. Would she?

'I'm staying just here.' He points at the pink stucco-rendered motel we're standing next to. 'The conference is putting me up. I'm the keynote speaker.'

We both look at the building.

'Very Mediterranean,' I say.

'Mediterranean with an outback influence.' Professor Brownlow points at the old carriage wheel suspended over the entrance arch. 'I'm supposed to be at the dinner, but, well ...'

'You'd rather go swimming?'

'Yes.'

'Is Belinda with you?' I am pleased with myself for remembering her name. Usually I think of her as Professor Brownlow's wife.

Professor Brownlow shakes his head but doesn't elaborate.

I hear a miaow and look down. A black cat winds between my feet. 'Kafka? Is that you?'

The cat miaows again, looking up at me with its lemon eyes.

I bend to stroke it. 'Gary's in the pub if you're looking for him,' I murmur, 'just up the road there.'

'Kafka?' enquires Professor Brownlow. 'As in *Kafka on the Shore*?'

I stand up and our eyes meet. For some reason I blush. 'It seemed to fit.'

'Do you want to come in for a drink?' asks Professor Brownlow. 'I'd like to talk to you some more about Japanese literature.'

He says this as if it is the obvious thing to do when running into your research assistant on the street. As if it is a natural extension of our pleasant working relationship. We talk about Japanese literature at work, so why not in his mock-Mediterranean/outback motel room? It seems churlish to refuse. What is more, I am grateful for the diversion. I don't want to be left alone with only my spiteful ants for company.

So even though I know going into your married boss's motel room is heavy with meaning and despite the fact that I have no more to say on the topic of Japanese literature, before I know it I find I have said, 'Yes. Why not?'

When I look down, Kafka has vanished.

Chapter Twenty-one

The behaviour of a human being in sexual
matters is often a prototype for the whole
of his other modes of reaction in life.

SIGMUND FREUD

Professor Brownlow opens his mini-bar. 'Beer, wine or
gin? Or would you prefer a cup of tea?'

'Gin, thanks.' I perch on the edge of the solitary
chair, wondering what I am doing here. There has been
nothing about our work relationship to prepare me for
the awkward intimacy of a Lighthouse Bay motel room.
I avoid looking at the bed, which is difficult as it takes
up most of the room.

My erotica and what Professor Brownlow does or
doesn't know about it hangs between us like a giant
snapping crab.

Professor Brownlow opens a beer and hands me a
gin. He eases himself onto the bed and puts his legs up.
'Cheers.'

'Cheers.' I down my gin in an effort to paper over the social gaps.

'So, which authors have you read apart from Murakami?' asks Professor Brownlow.

None, would be the correct answer, but why tell the truth when you can lie? 'Nori Toyota is one of my favourites.' I am careful not to look into Professor Brownlow's beautiful eyes as I need all my wits about me. I see his glasses on the bedside table. 'Can you see all right without your glasses?' I wish he would put them on.

'I can see well enough for this kind of thing.'

'For discussions about Japanese literature, you mean?'

Professor Brownlow gives me a quizzical look. 'Indeed. For discussions about Japanese literature with my talented research assistant.'

The giant crab snaps its menacing pincers. I retreat back into my chair.

Professor Brownlow smiles. 'I haven't heard of Nori Toyota.' He pulls a laptop from the bedside table towards him and opens it. 'Might just Google him.'

Damn Google to hell. Why wasn't I born into an era where fact-checking required more effort? A three-day journey on horseback to a rundown library with no Japanese books, for example. Don't these web nerds ever consider the consequences of their actions? 'He's not very well known.'

'Hmm, no, can't be.' Professor Brownlow scrolls down the screen. 'Who else do you like?' He looks up, fingers poised on the keyboard.

'No one else.' I am sullen. 'Only Nori.'

'You know, I like your writing a lot, Edie.' Professor Brownlow's voice is mild. 'You are an interesting woman.'

The giant crab attacks. Its pincers are sharp and strong. I gasp like a small fish being pulled towards its sandy burrow. I turn red, then white with terror. My mouth is dry and my hands are wet.

Professor Brownlow taps a few keys on his keyboard. 'It reminds me of the work of the late Nagasaki. I think you're filling a niche market there. You should do a pitch to the crab symposium. They'd love it.'

I am lost for words. Professor Brownlow is more deeply eccentric than I'd ever suspected. Lighthouse Bay could sink into the sea before I'd stand in front of an audience and discuss erotic literature. I tip my glass to my mouth, but there is no gin left. I feel as exposed as a crab larva under the microscope but not nearly so innocent.

'I'm serious. We could use some light relief in the program. You could team it with your drawings.' He double clicks on his mouse and an image fills the screen. It is my Hercule Poirot crab larva. He tilts his head to one side. 'I'm still trying to figure out a way to slip them into my presentation.' Looking up from his keyboard, he gazes at my face. 'What? You thought I'd be shocked? I'm flattered you think of me like that. Here I am – a boring forty-two-year-old academic. '

'It's not you.' I gulp. 'It's nothing like you. It's fiction.'

Professor Brownlow smiles. 'If you say so, Edie.'

I don't know where to look. You could sauté crab sticks on my burning face.

'I'm afraid I got you into my motel room under false pretences.' Professor Brownlow focuses the beam of his cerulean eyes on me.

Oh help. Those eyes should be classified as WMDs – Weapons of Mass Desire. My heart palpitates and sweat breaks out in my armpits. This is it – he's read my fantasies, now he wants to act them out. My eyes meet his and a tremor passes through me – I don't know if it's lust or fear. My body sways towards him like a charmed snake.

Professor Brownlow looks puzzled. He nods towards his laptop, breaking the charm. 'I could really do with some help typing up my presentation for tomorrow.'

My heart slows, but my cheeks grow hotter. How embarrassing. I probably looked like I was about to throw myself at him. Embarrassment is followed by indignation. He lured me into his motel room with Japanese literature, not to seduce me, but just so I could type up his speech? The cad. How dare he? I should slap his face and leave. That's what a Brontë heroine would do. That, or throw his laptop out the window onto the windy moors.

Instead I say, 'Of course, Ralph.' I hold out my hands for the laptop. 'I'd be happy to help.'

I am woken by the sun streaming into my eyes. As I open them I find I am looking straight into Professor Brownlow's face. I feel like I have hardly slept at all.

I am lying on top of the almost unruffled covers of his king-sized bed.

Professor Brownlow is sitting on the edge of the bed wearing his regulation short shorts and loafers. His glasses sparkle in the sun. Today he has added a tie to his button-up shirt. I wonder what Sally would say about this wardrobe addition. Personally, I find his lack of dress sense quite sexy. It shows he has more important things to think about.

'You look like Botticelli's Venus,' he says.

I am familiar with the picture; the naked, golden-tressed woman standing in a shell. And lovely though the image is, there is one aspect of it which troubles me – the nakedness. I glance down at myself and find I am still wearing my complete outfit – skirt, tights, T-shirt, all intact.

'I'm sorry.' Professor Brownlow smiles. He doesn't look sorry. 'I meant your hair – the way it's lit up in the sun.' He holds one lock up to the light. 'See what I mean?' It is an intimate gesture, and although his manner is more scientific than personal, my heart still quickens.

Fuelled only by teabags and biscuits in plastic wrappers, Professor Brownlow and I had worked until two in the morning. By this stage driving home had all the appeal of root canal surgery.

'You may as well stay. I'll sleep on the floor if you like, Edie,' he'd said, giving a big yawn.

'No, no, it's a big bed.' The mood between us was so comradely, so businesslike; I knew sleep was the only thing which was going to happen in that bed. There had not been even the slightest frisson between us as we lay down. Well, that's a lie, there had been a teensy frisson on my part, but I don't think it showed.

And it *was* a very big bed.

Professor Brownlow stands; laptop under his arm. 'Thank you for your help last night, Edie. I'm sorry I kept you up so late. I'll pay you overtime, of course.' He sounds brisk. There is no hint in his manner that our working relationship has breached any of the usual guidelines.

This is reassuring. Even though he has read my erotic fantasy about him, we have shared a bed, and he has compared me to a naked goddess, we are still all above board, shipshape and totally professional. Excellent.

He glances at his watch. 'I'd better be going. Will you stay here for a while?'

'No.' I slide my feet onto the floor and stand up. 'Things to do.'

This sexless bed-sharing seems to be turning into a pattern, I reflect. I yawn and follow him to the door. Am I really so unattractive no one wants to have sex with me? Apparently so. And I'd always been under the impression that men would have sex with anyone given the opportunity.

Anyone except me.

'Yo, Edz.' A voice hails me as we step out into the sun.

Tim the surfer boy gives me a thumbs-up as he rides by on his bike, surfboard under his arm. 'Surf's up in the

Bay,' he yells back to me. 'See you out there.' His eyes slide to Professor Brownlow and he winks at me.

'Friend of yours?' asks Professor Brownlow.

I look after him. 'Kind of. I'm starting to think he might be stalking me.'

Chapter Twenty-two

If you can't do it, give up.

SIGMUND FREUD

Sally is sitting on the verandah couch texting when I get home. She presses Send, then glances at her watch. 'What time do you call this?'

I look at my watch. 'Ten o'clock. Why?'

'Life coaching. Nine o'clock.'

I had completely forgotten my appointment with Sal. 'I didn't think we made a time.'

'Where have you been, anyway?' She smiles in a nudge, nudge, wink, wink way. 'Out on the town?'

'I don't want to talk about it.'

'You're going to have to tell me sometime. May as well be now.'

I shake my head.

'You're giving me your stubborn look, Ed. It's not going to work.'

'Okay, I'll tell you later. Some other time. Not now.' My voice squeaks.

'Bad night, huh?' Sally gives me a long look. 'I know what it's like.'

I doubt that Sally's bad nights are anything like mine.

'Some guys just don't know how to satisfy a girl,' Sally muses.

'No.' This is close to the mark but I suspect we are talking about two different things.

'Did you know that in Victorian times doctors used to treat female hysterics with genital massage?'

'Sally, I am not hysterical.'

'Did I say you were? I'm just telling you an interesting historical fact. You're the one jumping to conclusions. Later, they moved on to vibrators and water hoses.'

'Really?'

'Uh huh.'

'Good business to be in. I bet they made a motza out of that.'

'Mmm, I think Victorian women were a pretty hysterical bunch. All that lie back and think of England stuff. So, did you get your ten smiles in?'

I'd forgotten about the smiles. I add them up. 'I only got up to six.'

Sally frowns.

'But they were good ones.'

'I suppose that's not too bad. See how easy it is?'

I think of the doorman, Josh my school mate and the barman. Perhaps I was doing it wrong, but I don't want to repeat the lesson. 'Easy peasy.'

'Let's go,' she says.

I am confused for a moment, but then I see the cue

cards on Sally's lap. Could I perhaps stage an epileptic fit
or a stroke?

'Don't even try it,' says Sal.

Sally has seen my tricks before. There is no escape.
'Lead on,' I say.

Fifteen minutes later, Sally and I are leaning on the
fence at the beach. I have been briefed on my strategy.

'The fifth stranger.' Sally sidles away, just far enough
to look like she's not with me.

A couple of joggers go by. It's lucky I don't have to
talk to them as I'd have to catch them first. Next comes
a mother wheeling a baby in a pram. It is a pity they're
number three and four as I do a good line in baby talk. But
perhaps Sally hasn't been counting? I glance over at her.

She gives me a stern look. 'Next,' she mouths.

'A pleasant social interchange. A pleasant social
interchange,' I mutter to myself. I practise my smile, but
a smile without spirit is like a dance without music. Or a
capella singing. I've never seen the point of that.

A surfer picks himself up out of the water and begins
a lazy stroll towards me. Sally and I have workshopped a
number of opening lines. *How old is your baby?* would
have been perfect for the last two. *Do you know where
the toilet is?* was my all-purpose suggestion, but Sally
gunned that one down.

'Too bogan, boring, personal and difficult to move
on to something more interesting,' she said.

I disagreed. You could comment on the location. *Oh
so convenient/inconvenient!* Compare it to other toilet
locations you have known. *But not nearly as inconvenient*

as going to the toilet in India, so I hear. Or alternatively, *Not nearly as convenient as going to the toilet in Japan.* The toilet conversation would demonstrate my knowledge of other cultures. I was holding it in reserve.

As the surfer comes towards me, recognition dawns. *No way.* I turn to Sal and make a slashing motion across my throat. We haven't rehearsed, but I'm pretty sure this is a universally recognised abort mission signal.

Sally shakes her head and gives me a thumbs-up.

Is she mad? I shake my head and ramp up the slashing actions, like a scuba diver whose air-supply hose has been bitten in half by a great white shark. Sally doesn't realise who this surfer is.

There is probably one in every town – a person whose aura screams that they find you beneath contempt. Simply put, unfriendly-goatee-beard-man is my nemesis. There is no reason to this, no shared history of hostility; we are not Israel and Palestine or Serbia and Croatia. We are more like Sydney and Adelaide. I've never been to Adelaide and I'm sure it's a very nice place. Just like I'm a very nice person. But I can sense that unfriendly-goatee-beard-man thinks otherwise. I am nerdy Adelaide and he is cool Sydney.

Sally gives me her laser-beam stare. If I was a superhero I would be putting up my plutonium defence shield now. I am powerless to resist. Unfriendly-goatee-beard-man is coming closer. I give Sally my possum in the headlights look in a last plea for mercy.

She scribbles something on a piece of paper with a marker pen and holds it up. SURF!!! it commands.

Goatee-beard-man is five metres away, four, three, two ...

'H ... how was the surf?' I ask.

He keeps walking. I feel a bit sick as I watch him go past. I knew he was unfriendly, but I didn't realise he was *that* unfriendly.

A couple of metres past me he stops and turns, pulling a yellow ball out of each ear. 'Did you say something?' He holds up his hand. 'Earplugs.'

His voice is not what I expected; it is neutral, maybe even friendly.

Sally waves her sign behind his head like she is meeting an unknown guest at the airport.

'How was the surf?' I ask again.

He looks surprised. 'Good.' He half-turns to point at the break. 'That's the spot. You goin' out?'

Behind his head, Sally has changed her sign. It now reads BOOK. She jiggles it in an assertive way.

'I ... I would, but I'm in the middle of a very exciting book.'

He smiles.

This is good. I feel a surge of exhilaration. We are having a conversation. Or about to. We will talk about books! I can't wait. Books are my forte.

'I read a book once,' he says. 'It was about all these people killing each other.'

'Oh.' My mind goes blank. That's the trouble with this conversation thing, it's so unpredictable. You think you are proceeding happily in one direction then, whammo, they throw you a curve ball.

209

'Have you read it?' he asks, like it's the only book in the world.

'I don't think so.'

Behind him Sally is smiling and nodding like she thinks this is going swimmingly. That's because she can't hear what we're talking about. She doesn't realise we are now stuck in a conversational version of the Bermuda Triangle.

'Well,' he says.

'Well.' It now occurs to me that he has no idea how to extricate himself from this awkward social situation I have created. Could he be as socially deficient as I am? If so, this is a very dangerous state of affairs. We are in a quicksand from which neither of us has the skills to escape. We could be stuck here forever.

He coughs.

I smile like he has made an excellent point. *That cough reminds me of another cough I once encountered in South America* ... They could make a movie about us. You've seen *Die Hard,* now coming soon to a cinema near you – *Die Shyly and Awkwardly.* If I come out of this alive I want my part played by Scarlett Johansson.

We both shuffle our feet. I should have made a contingency plan when Sally and I were discussing this. *Ear scratch means ring me now.* But it's too late for that. I cast Sally a beseeching glance. She has abandoned me, leaning over the railing to chat to a surfer on the beach below. Their words flow like the Amazon in flood.

'Well.' A small drip escapes my conversational tap. *Well, well, well.*

'Hmm,' he says, displaying a wider range than me. He is a virtuoso of the monosyllables.

'Hmm,' I echo. I'm sure he is wishing he never took those earplugs out. I want to tell him he is dismissed, but it is beyond me. My mind scrabbles for something to say.

I don't know how long we stand there. It feels like forever – like I could have read *War and Peace* twice over. I have no idea how to break this deadlock and, apparently, neither does he. I have met my match. Like two tongue-tied cowboys, we are trapped in a duel. *This town ain't big enough for both of us and it isn't me who's going to leave.*

'Edie,' Sally calls at last.

Her voice comes to me like a life raft. 'Gotta go,' I say apologetically, like I would so love to stay and chat some more.

'Nice talking to you.' He sounds like he means it. It must be the relief of escaping.

'You too.' Already I have reframed the encounter in my mind as a pleasant social interchange.

'How did that go?' asks Sal when I wander over. 'Sorry, I got a bit distracted.'

'It was cool. We talked about books and surfing.' If I don't make it seem like a big success she'll force me to do it again.

'You see. All you need to do is give it a go.'

Sally and I walk home across the football field.

'I heard you on the radio yesterday,' I say as we reach my street. While I had been horrified at the time, given

211

that the sky hasn't fallen, it is possible I may have been over-reacting.

Sally shows no sign of embarrassment. 'Oh yeah, that was great. I got a new client out of it.'

'Erotic writing?' I still find it a bit hard to believe that people are getting off on my writing.

'She's an interesting one. She wants the erotic writing, but she also wants creative coaching. She says her inner muse has deserted her. She needs to reconnect.' Sally drawls this last word.

The inner muse thing rings a bell. 'It isn't Djennifer, is it?'

The way Sally looks at me, I know I am right. 'Client confidentiality, Ed.'

I smile. 'Djennifer with a D, right?'

But Sally's mouth is locked tight.

When I get home it is eleven o'clock. The house is quiet. I sneak past Jay's room. His door is closed. Maybe the long-legged leopard-print mini girl is in there with him. I wonder why he invited me to the gig. He must have felt sorry for me.

I continue upstairs and sit down at my desk. Today is an erotic writing day, so I switch on my computer and fill in my chart.

Tuesday: 52 days
Pain level: 8.5.
Location: Left side of chest
As the computer boots up I remember I was supposed to go running.

Today still doesn't feel like a running day. Murakami must have a much more structured life than me. I haven't given up on the idea of running though. Absolutely not.

Run at the next suitable opportunity, I write in my *Tips for self-improvement* section.

Having soothed my conscience on that point, I change into my writing outfit. For some reason I work best in clothing with no distinct boundaries. An extra-large T-shirt and track pants is good. I suspect a caftan would be even better and the next time I see one in a shop I'm going to snap it up. I will wear it with no underwear, leaving me with the sensation of being draped in a sheet. I've tried working naked, but it's not quite right.

I imagine Sooty, when she is not wearing her red satin dress, works in slimline black pants and a little black beret. She puts on bright red lipstick and sexy lingerie in case an unexpected lover should drop by. As I don't have a lover, this is not an issue for me.

My evening with Professor Brownlow has left me tired but contemplative. I feel on the verge of something which is eluding me – an epiphany perhaps.

My mind seizes on the word. *Epiphany*. I pull the dictionary towards me. 'Manifestation of Christ to the Gentiles as represented by the Magi', says the *Pocket Oxford*. Evidently it is not a good dictionary. I try the thesaurus instead – *revelation, illumination, inspiration*.

If I sat around all day waiting for an epiphany I'd never get anywhere, says the bonsai.

I look at the bonsai's stunted limbs and dried out leaves and it seems a bit cruel to state the obvious – that it's not getting anywhere. 'Each to their own,' I say.

The bonsai sniffs. *'Go on then, wait for an epiphany, see if I care.'*

'I will. Just watch me.'

My fingers hover over the keyboard, waiting.

While I wait, I gaze out the window at the sea. The sea and I have a curious relationship. It both lures and repels me. I can watch the waves all day but nothing would get me in there.

Ten minutes pass while I contemplate the way the foam flicks off the back of the waves. The bonsai is right; neither revelation nor inspiration strikes. I am not in the mood for erotica.

I think of Jay. 'Jaybird'. It must feel weird to have a chart-topping song named after you. I wouldn't like to have people think they knew me because of something like that.

I push my chair out from my desk and stand up. I don't quite know how it happens but I find myself sitting on the edge of my bed. Mum's notebook is in my hands and I am reading the line she has written on the inside front cover.

Is wanting everything the same as wanting nothing?

It is very similar to something Sylvia once said. Sylvia Plath, that beautiful genius who gassed herself at the age of thirty. In retrospect, an attraction to Sylvia was not a good thing.

*

I am ten and I am tired. I am tucked up in bed, my hair spread across the pillow. Mum is propped up next to me. She is wearing an old singlet and short shorts. Her pale legs stretch out endlessly along the covers. I lean against her and she smells like salt. This is familiar and safe. She reads to me. Poetry reading is our night-time routine. We don't only read Sylvia Plath. AA Milne and Spike Milligan are also popular but Sylvia is our favourite.

'I close my eyes ...' Mum hardly has to say any more. I know the words to A Mad Girl's Love Song *off by heart. I repeat the last line of each verse with her.*

'It's like that for me.' Mum smiles at me when she finishes. 'Sometimes I think I made you up inside my head.'

'Me too,' I say. And this seems a beautiful thing to me; we have made each other up out of nothing but dreams and fantasies.

We hold hands as my eyelids droop.

These days I realise how selective Mum was with Sylvia's poems. How much she knew but didn't say. I close the notebook and place it back in the chest, next to Mum's well-thumbed copies of *Ariel* and *The Collected Poems*.

I look out the window again at the waves flinging themselves against the shore, think how easy it would be to Google her name then shut down the computer before this happens.

It seems that today is not about either writing or running. I must venture downstairs in search of purpose.

Chapter Twenty-three

I cannot think of any need in childhood as strong as the need for a father's protection.

SIGMUND FREUD

A raucous laugh drifts up the stairs as I open my door. This is alarming. I was expecting a quiet house. My mind was turning to baking scones, maybe gardening, possibly spring cleaning. The fact I have never done these things before is no impediment to doing them now. Domestic routines could well be the key to happiness.

I am also affronted. This is my childhood home. I should be able to wander around it without having to encounter raucous laughter. I decide to go for a walk instead. If I sneak past quietly, the raucous person, whoever he is, will not see me.

I am almost out the front door when a loud voice calls my name. 'Edie.'

I turn. Gary Jaworski is waving at me from the kitchen. 'Come and have a drink.'

He sounds like he is in his house and I have dropped over. Clearly Gary is the sort of person who knows how to make himself at home.

'I've made a pizza for lunch,' says Gary. 'Why don't you share it with us?'

This is even more disorientating. Shouldn't I be asking him to have lunch with me, not the other way around? But his good host air is irresistible. As I trail towards him a miaow sounds at my feet and I look down. 'Hi, Kafka.' The cat sits down with its eyes on Gary.

'A cat philosopher, huh?' Gary opens the fridge. 'Beer?'

I glance at my watch. The hands have not even met at the top yet.

Gary catches this gesture as he turns around, two perspiring cans in his hands. 'You're not one of those no-drinks-before-sundown people are you?' He says this in a way that implies this is an uptight middle-class consideration.

Suddenly I don't want to be one of those types. I want to be a rockstar – a crazy, wild, live-for-the-moment artistic type. Or at least feel like one. I hold out my hand. 'Thanks.' The cold can reassures me. I am leading an exciting, creative life. Even if no one wants to have sex with me.

Gary puts his hand on the small of my back as he ushers me towards the lounge room. 'Look who I found.'

I stop in my tracks like a donkey sighting a snake. Jay is sitting on the couch with the leopard-skin mini girl from last night beside him. They obviously spent the night together. *Or did they?* My intimate-ometer measures the distance between them and comes up undecided. They are closer than friends, but not quite close enough to confirm them as lovers.

Jay eyes me as if I might bite. 'Hey.' He has a can of beer in his hand. So does leopard-mini girl. 'This is Tanya,' he says.

Tanya is pale. She looks young enough to be at school, but if I was her mother I'd give her the day off and tell her to buck up. 'Hi,' she says. She says this as if it costs her a lot; as if hi is a marathon she wishes she hadn't had to run.

I feel like tipping my beer over her. Instead, I consider my seating options. There are two solitary leather chairs and the couch on which Jay and Tanya have staked their claim. A leather chair would be the sensible option but the beer in my hand convinces me today is not a day for sense or sensibility. No, bugger Jane Austen, today is a day for recklessness, attitude and Brontë-style daring. *I cannot live without my life!*

I lower myself onto the sofa next to Jay. I am aiming for a Courtney Love or Amy Winehouse 'fuck you' attitude, but suspect my stained T-shirt and track pants may be detracting from my stage presence.

As soon as my saggy-bummed bottom hits the couch I realise I have made a terrible mistake. Beer or no beer, I am feeling awkward. A personal-space-invasion alarm is going off inside my head. I have breached the recommended approach distance for whatever class of relationship now exists between Jay and me.

I observe Jay out of the corner of my eye. He is looking awkward too. As well he should. I edge away from him, trying to reduce the volume on my alarm. The couch is not quite big enough for this to have much effect. Jay doesn't shift, but leans away from me. Or is he leaning towards Tanya?

Human interactions are so trying sometimes. Why don't we cut out the subtlety? Wouldn't it be much easier to just go outside and fight it out? A quick slap and punch and I'd feel much better.

Gary, oblivious to the tension in the room, settles himself on the leather chair opposite us. I am not surprised when Kafka wanders in and crouches, his shiny eyes on Gary. Once again we are in a nativity scene, our Jesus an ageing, but still sexy, rockstar. Gary has bleached-blond hair and a row of earrings up his left ear. He is snake-hipped in his brown leather trousers and still in possession of the charisma that had teenage girls fainting at his concerts in the eighties.

Tanya sips her beer through black-lipsticked lips and says nothing. Jay, still leaning towards Tanya, also sips his beer and says nothing. I take several large gulps of my beer and gaze out the window, searching for a suitable topic of conversation. If Sally was here she would know what to say.

'Was it a successful concert last night?' This sentence, which was smooth with an edge of irony in my head, comes out like a pompous librarian discussing a chamber music recital.

Jay's brown eyes flicker to me. He doesn't smile. 'Yes, it was … rather.'

His fake English accent is so faint I could almost pretend it wasn't there, except I know it was. I flush.

He notes this, I can tell.

Again, I wonder why I have ever felt Jay and I have a connection. Obviously this is not the case. He thinks I am an idiot. And he is right. Everything I say or do turns to sawdust in his presence.

'It was rockin',' says Tanya. 'Wasn't it, babes?' she adds, to Jay.

Jay smiles at her. 'Totally.'

I want to pinch him. Hard. And I wish I had said, 'Was it rockin' last night, babes?' That would have been a good thing to say. But I can't imagine saying that. Not without a script and a rehearsal.

'Well, this is fun.' Gary smiles from one of us to the other, his leathery skin crinkling up around his eyes.

I smile back, while thinking that covering myself with honey and rolling in an ants' nest would be much more pleasurable.

'Watcha doin' all the way over there, babe?' Gary says to Tanya.

Tanya rises, her beer in her hand. She glides across to Gary, perches on his lap and plants a long kiss on his lips. Gary's hands land on her leopard-skin bottom. The cat puffs out the hair on its neck. A low growl emanates from its throat.

Oh. So that's the way it is. A ray of sun pokes

through the damp fog which descended on me in the Top Pub last night. I straighten my leaning tower.

This is only a small action, but Jay looks straight at me. He smiles in a way which tells me he knows exactly what is going on.

I remember, again, what it is we have in common – intuition. Jay is attuned to the unspoken. This is rare, especially in a man. I smile back.

Gary and Tanya are locked in an embrace which is likely to lead to the bedroom. He is running his hand up her slender, pale thigh. I hope she is old enough for this. I hope her mother knows where she is.

Jay and I are sitting closer together than housemates but further than lovers. Our leaning towers are now angled towards each other. He puts his beer down on the floor and our shoulders brush, as if by accident. We catch each other's eyes, pause and look away. And I sense we have been leading to this moment for a long time, possibly a lifetime.

'What happened to you last night, Edie?'

I like the way he says my name, as if it is something to be cherished.

He rests his head on the back of the couch, inclined towards me.

I do the same. We are two heads on pillows with not much distance between us. It is like being in bed. I can tell by the languorous look in his eyes he is thinking this too. 'I turned up. But then I saw you. With Tanya.'

Jay and I glance towards Gary and Tanya. They seem to have forgotten we are here. Gary's hand has disappeared up her skirt and there isn't a lot of space up there.

Jay rolls his eyes. 'Let's go outside.'

We sit on the couch outside. Now, we are much, much closer than house-mates, but still not as close as lovers. I feel like we are oppositely charged magnets, held apart by sheer force of will. If I stretched out my hand I could touch … I look away at the sea then back down at his hand. It is resting at his side. I don't think I have ever found a hand quite so fascinating. Jay's hand is pale, but not as pale as mine. His nails are cut short, except for his thumbnail, which is longer. I imagine this has a guitar-playing function. I think it would be quite easy to slip my hand inside his. I think it would fit quite well.

'What are you thinking about?' asks Jay.

Our eyes meet and a pulse passes through me, pulling at my stomach. 'Nothing much.' I don't look away. 'How about you?'

'Same.' Jay half-smiles.

Silence falls. The tension is almost unbearable. No, it *is* unbearable. My hand reaches out, touches his. I am astonished at my daring, but it is easier to touch him than not touch him. He takes my hand, winds his fingers through mine, rubs my palm with his thumb, runs his hand up my wrist. A warm, languid feeling spreads through me. I could purr. Jay is very good at holding hands. I think he has done this before.

'So,' he says.

'So.'

'You know I'm more or less your brother-in-law.'

I think about that. 'Uncle-in-law. And only if Rochelle and Dad get married.'

'In-law things are bad. So I've heard.'

I can't tell if he is joking or not. 'You're not speaking from personal experience?'

'No.'

We are still holding hands. This feels very right. I wish time would stop – we could stay here forever, poised on the brink of possibility. But that isn't the way life works. You go forwards or backwards, you never stay still.

'I'm in no position to start a relationship,' he says, but he doesn't release my hand. His thumb still traces a curve across my skin. 'I'm ...' he seems to be searching for a word, 'resting.'

'That's fine. We don't have to have a relationship. We can just talk. And maybe hold hands. Holding hands is nice.' And I don't think holding hands has ever been this nice before. Right now I would be happy to hold hands with Jay for the rest of my life.

Jay smiles, his fingers twined through mine. 'I like holding hands with you.'

So we talk. Well, mainly I talk at first. And time does stand still. Before long I find I have told him things I've never told anyone else – big things and little things. How I have a freckle on my left hand that lets me know which hand is which, or else I'd never know. How many lovers I've had and which ones meant something to me and which didn't.

I don't know why I have never told anyone else these things. But then I think maybe I do. Jay is different.

He is interested in how I am – not just in how I could be if he trained me right, or in what I can offer him. Usually when I'm with men they do all the talking. It occurs to me that listening the way Jay does is a wonderful gift.

I tell him about Daniel. Seeing as I am in a confessional mood I don't hold back. 'You know what irks me?'

'What irks you?' asks Jay. 'Now that's an under-used word. I like it.'

I find I am shy again. 'He would never, you know ...' I wave my free hand vaguely.

Jay cocks his head, waiting.

'He was always so ...'

Jay raises one eyebrow, but still doesn't talk.

I take a deep breath and speak fast. 'He would never come first.' I can hardly believe I have said that.

Jay purses his lips. He looks puzzled.

'Don't you think that's just too ...'

Jay regards me with a steady look. 'We're talking about sex?'

I nod.

He smiles. 'He sounds like a man of high principles.'

'Can you have high principles about sex?'

'High principles start with sex. There's equality, fraternity ...'

'Liberty?'

'Liberty?' Jay meets my eyes.

A flash of chemistry darts between us. My heart beats faster.

'I think you probably sacrifice liberty for intimacy,' says Jay.

The concept of intimacy interests us both. I quote Jane Austen, 'It is not time or opportunity that determines intimacy. Seven years would be insufficient for some, while seven days are more than enough for others.'

'The funny thing is, you can find intimacy with unlikely people,' says Jay. 'Even people who seem quite unpromising at first.' He gives me a lop-sided smile.

I know he is talking about me. And suddenly I can see the value of old-fashioned courtship. Getting to know someone intimately before you jump into bed with them, rather than after is not a bad idea at all.

The sun moves on while Jay and I hold hands on the couch. It is like travelling through space with a single companion. The talk goes here and there; it stops and starts without a moment's awkwardness. I can say anything; anything at all and I know it will be just right.

'How do you feel about bonsais?' I ask.

'Hmm.' Jay considers this. 'I like the way they look, but ...'

'But?'

'Aren't they a bit like a caged animal?'

I nod. 'If a bonsai could talk, what do you think it would be like?'

'Well, if I was a bonsai I'd probably be all warped and twisted. The pruning would get me down. You'd have to end up with a chip on your shoulder, wouldn't you?'

'That's exactly what they're like.'

'Know a few bonsais, do you?'

'Just one.'

We smile at each other and my stomach skips. *He gets me.*

'Do you have any strange obsessions or, like, stuff I should know about?' I ask.

'Before we go any further, you mean?'

I shrug. 'It's good to get things out in the open.'

'What sort of things?'

'Strange jobs?'

'This from a girl who draws baby crabs for a living.'

'It's a perfectly respectable career choice.'

'I was a games host at Luna Park for three years.'

'Games host?'

'Laughing clowns, knock-em-downs, goin' fishin', you know ...'

'I've never met a games host before. Give me your spiel.'

Jay puts his spare hand to his mouth like a megaphone. 'Come try your luck. Knock 'em down and win a bear for your girlfriend.'

I smile. 'That's amazing. You sound so shonky and sleazy.'

'Years of practice. Your turn now.'

'What?'

'Give me your crab larvae spiel.'

'I don't have a crab larvae spiel.'

'You must have. What do you say to get them posing at their best? Yeah, baby, show us your ...'

'Mandibular palpus.'

'Sexy. What else?'

'Ooh, yeah, get those maxillipeds waving. Do it for Edie.'

'Sounds like a riot. Does it work?'

'Sadly, no. They're dead.'

'You draw dead crab larvae? That's macabre. I'd imagined them swimming around in a fish tank. How do you kill them?'

I mime a pistol shot, blowing the tips of my fingers. 'Formalin.'

'You're a scary woman.'

'Someone's got to do it. Damn critters'll take over otherwise.'

'Really?' Jay effects mock horror.

'You've seen *Attack of the Crab Monsters*.'

Jay smiles. 'Best movie I've seen in ages.'

'Too scary for me.' Inside the house, Tanya giggles. 'Do you think you're much like him?'

'Gary?'

I nod.

'More than I want to be. But I've seen what it's done to him. He lives in a bubble. No one tells him the truth. He's got people he pays to be nice to him.'

'You don't want to be famous?'

Jay shrugs. 'I used to think I did. He'd send me all these postcards. *Played Seattle today. Huge crowd! What a night in Tokyo! Just got home.* It seemed so far from life in the 'burbs. I totally bought it. I played guitar until my little fingers bled. Then when I was thirteen I stopped.'

'What happened?'

'I started to see through him. Every time I opened a music magazine there he was with a new girl. He got older, but the girls never did. He thought he was Peter Pan.'

'Still does, by the look of things.' I glance towards the lounge room.

'Good old sex and drugs and rock and roll.' Jay looks at me from under his fringe. 'Not that there's anything wrong with that.' He smiles. 'Giving up guitar was my form of teenage rebellion. I knew it would piss him off.'

'What made you start again?'

Jay hesitates. 'In Year Eleven, this guy ... Ben, came to my school. We clicked. He wanted to start a band. He knew about Gary of course, but he never said anything. Just kept asking me to play with him. Eventually I did.'

'How did that feel?'

'Oh,' Jay sighs. 'Incredible. Like being able to talk again. But I was doing it for myself this time, not for Dad.'

Chapter Twenty-four

How bold one gets when one is sure of being loved.

SIGMUND FREUD

Edaline and Jason talked about many things. They talked about love, they talked about sex, they talked about music and happiness and sadness. They also talked about words.

'Relinquish is one of my favourite words,' said Jason. 'I'm planning on writing a song about it.'

Edaline considered the word. 'What does it mean?' She knew, but asked the question anyway, just to see what Jason would say. She was in the grip of a fascination with his mind which knew no limit.

'To retire from, give up or abandon, to put aside or desist from, to let go, surrender, to cease holding physically.'

His words were like a symphony to her ears.

She stroked his hand. It was soft, except for the roughened pads on the ends of his fingers which he used to play guitar.

'Relinquish implies regret,' Jason added, almost as an afterthought.

I turn from yesterday's writing to the back of my notebook and contemplate my chart.

Wednesday: 53 days
Pain level: Non-existent
Location: Nowhere. A miracle!

Does this mean I have got over Daniel? My head feels fresh, as though a sea breeze has blown away those sad, repetitive Daniel thoughts. I feel almost happy. No, damn it; what the hell, live dangerously, I do feel happy. I smile. I had forgotten how that felt.

I sigh, stretching my feet in bed, remembering yesterday afternoon. Jay and I had talked for hours, holding hands on the couch like teenagers. In the end, it seemed by mutual agreement, we had relinquished each other.

'I'd better ...' said Jay.

'Me too.'

We had got to our feet and drifted our separate ways.

At the time, this had been perfect – a comma, not a full-stop – the hand-holding more than enough. But now ... I wasn't so sure. There is a gravity about sex which makes you say, this has happened; we are now something to each other we weren't before. Holding hands on the couch isn't the same.

And while I know sex isn't everything I want him to acknowledge there is something between us – we have meaning to each other. What if he never wants to hold hands on the couch with me again? But I know these kinds of thoughts are useless. Relationships are what they are. Even a marriage is not enough to keep some people together.

I'm pretty sure my favourite poet, Rilke, had something to say about this. The quotation lurks out of sight and then surfaces: *We need, in love, to practice only this; letting each other go. For holding on comes easily.* And I know this is what I need to do with Jay, open my hand, relinquish, let him come back if and when he wants to. Easier said than done.

I think about what he said, *I'm in no position to start a relationship.* But what do we have if not that? An ambiguous something or other?

My ringing phone distracts me.

I pick it up. 'Yo.'

'Yo? Since when do you say yo?' It is Sal.

'It's part of my new professional erotic-writer persona, S-dog.'

Sally is very quick; she must have been listening to hip-hop too. 'I'm down with that, E-dog, but what's with this talking stuff?'

'Huh?' She's lost me.

'"Relinquish is one of my favourite words," said Jason,' Sally reads. 'What's sexy about that?'

I am taken aback. 'I thought that was an extremely sexy scene. You are aware ninety per cent of sex happens

231

in the head, aren't you?' I am making this up, but I'm pretty sure it's a fair call.

'Edie, the scene is great, beautiful – personally I love it, but my clients pay for erotica, not a high-brow discussion between two poetic librarians. As far as I can see,' she shuffles paper, 'no bodily contact beyond hand-holding happened in this scene.'

I can't believe she doesn't get it. 'Oh my God, Sally, the whole scene is just dripping with sexual tension. I can't believe you don't get it.'

'Edie.' Sally is using her firm but fair voice. 'I need sex. Not hand-holding, not even foot-rubbing, though that would be an improvement. Sex. S-E-X.'

'Oh. I didn't think it needed to be so literal.'

'They can talk while they're having sex if you want,' says Sally, like this is some kind of compromise.

I consider this and decide it may have possibilities. *Oh yes, darling, just like that. Now tell me, what do you think of the state of the economy? No, don't stop ...*

'Speaking of which,' says Sally, 'you're not interested in some extra work, are you?'

'What sort of work?'

'One of my clients is interested in a bit more ... interactivity.'

'You interact with them, don't you?'

'Mmm, but not in the particular way in which um ...'

Sally is being very circuitous. This is unlike her. It makes me uneasy. Usually she gets straight to the point. 'This work, Sal. Is it something ... distasteful?'

'No, no, no, no. Just phone sex.'

232

These last words are muttered so fast it takes me a while to process them. 'Phone sex? You want me to have phone sex with your clients?'

'Just one client at this stage. He's really into your writing. He'd go crazy for a sexy chat with you.'

'Sally! I am not having phone sex.' Even the meek have their limits.

'You could just read your writing to him over the phone. You wouldn't need to make it up on the spot.'

Sally makes it all sound so reasonable. It almost seems mean not to oblige. But the trouble is, if I give in on this point, she'll be asking for costumed re-enactments next.

'I'd charge him a hundred bucks for fifteen minutes and give you sixty.'

'No.'

'Okay, seventy.'

'It's not about the money. I ... am ... not ... having ... phone ... sex.'

'I'll talk to you about it some other time. When you're in a better mood. I'm planning the next stage of your life coaching too.'

'I thought I'd finished.'

'Life is a work in progress. How can you be finished?' Sally sounds astonished.

This is a depressing prospect. 'I was looking forward to graduating one day.'

'It's like playing sport. No matter how good you get, you can still get better.'

'I wouldn't know.'

'Self-improvement is a personal journey, Ed. If the sport analogy doesn't work for you, think of it as a road trip. Sometimes there are freeways and you go fast, sometimes you get stuck in traffic, sometimes there are crossroads and you have to make a choice ...'

'Sometimes you get sideswiped in a supermarket car park.'

'Exactly. Keep that analogy in mind. We'll talk about it next time.'

After Sally hangs up I look at my watch. It is seven-thirty. I don't need to leave for work until eight-thirty so I have no excuse not to go for a run. My mind flutters around trying to find some urgent alternative, but I will not be distracted. Murakami says that it's all about the pain. And Murakami is one of the world's greatest living writers. If the pain is the point for him, then it will be for me too.

I pull on my shorts and lace up my runners. Murakami runs ten kilometres every day but that will take some building up to. Five kilometres might be achievable. A short road trip. I will run to the top of Darling Point and back. I walk down the stairs, thinking I should run. But a warm-up is important, after all. I walk down the street, thinking I should run. Finally, at the end of the street, I can put it off no longer. I start to run.

I am running. I am running towards the beach. I would like to say I feel inspired, free-flowing, at one with my body, but in fact I feel an almost overwhelming desire to stop. *It's all about the pain, it's all about the pain*, I chant inside my head. This hurts so much it has to be doing wonders for my erotic writing. I make it to the beach. I think my legs must be a lot heavier than Murakami's. There is no way he could keep this up for ten kilometres if he had my legs.

A lean and sinewy man overtakes me as I run down the ramp to the beach. I am consoled by the fact that he does not know as much about pain as I do. I shuffle down the beach, only marginally faster than a walking pace. Darling Point seems to recede, mirage-like, as I approach it. I had planned to go to the top, but now even the bottom seems unlikely. This road trip would be easier if I had a better car.

As I run I think about Jay. What did we talk about for so long? Now that I think about it, I still know so little about him. I feel like I have been in the hands of a skilled interrogator. Jay knows everything about me, but what do I know about him? Almost nothing. He gave up playing guitar for a few years, then took it up again. That's it.

Who are his friends? What is his favourite colour? What does he like to eat? I can never admit to Sally that I know none of these things. I am a failure as a conversationalist. *And yet ...* We talked. Could it be that we skipped both shallow and medium and went straight to deep? Or did I go deep while Jay stayed shallow? Did I really tell him that Daniel never came first? *Surely not.*

These thoughts distract me and I am halfway to the Point before I realise that if I do make it there, I will never make it back. I make a u-turn, and push my trembling legs back to the house, panting and sweating. When I look at my watch I see I have been running for twenty minutes. I have to clutch the railing to help me climb the stairs.

Perhaps I have chosen the wrong role model with Murakami? I wonder if there are other writers I could model myself on – ones who are into chocolate, gin and spa baths maybe. Some research may be required.

Before I go to work, I summon my resolve and print off the love scene that Sally rejected.

I wouldn't do that if I were you, says the bonsai.

I stick my fingers in my ears and hum loudly.

Don't say I didn't tell you, it says as I walk out the door.

Jay's door is still closed when I come downstairs. *A crossroads. He likes my writing*, I tell myself. My heart is thumping, but I am determined to take the road less travelled. Leaning down, I push the papers beneath his door. *I will woo him with words.*

Exercise daily. Walk with God. Run from sin, says the church sign today. The priest waves at me from the door as I drive past. I pretend I haven't noticed, but I must admit he's got me worried. Can the alarming relevance of his signs be mere coincidence? Yes, it must be. He knows nothing about me. But I can't shake a feeling of unease. Am I a sinner?

Professor Brownlow is bent over his microscope when I come in. He looks up and smiles.

I smile back. 'How was the crab symposium?'

'Dull. But I did have an interesting chat about Japanese literature in my motel room on the night of the opening. And thank you for your help with my presentation.'

We smile at each other again. I wait for the usual symptoms to strike. But wait – my heart isn't pounding, my brain isn't turning to jelly. I think, perhaps, he could even take off his glasses without overwhelming me.

I am over my infatuation. How strange – the rose-tinted aura of sexual longing has dissipated. How did that happen? Now he is a good-looking man in short shorts who is almost twenty years older than me and loves his wife. In a way, I am disappointed. I miss my crush. It was intense while it lasted.

'You're right about Nori Toyota,' says Professor Brownlow. 'A very distinguished author.' His face is serious and I almost think I have lucked out with a name that matches up until I catch the twinkle in his eye. He laughs. 'Did you even read the Murakami?'

'Of course I did.' I snort. 'I lie, but only out of necessity.'

'We all do that. I liked your last piece of writing; the Jason one.'

'You've read that?' I blush. I have got to tell Sally to take him off her client list.

Professor Brownlow nods. 'It was more … intimate than the others; more romantic. You've changed subjects too. I think that's a good thing.' His eyes are intent and I know he has registered that I've moved on.

I am still more than a little uncomfortable discussing erotic writing with my boss, but he seems fine with it. It

237

occurs to me I might be able to enlist his support against Sally. 'Do you think just talking is sexy?'

Professor Brownlow nods. 'Just talking can be very sexy. But ... are you talking about erotic literature?'

I nod.

'Well, I'm not sure if just talking would classify as erotic literature. Talking is intimate, often more intimate than sex, but erotic?' He pauses.

'It would be if they were talking about sex.'

He nods. 'Talking about, but not doing, yes, that has potential; the growing charge never released, that sort of thing.'

In my mind a light bulb goes on.

'The "Song of Songs" for example,' Professor Brownlow continues. 'But you'd know about that, of course.'

I rack my brain. 'I'm not sure I do.'

'You must do – it's one of the earliest examples of erotic literature.'

My confused look prompts him to continue.

'It's from the Old Testament, a series of speeches between a woman and her lover. Some people say it is representative of God and Israel, but ...' He takes a deep breath, gazes out the window and lowers his voice an octave or two. 'Thy two breasts are like two young roes that are twins, which feed among the lilies.'

'For a zoologist you certainly have a way with poetry, Ralph.'

He turns back to me. 'Does that sound like something God would say to Israel?'

238

I shake my head. 'No way. It's totally a guy with the hots.'

Professor Brownlow looks taken aback for a second, then he laughs. 'Indeed.'

Suddenly I am desperate to get to work on my erotica. 'The crab larvae await me.'

'Take thee to thy desk,' says Professor Brownlow. His gaze lingers on me. I remember the naked goddess comment and I wish, for a moment, we had met in a different time-space continuum and made passionate love. But that is something I will have to leave to our alter egos, Edaline and Professor Brown.

'Why are you walking like that?' he asks as I head for my desk.

I stop and turn. This takes a little while. 'Like what?'

'Like you're wearing leg braces.'

'I ran this morning.' I say with a nonchalant air. 'Went a bit further than usual.'

'I didn't know you were a runner.' Professor Brownlow sounds surprised.

'Yeah, I run. I like the pain.'

Professor Brownlow's eyes meet mine. 'Ah, yes – the pain. Only a runner understands.'

We are like two freemasons exchanging a secret handshake.

'You run?'

'Every day. Ten kilometres,' he says.

'Like Murakami.' That explains the sexy legs.

'Exactly.' Professor Brownlow gives me a nod of complicity.

A glow of achievement warms my chest – my first comradely running chat. I hobble off and do at first continue with the job I am being paid for. One crab larvae, two crab larvae, three crab larvae, four ... But then Professor Brownlow disappears to give a lecture and I dart to the keyboard.

'What do you think about when you think about me?' asked Edaline.

Jason looked at her for a long time, his brown eyes steady, but he didn't speak.

Edaline blushed. 'What were you thinking about just then?'

'I was thinking your lips are the colour of crushed strawberries.'

'Why don't you kiss me?'

'And then we'll see how important you are?'

Edaline nearly swooned with delight. He was paraphrasing Sylvia Plath. She had never met a man who had read Sylvia before. She nodded.

Jason leaned over and brushed her lips with his. 'Mmm, you are clearly very important.'

'How important?' Edaline's lips were tingling.

'Foreman material.' Jason smiled.

'I think we need to try that again.'

Jason put his hands on her shoulders and brought his face close, so their noses were touching. Inclining his head, he brought his lips to hers.

Edaline closed her eyes, lost in sensation. Her lips parted and she pressed her tongue against his. Time passed. She wasn't sure if it was seconds, minutes or hours. She was only conscious of his lips and the thumping of her heart.

When at last they separated Jason looked dazed, like he had woken from a long sleep.

'I was wrong. Presidential material,' he said. 'Definitely.'

'Still not erotic,' says a voice over my shoulder. 'Intimate, but not erotic.'

Chapter Twenty-five

The poor ego ... has to serve three harsh masters.

SIGMUND FREUD

I jump, swivel in my seat, almost scream at the sight of Professor Brownlow. Oh God. Sprung. My road trip has hit black ice and I'm spinning wildly off course. Is there any way I can make writing erotic fiction on Professor Brownlow's time seem like a reasonable thing to do? Maybe if my scene was crab larvae related, but I do not even have that weak and ridiculous excuse.

I close my file, blush hotly and try to think of something to say. 'I ... I needed to strike while the muse was hot,' I stammer.

Professor Brownlow looks stern. I wish he wouldn't. It makes me feel bad. He folds his arms and looks me in the eye. He is waiting for a better explanation.

'I've got a tight deadline.' Oh, I wish he wouldn't look at me like that. Professor Brownlow is my friend. We have history. I feel like I have betrayed him.

His eyes flicker to the beakers of crab larvae and back again. 'I do too. I've got a paper on the Japanese Brine Shrimp due next week.'

Japanese Brine Shrimp? Is this a coded reference to my erotic writing? If it is, what is he saying? Suddenly I feel sleazy and tainted. How have I managed to avoid realising what I am doing is tacky and wrong? Subconsciously I've known all along, but I've been like a frog in a pot of water. The temperature has been raised degree by degree and I haven't noticed. Why didn't I jump out before the water boiled? How did I let it get to the stage of Sally pimping my pornography around the town? And now the quality of my crab-drawing work, which I didn't think could get any worse, has.

Tears spring to my eyes. I want to be washed clean, redeemed and forgiven. The priest with his church signs was right. I need to run from sin.

'I'm sorry, Professor Brownlow.' I forget I'm supposed to call him Ralph. 'I'll never do it again. I don't want to write erotica anymore. It's making me feel dirty. I'm so sorry.' I resist the temptation to fall to my knees and kiss his feet.

Professor Brownlow looks taken aback. 'It's not that bad, Edie. I like your erotica. I'd just prefer it if you wrote it in your own time.'

But there is nothing he can do to make me feel better. 'No. It's all wrong.' I pull at my hair. 'I don't know what possessed me. I've been going through a difficult phase. I'm not like this usually. It's Sally's fault. She made me.'

Professor Brownlow makes soothing noises. 'There, there.'

Perhaps he's a saint.

Just then there is a knock at the door. Professor Brownlow and I look up. A man steps into the lab. He is fortyish, overweight and wearing a tweed jacket over blue polyester pants. His stringy black hair is combed over a pale, balding scalp.

'Can I help you?' asks Professor Brownlow.

'I'm looking for the crabsexinstute.' The last word comes out in a muttered rush. The man's eyes shift from side to side.

'Pardon?' replies Professor Brownlow.

But I have understood. This has something to do with my erotic writing. I don't know what, but I know I am right. I am horror-struck. Why is he here? It is like my debauched and sinful alter ego has turned up to accuse me. This is one car I don't want on my journey. The man must be dispatched before Professor Brownlow catches on.

'Gideon Building, G8. Over there.' I point out the window towards the rest of the university.

The man frowns. 'No crabsex here?' Again the word escapes him in a guilty rush.

'Definitely not,' I say.

The man backs out the door.

Professor Brownlow, bless his pure unsullied heart, looks bewildered. 'What did he want?'

I flap my hands. 'God knows. I just wanted to get rid of him. He looked like a sleaze.' I am having the most awful sensation that my life is turning into a disaster. 'I'd better do some work.'

I draw crab larvae for the rest of the day as if paying penance. A pilgrim crawling on their knees to Rome could not be any more humble. When Professor Brownlow is ready to leave at five o'clock I am still at it.

'You can stop now, Edie,' he says.

'No, no.' I mentally smite my forehead in the dust. 'They're not done yet.'

Professor Brownlow pauses at the door. 'Don't beat yourself up, Edie. I know it's not the most exciting job in the world.'

I can practically see his halo glowing. 'I just want to finish these few.'

After he leaves, I enter a strange place. It is absolutely imperative that I make amends. I can no longer stand the fact I've been doing my job in such a slap-dash fashion. Professor Brownlow's reputation could be ruined forever by my sloppiness. I finish the larvae I am working on then run to the cabinet where he keeps my drawings.

I pull out the first one, then find the glass slide with corresponding larvae on the shelf above. Slipping it under the microscope, I double-check it against the drawing.

Two maxillipeds and three plumose hairs are missing. I fix this with a few pencil strokes and move on to the next. And then the next. A strange exaltation strikes me around the tenth drawing. I am washing myself pure in the formaldehyde of the crab. I will be reborn.

I don't know what time it is when my phone rings, but it is dark outside.

'Where are you?' Sally asks. 'I just went round to your place.'

'I'm at work. I'm busy.'

'Writing erotica I hope.'

'I'm not doing that stuff anymore.'

'What? But we have a deal. I need it. I've got clients waiting.'

'I'm going to be good from now on.'

'But your erotica is good. It's very popular.'

'I mean good – as in moral, upright and conscientious. People shouldn't need erotica. They should just get over it and only have sex when they really need to.'

'But Edie —'

I hang up and turn my phone off.

The lab is quiet after talking to Sally. I turn on the radio and tune it to the university radio station. The stoned-sounding DJ is ranting again. Or perhaps it is a different one who is also stoned.

I pull out the next crab larvae and check it against my drawing. Several errors leap out immediately. Strangely, now that I have put my mind to it, I am finding this crab-drawing thing quite engrossing. Perhaps I have found my true vocation after all. What a blissful thought. I have been called, not by God, but by zoology. Perhaps I will become a crab-drawing nun – a singing nun even. *High on a hill was a lonely larvae*, I hum. I am lost in telsons, maxillipeds and plumose hairs when I hear Jay's voice. I stop humming.

You looked at me
  As if I was the answer
  Though you didn't know the question ...

I stop drawing and look around – it is just the radio. I sigh, feeling an achy tug in my chest. And other places. I would, of course, have to renounce these sorts of carnal feelings if I was to become a singing nun.

His voice reminds me of how little I really know about him. How can I feel like I understand him at all, when he has told me practically nothing? And yet I do.

I return to my drawing while Jay croons about being in love – with someone who isn't me. I think about all the topics we discussed on the couch and somehow this wasn't one of them. Our conversation was like a spiral, going around and around an unspoken centre.

And now love and pain are the only things I want to talk about. But because I made such a mistake with asking Jay about his scars last time I am scared to go there again. Perhaps we can get there slowly, circling nearer and nearer until we are so close we hardly notice the moment of touchdown.

'Hey.'

I am thinking about Jay and hearing his voice on the radio, so it doesn't register that he is now talking to me in person.

'Hey,' he says again.

I look up from my drawing. Jay is standing in the door of the lab. Somehow I am not surprised to see him. 'What are you doing here?'

He shrugs and smiles. 'I don't know. Visiting you?'

I smile back. My smile goes on and on. I probably look like one of his sideshow-alley clowns. With an effort, I stop.

'I liked your story,' he says. 'Thanks.'

He liked my story. My smile starts up again. My heart dances a happy jig.

'Relinquish *is* a good word. I don't know if it's my favourite, though.'

'You have a favourite?'

'It changes. At the moment it's something beginning with *E*.'

I purse my lips, thinking.

'E-d.' He pauses. 'E-d.'

We smile at each other again as I get it.

'Working late?' he asks.

I gesture at all my drawings, laid out on the lab bench. 'I've ...' I don't know how to describe the epiphany that has just taken place in my mind. 'I've decided to be good.'

Jay steps inside the lab. He gazes at my drawings, his hair falling across his eyes. He nods, then looks up at me. 'Tell me about it.' His voice is both gentle and masculine. I could listen to it all day.

I resist an urge to smooth his hair back from his face. 'There's just been too much ... wrongness in my life lately. The erotica, the way I'm so crap at my job ...' I flap my hand. 'I'm turning over a new leaf.'

Jay perches on a lab stool. 'You're sounding a bit born-again, Edie.'

248

'That is exactly it, Jay.' I nod. 'That is what I want. To start again and do it better this time. Don't you ever feel like that?'

He rolls his eyes. 'All the time. All ... the ... fucking ... time.'

My chest lurches. He understands. He really understands. We gaze into each other's eyes and I get the strange sensation that I'm falling into him. *Going, going, gone. Oh God, I think I might just have fallen in love.*

I hold up one of my drawings. 'Look – five plumose hairs missing.' I hand it to him. 'This one, the endopodite is just wrong.' I hand it to him as well.

'This one ...' I look at the drawing in my hand and try to slide it to the bottom of the pile.

Jay takes it from me and laughs.

It is a crab larva in a low-cut T-shirt, which displays its most un-crustacean-like breasts. A speech bubble says: *Would you like to take a look down the microscope, Professor?* 'I don't know who did that.' I blush and bite my lip.

Jay puts his head on one side. 'The plumose hairs seem all accounted for on this one.'

'You'd know, Professor.'

His eyes flicker towards me. 'Maybe I should take a look down the microscope?'

A tug of most un-nun-like yearning strikes without warning. I take a deep breath and slide the next drawing across to him. 'On this one, the maxilliped's all wonky.' 'Don't you see? They might only be crabs, but they're important. They're important to Professor Brownlow and I've turned them into crap.' I blink as tears well in my eyes. I try to stop them, but they flow on regardless.

Jay stands up, the drawings still in his hands and walks around the bench towards me. He comes closer until he is facing me nose to nose, then wraps his arms around me. He pats my back and makes soothing *shh* noises.

I lean into his chest, breathing him in. He smells like freshly sawn wood. His cheek presses against mine. It is slightly rough and makes my face tingle. I can feel his heartbeat. I want to stay like this forever.

'You already are good, Edie.' His hands run down my back.

'I knew this was the Crab Sex Institute,' says a voice behind me.

Chapter Twenty-six

I have found little that is 'good' about human beings on the whole.

SIGMUND FREUD

Jay and I jump apart, our tender laboratory moment in tatters. Mr Sleazy – my worst nightmare, my dirty secret – has reappeared.

'Go away.' I make a shooing action. 'I've already told you, you've got the wrong place.' I just want him out of here so I can be alone with Jay.

But this is one car that won't get off the highway. Mr Sleazy steps inside. He is perspiring in his tweed jacket and his eyes are on the drawings in Jay's hands. 'Give me a look.' He snatches the drawings before Jay can protest. Holding them in his plump, white hands, his eyes devour the pictures. He studies them, his face lighting up. He smiles, revealing a mouth full of snaggle teeth. 'You've been drawing these wrong, you little minx. You deserve a good spanking.'

I back away. *Minx*. I was right; he has been reading

my stories. But how did he find me? Sally assured me I was anonymous.

Jay backs away with me. He pulls his phone out of his pocket. 'I'm calling the cops if you don't leave now.'

'You make it up as you go along, don't you?' Mr Sleazy is quoting from my Mount Vesuvius sex scene. 'That was one of my favourite parts. Are you interested in metaphysics?' he adds. 'Take me now, you sexy fiddler crab.'

He steps towards me. 'You are a crab sex goddess.'

'I don't know what you're talking about.' My voice is a whisper.

Jay and I take another step backwards. Jay puts his arm around my shoulders.

'I'm a big fan of your writing.' Mr Sleazy pulls a crumpled wad of paper from his pocket. It is one of my erotic stories, stained with coffee and other stuff that doesn't bear thinking about. He thrusts it towards me. 'Can you sign it for me?'

My first fan. Should I be flattered or nauseated? If this is what being a celebrity is like, I don't want it.

'What's happening here?' asks a voice from the door. It is Professor Brownlow. 'I was driving past and I saw the light on.' His eyes swivel from me to Jay to Mr Sleazy.

I feel like he has caught me in the middle of an indecent act.

Mr Sleazy smiles a long, slow smile. He raises his eyebrows. 'Professor Brown, I assume? How are your volcanic eruptions?' He cackles.

Professor Brownlow looks appalled. His eyes move from Mr Sleazy to me. He steps inside. 'Edie? We need to talk.'

'I think there might have been enough of that,' says another voice from the door. It is Professor Brownlow's wife.

I can't believe it. This is like a French farce. Is there anyone else we can squeeze in here?

If this was a French farce Professor Brownlow's wife would be playing the role of the French maid. But instead of a frilly apron, she is wearing a short white tennis dress which sets off her well-toned golden legs. A small backpack is slung over her shoulder and a tennis racquet dangles from one hand.

Mr Sleazy's eyes light up. 'This is even better than I thought it would be,' he snickers. 'I'm sensing a stirring in an underground chamber. I wish I'd found this place years ago. Come on in, darling.'

Professor Brownlow's wife's eyes slide over Mr Sleazy and her mouth curls. 'Ralph.' She steps towards him, her tennis racquet held as if ready to return a serve. Her voice is like ice. 'I just played tennis with Jackie. She was in Lighthouse Bay yesterday morning. She saw you. Both of you. Coming out of the motel room.' She looks at me like I am a ten-day-old piece of chewing gum stuck to her shoe. 'I thought I'd find you here.' She takes another step towards Professor Brownlow. 'You said you were at the crab conference!'

He steps backwards, his eyes on the tennis racquet.

'How could you do that, Ralph? In a Lighthouse Bay motel room.' These last words are wailed, as if the motel room is the worst part. She bangs the tennis racquet down on the lab bench.

Professor Brownlow jumps.

I suppose I can see her point. A motel room *is* sleazy. A cold vice grips my stomach. I feel like throwing up.

'Hit me with your tennis racquet, baby,' says Mr Sleazy. 'Hit me here.' He slaps his polyester-clad bottom.

Professor Brownlow's wife doesn't even deign to look at him. She is way too classy for that.

She saw us come out of his room. I am, of course, pure and unsullied, but who's going to believe that? The trouble is, I feel far from pure. My Professor Brownlow fantasies are out there in the public domain. And even though I haven't enacted them, perhaps I may as well have. After all, we did share a bed.

Jay's arm drops from my shoulders.

I can't bear to look at him.

'Belinda.' Professor Brownlow steps towards her, his eyes still on the tennis racquet. 'We were just working.'

Mr Sleazy cackles. 'I want some of that work.'

Belinda's eyes dart from Professor Brownlow to Mr Sleazy to me. 'I don't know what you've got going on here, Ralph.' She opens her backpack and pulls out some paper. 'This stuff you've been bringing home.' She reads, '*Professor Brown flicked noisily through Edaline's drawings. Today he seemed to be channelling some deeply repressed emotions.*'

'That's a good one too,' says Mr Sleazy. Then quoting from memory, '*His usually sanguine air had been disturbed by something darker.*'

I am almost flattered that he knows my work so well.

Belinda ignores him, drilling Professor Brownlow with her eyes. 'It's her, isn't it? She's written it. About the two of you. I don't know why I didn't realise before. How could you bring this, this ... pornography home?'

I sink onto a seat. If I dropped to the floor, rolled under the table and crawled out of the lab, would she notice?

'Edie,' calls yet another voice from the corridor. 'I just can't accept you're not doing any more erotica.' Sally's face appears at the door. She blanches at the sight of the crowd inside. 'Oh, sorry ...'

I scream with anguish. 'Oh, for God's sake, come in and join the party.' Pushing past her, I run out into the night, leaving a smoking five-car pile-up behind me.

Out in the car park I see a familiar shape striding towards the laboratory – Djennifer. At first I am baffled, but then I remember; Sally said she was a client. She must be looking for the Crab Sex Institute too. Make that a six-car pile-up.

I turn and walk swiftly in the opposite direction before she sees me.

Chapter Twenty-seven

Life is not easy.

SIGMUND FREUD

Thursday: 54 days
Pain level: 9.9
Location: Everywhere

The morning after the Crab-Lab showdown I wake thinking of Jay. I say *wake*, but I am not sure that I actually slept. I am thinking about the parallels between his life and mine.

In Darling Head I'm pretty sure Dad's name has a much higher recognition factor than Gary Jaworski. I might not have been made into a song, but the coffee table book *Australian Surfing Legends* features a large picture of me as a toddler in my father's arms. *Dave McElroy with the next surfing legend?* reads the caption.

This book is as ubiquitous as board wax in Darling Head households. Even if I'd been a sporty kid it would have been hard to live up to. As it was, it was impossible.

Here's the next surfing legend, kids would snigger at the school swimming carnival as I hauled myself out of the water five minutes after everyone else had finished.

I wonder if Jay got taunted with 'Jaybird'. I imagine he probably did.

My legs scream as I pull myself out of bed. I lower them to the floor and stagger to the computer with difficulty. There is no way I am running today. I'm sorry Murakami, but I will have to find an alternative mentor.

I check my emails. I am looking for a miracle – something to drag me out of the meltdown my life has become. After deleting five messages offering me Viagra and penis extensions (why can't people think about anything except sex?) I come upon the reminder from Jetstar – I need to pay for my ticket to Tokyo today or forfeit it.

Going to Japan now, are you? The bonsai sighs. *Nice for some. Oh, to be back in Kyoto in autumn when the leaves are turning gold.*

'I thought you were, um, grown in Sydney?'

Japan is my spiritual home, says the bonsai. *The elegance, the simplicity, the refinement ... You're not going to fit in at all over there, you know.*

'Well, I don't really fit in here either.'

Oh, the tea ceremony, the parasols, the flower arranging, the origami ...

I leave the bonsai to its musing, whip out my credit card and punch in the details. Thank goodness I had the foresight to do something right. Only nine days to go until I Jetstar my way far from all my troubles. Perhaps

I can stay in my room until then? Maybe I can order in takeaway and make quick trips to the bathroom in the middle of the night when no one is around. I glance around my room – I can wee in the wastepaper bin, that's one thing taken care of.

There is also a message from my beloved Nigerian, Philip of the very short memory. His inability to remember that we already know each other each time he emails is now explained. Poor Philip has suffered a stroke due to a brain tumour and his parents, who I thought were already dead, have now been brutally murdered by rebels. This certainly puts my problems in perspective. I should send him a message of support, but I haven't got the energy. While my problems are nowhere near as devastating as Philip's, they are still weighing me down.

Professor Brownlow's wife thinks I have been sleeping with her husband. This feels bad. It feels murky. Jay thinks I have been sleeping with Professor Brownlow too. I wish my life was less fucked up. I wish I was a singing nun with no need for male company. If I had been confined to a nunnery I might not have become the type of person who writes erotica about married men. How did that happen?

I desperately need to do something to cheer myself up.

My seized-up legs are a persistent reminder that I am no Murakami in either the writing or the running stakes. Who else can I turn to for sources of inspiration? I call on Google.

Alcohol and drugs, it turns out, are a much more popular source of stimulation among poets and authors than running. No big surprise there. Hemingway, Hunter S. Thompson, Raymond Chandler, Dylan Thomas ... The list of enthusiastic drinkers goes on. Most of them died young, but they did produce a lot of good work before their livers packed up.

Tolstoy favoured smoking to *stupefy the critic within*. Balzac, the famous French author, drank up to fifty cups of coffee a day. If coffee wasn't available he would chomp on coffee beans. He died early, at the age of fifty-one, after suffering from an enlarged heart, stomach cramps and high blood pressure. In contrast, yoga and swimming are favoured by some lesser known, but probably longer living authors. My legs tell me I may be more suited to the debauched live-hard, die-young end of the spectrum.

There is something attractive about that. Perhaps I will be the female version of Dylan Thomas, reciting poetry, whiskey in hand, a kerchief tied artistically around my neck. I will cultivate a Welsh accent and write poetry in a boat shed with —

My phone rings. I look at the number. Sally — wanting erotica no doubt. Well, she'll just have to find another supplier. *This shop is closed, baby.* I turn off my phone and put it under my pillow. This doesn't seem decisive enough. The phone might be turned off, but it is still taking messages. I don't want messages. I would prefer it if people could just forget I ever existed.

I pull out the phone, put it on the ground and stomp on it, but it is surprisingly tough. I put it on top of a hardback book and whack it with another hardback, but it still sits there, no doubt taking messages from one of the many people who now hate me. I walk over to the window and look out. Beneath me is the Japanese garden and fishpond Rochelle has lovingly created. I take careful aim and let my phone go. A satisfying splash tells me it now lies among the fishes.

Once I have done this I am, suddenly, extremely hungry. I remember the box of chocolates in my cupboard I got for my last birthday. I devour half, feeling the sugar and caffeine surge through my bloodstream. I haven't heard of any writers who use chocolate for inspiration, but I know they're out there.

The chocolate stirs up a dark and sinful energy. Didn't the Aztecs used to drink chocolate before killing their human sacrifices? I can almost imagine doing that myself right now. Already it is hard to remember the calm singing-nun persona I wore so briefly last night. I am angry, restless, ready to pick a fight with anyone. And, damn it, I am still hungry. No one is going to stand between me and something to eat.

I open my bedroom door and feel even angrier. Gary Jaworski is laughing loudly downstairs. What is he still doing here? Doesn't he have a hotel room to trash? Groupies to shack up with? Paparazzi to avoid?

I stomp down the stairs, my legs screaming, my mind on food. I open the fridge and pull random items from the shelves. *Cheese?* Yes please. *Chicken?* Definitely. *Mayonnaise?* Absolutely. I am in the middle of creating an enormous sandwich when I hear Jay laughing in the lounge room.

I freeze. I have been doing a fairly good job until now

of not thinking about Jay. Not thinking about how he knew what I meant about starting afresh. Not thinking about that feeling of falling into him. Not thinking about holding him in the laboratory and how good it felt. Not thinking about the way he looked at me after Belinda's revelation. Not thinking that he is the only person I have ever told about the freckle on my hand and how I may never meet anyone else who wants to know this piece of trivia about me. I have been not thinking until it almost made my brain explode.

And there he is. Laughing. Not thinking about me at all.

It tears me up, the feeling I get when I hear him laugh. If this is love I don't want it. It hurts and I hate it with a vengeance. How do I make it go away? *Get angry.*

It isn't hard. I am already angry. In fact, I am furious. Does he really think I was sleeping with Professor Brownlow? Shouldn't he know me better than that? What's it to him anyway? If he hadn't let Tanya kiss him, I wouldn't have even been there in that motel room. And why didn't he give my name to the doorman at the pub? I never had any explanation for that. Now I think about it, this whole mess is totally his fault.

Gary and Jay are playing guitar now. I bite into my sandwich and listen. They sound good together – very slick – but I like Jay by himself better. *Men with guitars. There should be a law against it.*

'Not like that, like this, mate,' says Gary.

I edge around the corner where they can't see me and watch. They are sitting close together on the couch.

Gary leads, demonstrating some fancy finger work. Jay watches, then follows. Kafka the metaphysical cat lies on the coffee table, his yellow eyes intent on Gary.

If I wasn't so angry it would be nice to watch. For the first time I can see the father in the son. They have the same dexterous hands, the same look of concentration on the sound that flies from their fingertips.

It occurs to me that this is what my father would like to be doing with me – passing on his knowledge. Not of guitar, of surfing. Nothing would please him more than to have me next to him in the line-up. He could show me where to sit, how to paddle, how to catch waves. It would be a basic fatherly pleasure. Seeing Gary and Jay together makes me realise more than ever how much my father has missed out on not having a child who follows his interests.

'Yeah, good one.' Gary nods as Jay executes what sounds to me like a tricky little number. I can see why Jay called him a Peter Pan. From a distance he could still be twenty.

Jay doesn't respond, but I can tell he is pleased.

The tune to the Grafters platinum hit, 'Crush Me Up in Love', blares out, interrupting them. Gary leans backwards in order to extract a tiny phone from his skin-tight pants.

He barks out a series of sharp commands. 'Yeah, Moët. Make it seven. Get Derek onto it. Okay, sound-check at six.' He folds the phone and tosses it down beside him. 'Fuck knows what I pay her for. I've gotta go, mate. Sorry. They need me in Sydney.'

Jay looks up from his guitar. He has been practising a single riff over and over, while Gary was on the phone. He shrugs. 'Whatever.'

'That thing we talked about.' Gary stands, picking up his guitar by the neck. 'I'll sort it.'

Jay's face is closed, guarded. He nods, then drops his head to his guitar.

Gary punches Jay on the shoulder. 'Good to catch up, eh? We won't leave it so long next time.' He struts from the room so fast I don't have time to duck back in the kitchen. 'Hey, Edie.' He winks. 'Take good care of my boy, won't you?' He is out the door before I can respond.

Kafka leaps from the table and stalks after him, tail in the air.

Jay looks up.

I swallow my mouthful of sandwich and raise my hand in an ironic greeting.

Jay looks at me for a long time.

'What?' I am in no mood for subtlety.

If Jay's face was closed when he was with his father, it is now boarded up, impenetrable and totally unwelcoming.

I know I should just go away and leave him to it, come back when we both feel better, but for some reason I am unable to do that. I want to rip off those boards and make him show me what's inside. How can he come and go like that? We held hands on the couch, damn it; don't I have rights? 'Have I done something?'

The corner of Jay's mouth rises, but it isn't a smile. 'Apart from fucking your boss, you mean?' He sounds like no one I've ever met before. He sounds like all the other guys I've known. There is nothing in him that answers to anything in me.

The breath rushes out of me. 'What would you know? You think you're so cool. You and your rockstar father ...' I don't know what to say. I don't even know what I mean. I want to shake him until he stops looking at me like I'm someone he might have met once, but he isn't sure where.

Jay waits, like he is there to take my lunch order.

'You're just some guy in black clothes. I hate you.' I stomp from the room before he can reply to my devastating critique.

Chapter Twenty-eight

The intention that man should be happy is not in the plan of Creation.

SIGMUND FREUD

After climbing the stairs, I sink onto my bed and gaze out the window, blinking back tears. I hate you. I hate you not. My brain is like a computer hit by lightning; its circuitry useless. Now I've told Jay I hate him and yet all I can think about is how good it felt to touch him. I open and shut my hand, put it to my cheek. I wish I had never held hands with him. Now I know what I'm missing.

My short-circuited mind returns to Gary – Peter Pan. *Peter Pan* was one of my favourite books as a child. But I didn't know the story behind the story then. *That terrible masterpiece* is what the book's namesake called it. *Peter Pan* is not a good story to be thinking about right now.

At times like this I understand how Mum felt – how your brain turns against you. What would it be like to feel so sad all the time, not just when things go wrong?

I only heard Mum crying once. It was late at night and I'd got out of bed to go to the toilet. Her sobs carried up the stairs. She sounded wounded.

'It's all right, Jenny; it's all right.' Dad's voice was a low murmur.

I peered over the banister and saw them sitting at the table. They were holding hands.

I wanted to go down, to find out what was wrong, but I sensed it was private so I sneaked away. The next morning Mum was smiling and laughing again and I thought perhaps I'd dreamt it.

She must have been trying so hard.

I go over to my chest and pull out her notebook. Being in a melancholy mood, I open it near the end and read:

When the black dog sits on my shoulder, the colour washes out of the world. Relationships I thought were working are revealed to exist only in my head. My whole life feels like a complete waste of time – like I've drifted through experiences others would have made something of – slid past people I should have connected with, somehow missed the whole point. It seems to me that everyone else does it better – finds meaning in things that are meaningless to me. I don't want to feel this way.

That is exactly the way I feel right now – like I'm missing the whole point. It worries me to find my thoughts are so close to Mum's.

On the other hand, Jay was in the wrong too. There was no need for him to go all cold and hard. He should have let me explain. Perhaps I let him off too easily? Now that I think about it, I almost feel ready for another round.

There is a knock on the door and before I can snarl, *go away*, it opens. Sally comes in.

I stuff the notebook away and sit up straight.

'Hi.' Sally sounds wary.

'Hi.'

Sally sits down on the bed next to me. 'What's up with Jay?'

I shrug. 'Why are you asking me?'

Sally touches my arm. 'Hey, I'm your friend. I know you two have got something going on.'

'No we —'

Sally talks over the top of me. 'So why's he down there, looking like Doctor Evil and you're up here ...' she glances at the chest, 'doing a Sylvia Plath number.'

'I'm not doing a Sylvia Plath.'

'Yes you are, you've got that no-one-understands-me look.'

I glare at her. 'This is not a no-one-understands-me look. This is a don't-mess-with-me look.'

Sally raises her eyebrows. 'That time of the month?'

'That has nothing to do with it,' I snap. 'He thinks I slept with Professor Brownlow. Not that it's any of his business, seeing as we —'

'You did, didn't you?'

'*Slept*. I slept. That's all. Just slept.'

'So … You slept with him, but you didn't *sleep* with him.'

'Exactly. We talked about Japanese literature. I helped him with his crab conference presentation. Then we got tired.'

Sally looks sceptical.

'It was the same with Jay.'

'What, the crab conference or the Japanese literature part?'

'No. I slept with him, but I didn't *sleep* with him.' I flap my hands. 'We were bed buddies.'

'Bed buddies?' Sally's brow creases.

'Yeah. You got a problem with that?'

'No, no, no problem. Bed buddies is cool.' Sally's voice is soothing. 'It's just that this is a new concept you're presenting here. How does it work, this bed-buddy thing?'

'It's like a sleepover. Without the pillow fight.'

'Lollies?'

'No lollies.'

'Chick-flick DVDs?'

I shake my head.

'Hmm.' Sally looks thoughtful. 'Gee Ed, I don't think I've had a sleepover with a boy since I was ten. If I sleep with a guy these days, I *sleep* with him.'

'Well, I like to mix it up a bit. Sometimes sex, sometimes just sleep. It keeps things interesting.'

'Ed, I've got to say, this bed-buddy thing – I don't relate to it.'

'I think being with me makes men sleepy.'

Sally gives me some significant eye contact and slips into counsellor mode. 'Does that bother you?'

'What, being a human cure for insomnia? Why should it bother me? A good night's sleep is very important. They should market me. Troubled by a disturbing need for sex? Don't worry, one dose of Edie McElroy and you'll be sleeping like a baby.'

'I'm sure it's not like that. It's a compliment really; they feel comfortable enough with you to go to sleep.' Sally sounds less than convincing.

'Oh yes, I drive them wild. With a desire for some shut-eye. Scarlett Johannson has the same problem, I hear. Javier Bardem, Eric Bana, Josh Hartnett, all they want is sleep, sleep, sleep —'

'Funny night, last night.' Sal changes the subject.

'Ha. Ha, ha. Yeah, it cracked me up too. What happened after I left the lab?'

'It was a bit like being at a birthday party and the birthday girl leaves. We all stood there looking at each other for a moment, then Belinda slapped Ralph and took off.'

'At least she didn't hit him with the tennis racquet.'

'I think she was going to, but she changed her mind at the last minute.'

'How did he take it?'

'I felt sorry for him. He looked like a sick kitten that's just had a bucket of water thrown over it.'

'Oh, that's sad. Poor Professor Brownlow. So then it was just you and Jay and Professor Brownlow left?'

'And that creepy guy.'

'Oh yeah. Him.'

'He was really excited by it all.' She screws her nose up. 'Anyway, then Jay just kind of walked out, looking like he was about to do a Kurt Cobain ...' Sally catches my eye as she says this. 'Sorry, Edie, it's just an expression, I didn't mean ...'

I wave my hand. 'So then it was just you and Professor Brownlow?'

'And the creepy guy.'

'Right.'

'I thought I'd better give Ralph some counselling at that stage. He was looking totally stressed out and I am his life coach, so I told him people always regret not doing things much more than they regret doing them. I mean, I thought he'd been sleeping with you, in the normal sense of the word, so it might make him feel better.'

'How did that go down?'

'He just muttered something like "this is worse than Moorookami" and took off. I don't know what that meant.'

'Oh,' I finger my hair, wondering which part of Murakami's stories Professor Brownlow was thinking about. 'So then it was just you and the creepy guy.'

'Yeah. Turns out he's a client of mine.'

'I knew it! He's the phone-sex guy, isn't he?'

Sally jumps. 'There's no need to yell, Ed.' She looks embarrassed.

As well she should. 'Does the term Crab Sex Institute mean anything to you?'

'I didn't expect anyone to think it was real,' says Sal. 'It was just a marketing ploy – you know, hot stories from the Crab Sex Institute. I didn't identify where it was or anything. It was just to give it a bit of cachet.'

'But it was obvious it was at a university.'

'Not really.'

I glare.

'It may have been.'

'How many universities are there around here, Sal?'

Sally looks at me as if I am being unnecessarily pedantic. 'I don't know, how many universities are there?'

'One.'

'Only one?'

'You knew that, Sal.'

'I may have done.' If Sally wasn't a life coach, she would have made a good lawyer.

'Jesus, I hope I'm not going to get a whole procession of weirdos sniffing around.'

'I'm sure most of my clients aren't like that. Speaking of which, I really need some more erotica.'

'I told you, I'm not doing that anymore.'

'I'll double your money.'

'I can't. I'm completely off sex. I can't write about it. I don't even want to think about it. It's more trouble than it's worth'

'Edie.' Sal is about to use all of her famous powers of persuasion on me. 'You're so good at it. Just a couple more, while I look around for another supplier. Isn't it like a recipe for you now?'

I think about how expensive it's going to be in Tokyo and whether I can ever return to my job in the lab.

Sally bats her eyelashes at me. 'Come on, Ed, puleeese?'

'Oh, fuck, Sal. Don't look at me like that. Okay.'

Sally smiles. 'That's my girl.' She gives me a hug. 'Hustle, hit and never quit. Remember, if you're given lemons, make lemonade.'

'You want a story with lemons in it?'

'It's a metaphor. It means turn negatives into positives.'

'Okay, got it. Get that car back on the highway, right?'

'Vroom, vroom,' says Sal.

Creamy tuna pasta. I have ventured into the kitchen in search of inspiration. Mum's old cookbook is open in front of me. Like Sally said – erotic writing is just a recipe. Creamy tuna – now there's a whole lot of double entendre already. I take the book back to my lair and read through the recipe.

Cook pasta in boiling salted water until al dente. Drain and toss with half the oil.

Is it just me, or are cookbooks kind of like soft porn for everyone? I boot up my computer and summon my inspiration.

Edaline was boiling, salty and sticky. She poured olive oil over herself, feeling it trickle

272

viscously into all her crevices. Her skin was slippery and slick to the touch. Jason's body would slide over it with no resistance, no friction.

This has definite possibilities. I read on.

Over medium heat, heat remaining oil in a large fry pan. Add onion and cook for 2–3 minutes or until softened.

Goodness. Pretty sexy stuff.

She lay in the sun naked, cooking, softening, her eyes closed. There were footsteps and a round object was pressed against her lips. Without opening her eyes, she bit into it. It was an onion.

Add garlic and cook for 1 minute. Stir in cream and tomato paste, add tuna and peas. Heat gently for 1–2 minutes. Stir in half the parsley along with the tomatoes and capers, add pasta and season. Stir until heated through. Serve sprinkled with remaining parsley.

I carry on, my fingers flying across the keyboard. Edaline and Jason cavort wantonly with tuna and peas, parsley and tomatoes. They roll about on a white leather sofa and smear lavish amounts of tomato purée across a pool table.

At last, after it was all over, Edaline opened her eyes. Jason lay beside her. A sprig of parsley decorated his hair. She removed it, placing it between her sharp, white teeth.

'What shall we have for dessert?' asked Edaline.

I finish this piece and straighten my back. Part of me is guilty that I have reverted so swiftly to this seedy enterprise. On the other hand, I have to admit it has cheered me up; the world doesn't seem as bleak as it did an hour ago. Maybe I'm not over sex after all.

'Oh, my,' says Sal, in response to my email. 'Sigmund Freud isn't in it. I can't wait to see what you do with chocolate mudcake.'

Chapter Twenty-nine

The doctor should be opaque to his patients.

SIGMUND FREUD

Friday: 55 days
Pain level: 7.5
Location: Chest (business as usual)

Friday morning presents me with a dilemma. It is a work day, but will Professor Brownlow want to see me? Perhaps he would prefer it if I stayed away? On the other hand, I need the money. I also need to tell him I will be leaving at the end of next week.

My legs are even stiffer today, so running is out of the question. Perhaps I will disown Murakami and down a few whiskeys tonight instead, a la Dylan Thomas.

Tips for self-improvement: Find myself a stylish neck kerchief and a boat house.

As I get dressed I hear Dad and Rochelle talking.

Rochelle sounds annoyed. Are they having an argument? That would be a first.

'You have to tell her,' says Rochelle.

Dad mutters something incomprehensible in reply.

Tell who what? *Me?* Are they arguing about me? I don't like the sound of it. I also don't want to get involved. I loiter in my preparations and by the time I come downstairs they have gone to work.

I drive to the university, averting my eyes from the church sign as I go past. I am a confirmed sinner now. I am not open to salvation.

When I arrive, Professor Brownlow is at his desk, poring over some papers. My social barometer is firmly set to awkward. I stand at the laboratory door for a moment, reliving the horror of Wednesday night. I cough.

Professor Brownlow looks up. His eyes are bloodshot and he needs a shave. We lock eyes, but he doesn't say anything for a little while. Then he pushes out the chair next to him and gestures to it. 'Come in, Edie.'

I sit down, wheeling the chair back until I am sitting well outside lover or even friend distance. On reflection, I edge back a bit more; even co-worker distance is probably pushing it, should Belinda make a surprise appearance. At three metres, I feel I have struck the right note; very distant acquaintance.

Professor Brownlow slides an article across the desk towards me. 'Sally gave me this. It's very good.'

I lean forward and take the paper, being sure not to brush his fingers with mine. I look at the title: 'The secrets of happiness'. Running my eyes down it, I read the headings out loud. 'Be positive, be brave, meditate, be kind to yourself, put your pessimism to work, find a calling, act happy.' *Act happy*. I attempt to smile. 'Sounds terrific.' Funnily enough, it kind of works. Acting happy makes me feel better. 'Is it working for you?'

Professor Brownlow smiles. 'It's a work in progress.'

'How are things panning out for you after ...'

'Belinda is giving me the benefit of the doubt. That might be the best I can hope for at the moment.'

'Would you rather I left?'

'No, no.' Professor Brownlow shakes his head. 'I need you.' He gestures towards the cabinet where my drawings are kept. 'I've been having a look. You did a fantastic job the other night. I think you're coming into your own with this work.'

He needs me. Now I find I'm unable to tell him about Japan. I almost destroyed his marriage and he needs me. Next week will have to do. I stand up, 'I'd better ...'

'You know Belinda wasn't totally wrong about you.' His voice is low.

I turn. 'What?'

'I *am* very drawn to you.'

'You are?' I am thinking of the motel room and the sexless bed-sharing.

'I'm a lot older than you, Edie, not as spontaneous. I've learnt just because things seem like a good idea at the time, it doesn't mean they are.'

I glance at his article. 'What about being brave?'

'I've learnt to temper bravery with an assessment of the consequences. It doesn't mean I'm not tempted.'

Professor Brownlow's eyes twinkle for a moment behind his glasses. Then he pulls a beaker from his cabinet and proceeds to pour chemicals into it as if I wasn't there.

After a couple of seconds I am convinced that sexually charged moment never happened.

Saturday: Day 56
Pain levels: 8–9
Locations: Everywhere except my toes

Saturday is a carnival of awkwardness. Jay and I bump off each other like dodgem cars. Every time I see him a silent scream erupts inside me. He, meanwhile, is cool and polite. We catch each other in the kitchen in the morning; me heading for the toaster, he for the kettle.

'Excuse me.' He steps aside to let me pass.

I try to match his demeanour, but probably look sulky. As he leaves, I notice he has the same sinuous rockstar glide as his father. I think of Tanya and what else they might have in common. I wonder if he ever meant a word he said to me or if it was just meaningless banter.

It seemed meaningful. But then, I do have a tendency to take people at face value. I need to learn. My heart should have toughened up by now. I can't keep doing this all the time; can't keep going back for more.

It would be better if he was rude. Then we could fight. But his coolness is impenetrable, like he has switched off. I no longer exist for him as a person, only as an object in his path. I seethe with unspoken retorts, rude comments and taunts that I will never utter. Retorts and taunting are not my forte.

With every encounter in the kitchen, lounge room or on the verandah, I become more shaken and tearful, but I don't let him see this. I clench my teeth, walk past, presenting an exterior so at odds with my interior it is a wonder it doesn't slough off like a snake skin. I am relieved it doesn't. I manage to keep myself together, patched up with a fragile thread of determination to not let him see me cry.

I consider running, but eat a lot of chocolate instead. This requires frequent trips to the shop so I can pretend to myself that I am only eating small amounts of chocolate. While standing in line to buy very small chocolate bars I read a succession of women's magazines. I learn how to get a flat stomach, hold fabulous dinner parties and get the latest Hollywood look. I also learn that you should never leave the house unless you are looking so fabulous that you would not be embarrassed to meet an ex-boyfriend. Who has time for this stuff? There has got to be a market for trendy burqa-style outfits to wear on days when you need to buy milk, but haven't got two hours to get dressed.

As I munch my way through Cherry Ripes, Mars Bars and Kit Kats I decide that if I ever become a famous erotic writer I will tell my fans that everything I have learnt about writing, I have learnt from eating chocolate. I wonder what those things are. *How it can make you feel bad when you indulge too much. How it can make you feel good when you do it slowly with intention.*

How some chocolate is better than others. None of this seems any more of a long-bow than running.

In the afternoon, I buy myself a red silk scarf from the pre-loved clothes shop. On my way home, I pick up two mini-bar-sized bottles of whiskey. Getting a whole bottle would be tempting fate. That evening, I tie the scarf around my neck, then drink the first bottle. Standing near the window, I imagine I am Dylan Thomas in his boatshed.

It rains a lot in Glenorchy ...

When I spoke this line in Gleebooks, I had the crowd on tenterhooks. A bold start – but how would I follow it up in rhyming verse? *Corky? Dorky?* I unscrew the lid of the second bottle ...

And even the deer are quite gawky.

I take a sip of whiskey and try to remember what comes next but my mind is blank. I can't believe I've forgotten it. I adlib.

The shifting mist
Makes you want to get pissed.
And you'd kill for a sausage that's porky.

I'm sure the original poem was much more spiritually uplifting. It certainly seemed that way at the time. I finish the bottle, collapse on the bed, pull out my notebook and write under *Tips for self-improvement:*

Never write poetry again.
When buying whiskey, get the large bottle.

*

'Eddie.' Dad calls up the stairs.

'What?'

'There's someone on the phone for you. Jennifer.'

Jennifer? Do I know a Jennifer? Standing up seems too hard. Let alone going down the stairs and talking.

'Tell her I'm not here. She can call my mobile.'

This seems to do the job, as I am left in peace. After a few minutes I remember that my mobile is in the fishpond. Never mind, she's probably from the bank or Optus and I can do without those calls.

Despite my resolution, I can't resist one last poetic utterance before I close my eyes.

Men with guitars

Should be put behind bars.

My ticket to Tokyo sits on my bookcase like a lifeline.

On Sunday morning Sally comes around for the next phase of my life coaching.

I am sitting on the couch outside when she arrives. Jay has gone out so the coast is clear. I swallow my Mars Bar and stuff the wrapper down the back of the cushions before she sees it. 'I hope this isn't going to be strenuous. I'm not in the mood for talking to strangers.'

She smiles. 'Well, it's your lucky day. I'm going to try something different. We'll do it in your bedroom.'

'Good.' This sounds promising.

Sally is unusually dressed today. Her hair is tied back and she is wearing a neat skirt and a startlingly white T-shirt.

'What's with the primary-school teacher look?' I ask.

'I'm trying for a more professional persona. Like?'

'Like.' We climb the stairs. My room is fuggy as I have been spending a lot of time lurking in it with the curtains drawn.

'You lie on the bed.' Sal moves to the window, draws the curtains back and opens the window. 'There, doesn't that feel better already?'

I brush the chocolate wrappers off the bed and lie down. Lying down is good. 'Are you going to give me a massage?'

'You wish.' Sally wheels my writing chair over to the bed and sits down beside me. She bends over and picks up a Cherry Ripe wrapper. 'Bad sign, Ed. It's lucky I came round to help you out. This is going to do you so much good.'

I'm not sure that I like the sound of that. 'What are we doing exactly?'

Sally pulls a notebook out of her handbag. 'I've been having a look back through my university notes. I think I'm ready to get into some Freudian therapy now.'

This is not very confidence inspiring. 'Sure you don't want to try a bit of brain surgery while you're at it?'

'You should be grateful. People pay a lot of money for this.' Sally sounds reproachful.

'Sorry.'

'You're getting this for free, remember?' Sally riffles through her notes. 'Right, just to bring you up to speed, you need to know that the personality is like an iceberg divided into three sections. Our conscious mind, the ego, is just the tip of the iceberg. Lurking beneath the water is the subconscious, made up of the id and the superego. Got that?'

'Ego, id, superego. Got it.'

'Freud says that when the ego loses control and the id goes on a rampage it causes anxiety.'

'Tell me about it.'

'The purpose of this therapy is to find out what is going on in your subconscious, because your subconscious affects your behaviour. This is called making the unconscious, conscious.'

'Did you pass this subject?'

'Edie, I am a highly trained therapist. In fact, if I were you I would be careful what you say around me. For example, when you questioned my competence – that is called transference. You are projecting feelings about someone else onto your therapist. So, tell me, whose competence do you really doubt?'

'My own?'

'Aha.' Sally's pen scratches on paper. 'Interesting. Very interesting.'

'That's good, Sal. I like the way you say that.'

'Do you?' Sally smiles. 'Thanks. I'm trying for a kind of pondering psychoanalyst thing. It's working?'

'Yeah, it's good. I'd throw in the odd "I see, I see" too if I were you.'

'Mmm, great idea.' Sally's pen scratches again. 'Okay, lie back and relax. Don't look at me.' She wheels the chair back so I can't see her without twisting my head. 'There. Now I am a blank slate on which you can project your subconscious.' She sounds like she is reading from lecture notes. 'Now, Edie, some free association: what do you think of when I say ... worms.'

'Worms?' I squeak. 'Why worms?'

'Vy not vorms?' Sally puts on a German accent. 'Vat are you trying to avoid?'

'Have I ever spoken to you about worms?'

'Only once. In an email you sent after you and Daniel broke up. You said, and I quote, "the worms came between us".'

'It was a typo. I meant *words*.'

'Aha. A Freudian slip, then. Why do you think about worms when you mean words? I still sink ve should talk about vorms.'

'I don't want to talk about worms.'

'I see, I see.' Sally's pen scratches. 'I note that the patient does not want to talk about worms. Penis envy.' These last words are murmured.

'Pardon? What did you just say?'

'Penis envy. Worms are a phallic symbol.'

'What's phallic about worms?'

'In Freudian therapy anything long and slender is a penis.'

'Sally, is this ethical, for you to be doing therapy on me? I mean, you're my friend.'

'Since when were you concerned with ethics? Okay, if you don't want to talk about worms, tell me about your dreams.' Sally's notebook rustles. 'Recurring dreams are particularly significant. They mean your subconscious is trying to work something out.'

'Well, as it happens ...' I fill Sally in on my recurring nude hiking dream.

'Strictly speaking,' says Sal, 'this is a nude tramping dream. They call it tramping in New Zealand, not hiking.'

'Is that relevant?'

'I will decide what is relevant. Now, let's see ...' She leafs through her notes. 'Nudity means that you have a fear of exposure. Does that resonate with you?'

'Mmm.'

'However, the fact that this man doesn't worry about your nudity means that you may be unnecessarily concerned. Do you recognise him?'

'I'm not sure that I've even looked at his face.'

'Well, try and take a look at his face next time. Your subconscious is telling you that you don't need to be scared of exposing yourself in front of him.'

'Oh. Thanks. That is surprisingly useful. You're worth more money.'

'See,' says Sal. 'Psychoanalysis is easy. I just needed to get warmed up.'

Freudian analysis over, Sally and I chat for a while. 'So what's happening with you and Jay?' she asks.

Hearing his name makes my chest ache. 'We're not talking.'

Sally frowns. 'Why don't you tell him that that you and Ralph never, you know ...?' Sally makes it seem so uncomplicated. She just forges ahead and obstacles vanish in her path, while for me they sprout like mushrooms.

'I can't,' I say. 'It's not like Jay and me were … in a relationship or anything. I'd end up sounding stupid. Nothing happened between us.' That is not true – plenty happened, but now it seems hard to define.

Sally squeezes my hand. 'Plenty of fish in the sea.'

But it's never seemed that way to me.

Once Sally is gone I open another Mars Bar then Google 'fear of worms'. There is even a name for it: vermiphobia. Freud says that vermiphobia is related to a fear of death and dying. Freud says a lot of weird stuff. At least it isn't fear of penises. Sally had me worried there for a while.

I finish my chocolate. Talking to Sally has cheered me up a little, but not enough. I think perhaps I need to talk to someone who knows what it is to suffer. I drum my fingers on the keyboard. Yes, the time has come to enter into an email correspondence with my beloved Nigerian, Philip.

Do what you want, says the bonsai in a weary tone. *I know you will anyway.*

I decide to take that as an endorsement. My fingers race over the keyboard.

Dear Beloved,

    I hope you don't mind me calling you Beloved, as you have me. Although I have never replied to your emails I have read them with interest. It must be very sad for you that I am the only person you can trust. Unfortunately, I am not in a position to take care of your fortune but I am happy to talk to you if you need a friend.

I am in need of a friend myself. I fear that my
best friend, Sally, is exploiting me for her own ends
and I think that I might be in love with my uncle-
in-law. Does this kind of thing happen much in
Nigeria? My uncle-in-law now seems to hate me
due to a misunderstanding and is in a very bad
mood. You and I may have much in common in our
misery.

   Be blessed my beloved,
   Sooty Beaumont

I check my emails about twenty times over the next couple
of hours, but there is no reply. This is discouraging. I had
been sure that Philip, if no one else, would be pleased to
hear from me. Men – there's no working them out.

On Sunday night when I go to water the bonsai I
see that it has not one leaf left on its spindly branches.
I contemplate it for some time, then pick it up and place
it in my rubbish bin. I don't know if I am happy or sad
to see the end of it. I have a strange feeling that, given
time, I might have grown to like it. An ache in my chest
reminds me that I haven't filled out my pain chart today.
I pick up my notebook and open it at the chart, click my
pen open and shut and open again, start to write, then
scribble it out. Then, on a sudden impulse, I tear out the
chart, rip it into little pieces and scatter it like confetti
over the bonsai. I have lost interest in my research.

I look at the brittle skeleton in my bin and decide
that a speech is in order. 'Vale bonsai. I didn't like you
much, but you were a good tree in your own way, if a

little harsh and judgmental. I salute your elegance, your spirit, your unerring judgment and your stoicism in the face of adversity.'

I wonder if I should let Daniel know that his tree has gone to better pastures. I decide not.

On Monday, I decide that I must take the crab between the pincers as it were. I cannot delay telling Professor Brownlow about my impending departure any longer. I stop by his desk on my way in and give a light cough.

Professor Brownlow's glasses glint in the fluorescent lights as he looks up. I am glad he is wearing his glasses – this would be so much worse if I had to gaze into his eyes.

'I'm sorry, but ...' I chew my lip.

Professor Brownlow waits.

'I'm leaving on Friday.'

He cocks his head. 'Leaving?'

I nod. 'I'm going to Japan. I'm going to get a job teaching English.'

Professor Brownlow frowns. 'This isn't because of ...' he taps his fingers, 'the motel-room misunderstanding?'

'No. I bought the ticket before that. I need a change. Everything's been a bit strange here. The writing, and ... other stuff.'

Professor Brownlow takes off his glasses and rubs the bridge of his nose.

I want to scream, *Don't do that, don't make it any harder than it has to be.*

'The young man who was here the other night?' he asks.

I nod. 'That's one of the things.'

'It wasn't because of the fracas in the laboratory, was it?'

I shrug. 'Partly. Maybe. But, you know, if that's the way he is, it's better to find out sooner rather than later, right?'

Professor Brownlow sighs. 'Have you tried explaining it to him?'

I shake my head. 'No. I can't talk to him. I don't even want to. He's turned into a different person.'

'Oh,' says Professor Brownlow. 'That's hard to deal with, isn't it?'

'Yeah, it is. But the Tokyo thing; that was planned ages ago. And anyway, I don't want my life to be ruled by other people anymore. I'm just going to let it go.'

'We only need to practise letting go,' says Professor Brownlow.

I smile. The depths of Professor Brownlow's literary knowledge astound me. 'You read Rilke too. For a zoology lecturer you'd make a good literature teacher.'

'Zoology is the what. Literature is the why. By the way, did that woman, Jennifer, catch up with you?'

'Jennifer?'

'Black hair, like this.' Professor Brownlow gestures with his hands to indicate one side higher than the other.

'Oh, her.' I remember now that Djennifer was heading for the lab the other night, I assumed in search of crab erotica. 'No. What did she want?'

'I'm not sure. I ran into her in the corridor as I was leaving. She was looking for you. It was all so hectic ...'

'That's one way of describing it.'

Professor Brownlow smiles. 'That strange man was a big fan of yours, wasn't he?'

I roll my eyes. 'I suppose Djennifer wants an autograph too.'

Professor Brownlow looks doubtful. 'Maybe. She said something about the divine feminine. I didn't know what she meant.'

'Oh. Well, I guess she'll find me.'

'I hope you're going to take the opportunity to expand your knowledge of Japanese literature while you're over there.'

'I might.'

Professor Brownlow gives me a long look.

'Okay, I will. Definitely. Can't wait.'

He smiles. 'There'll be a test.'

'You mean I can't fob you off with Nori Toyota?'

He shakes his head. 'You'll be back, won't you? I'll keep your job open for you.'

'I don't know.' A stab of loneliness pierces me at the thought of Tokyo. I wonder if my *Where is the toilet?* conversation starter will come in handy there. *Toire wa doko desu ka?* Sadly, my limited Japanese means this line is unlikely to lead to a rewarding chat.

Tokyo. Thirty-five million people and not one of them I know. Sally would say that's thirty-five million opportunities to get to know someone new.

But I am not Sally.

Chapter Thirty

Neurosis is the inability to tolerate ambiguity.

SIGMUND FREUD

Tuesday is a lonely day. I check my emails as always, but even My Beloved seems to have struck me from his email distribution list. This is the final blow. Sally is still trying to coax erotic literature out of me. She sends me enticing recipes: toad in the hole, bombe Alaska, tiramisu. They all have possibilities, but I am too sad to deliver.

Sally calls on Wednesday before work and gives me a pep talk. 'Edie, you are on a carousel going round and round. You need to find a horse that's going to take you somewhere.'

'One that isn't attached to the merry-go-round, you mean?'

'Exactly.'

'I think I might be on one of those merry-go-rounds that have ducks and boats instead of horses.'

'Ducks, boats, horses, the principle is the same. You need to take responsibility, kick some butt.'

'I would if it wasn't so tiring,' I sigh. 'I'm flat out just going round and round.'

'The music's going to stop soon, babe.'

This sounds ominous. 'You mean I could be stuck on a duck out of luck?'

'Ha ha,' says Sal.

I open my self-improvement notebook after Sally hangs up. *Get off the duck*, I write.

I do wonder sometimes where I am going with this self-improvement thing. I don't really know what I hope to achieve. What is success? What is failure? The more I think about it, the more it recedes.

And one of the problems with this question is that there is something I am avoiding. This something is so dazzling, so dangerous, that to tackle it would be like looking into the sun. I wonder how much longer I can hold out before I crack.

On Thursday, in an effort to get off the carousel, I decide to run again. I move quickly before I can change my mind. Sliding out of bed, I pull on my runners. I then realise I am still wearing my bed shirt. This is an oversized Garfield T-shirt which hangs to mid-thigh. I root around in my cupboard for shorts, but can't find them. My sole pair of shorts is in the wash.

I could wear long pants? *No, too hot.* Or a dress? *Too ridiculous.* I could just give up ... *No. I won't give up. I will run.* I glance at myself in the cupboard-door mirror. I look a little odd, but I think I'll pass. Who am I going to see, anyway?

Kafka the cat is sitting on the footpath at the bottom of the stairs. He looks at me as I come down then coughs and spits out a furball in disgust.

'Sorry Kafka, it's just me. Gary's gone. No rockstars here.'

The cat stands up and stalks away.

'I can read you some poems,' I call after him, but he doesn't turn his head.

I set off. No one I pass seems surprised by my choice of running outfit. It is very practical, breezy. A little too breezy occasionally, but I am wearing big knickers, so that's not a problem. I am running strongly. I am surprising myself. I run and run. I am a cheetah. I am Cathy Freeman.

Then, all of a sudden, I am no longer surprising myself. Halfway to Darling Point I hit the wall. How can it happen like that? One moment I am running the one-minute mile, the next I am ready for a retirement home. My energy has drained out as if a plug has been pulled.

I turn and stumble homewards, gasping like a high-altitude climber. The oxygen levels in the air seem depleted. There are lead weights in my shoes. Running is stupid. I am never doing it again. I know more than enough about pain anyway.

As I limp up my street I spot a small blue car parked at the bottom of the stairs. Getting closer, I see an *Airport Rentals* sticker on the back. A man is sitting in the driver's seat watching me in the rear-view mirror. The back of his head is familiar. I freeze.

Two weeks ago the sight of that head would have made my stomach erupt in a locust plague of excitement. I test my reactions. No locust plague. I feel ... curious, but also slightly alarmed. What on earth is Daniel doing here?

The bonsai. He's come for his bonsai. My eyes dart to the bin outside our garage. Thursday is garbage collection day.

Daniel steps out of the car. His eyes flicker over me.

Even though I think I am no longer in love with Daniel, I still wish my legs weren't so red, my Garfield T-shirt wasn't so sweat-soaked, my hair so unattractively sticking to my head. Too late, I remember the article I read in the women's mag while I was in the queue at the supermarket. *Damn*. Those women's mags are more prescient than I give them credit for. Where is the trendy burqa when you need it?

Daniel, of course, is immaculate. He looks like he has just stepped out of the shower. He is wearing a light-blue, long-sleeved shirt, rolled up to expose his forearms. Light-brown pants and polished brown shoes complement this smart-casual lawyer look. His dark hair is cut shorter than it used to be. It suits him. I had almost forgotten how handsome Daniel is, but I still don't think I am in love with him.

'Hi,' I say.

Daniel's reply is drowned out by the roar of the garbage truck.

I try to distract him by saying, 'What?' in a loud voice, but he is riveted by the sight of the truck.

It is no exaggeration to say that Daniel is a garbage Nazi. Our weekly throwaway garbage never exceeded the size of a shopping bag. Not that we had plastic shopping bags. If I was ever unable to turn down a bag when shopping – you know how forceful some sales assistants are – I made damn sure I got rid of it before arriving home.

Knowing Daniel, he is now waiting to see if I have separated my recycling correctly. I never realised how much was involved in recycling until I met Daniel. It is not enough just to separate paper from plastic, you need to know the different types of plastic and wash them out thoroughly. And, of course, your food and vegetable waste must never go in the garbage; it must be put in a compost bin.

Or fed to worms.

The combination of Daniel and the garbage truck forces me to think of something I would rather forget.

In Daniel's flat, which became our flat, lived a big black plastic box filled with earthworms. Their function was to eat our scraps. At night I was sure I could hear them munching on apple cores and passing leftover broccoli through their digestive tracts. I tried not to listen, but I couldn't help it.

I'd nudge Daniel awake, 'Can you hear that noise?'

'What noise?'

'The worms.'

'Worms don't make a noise.'

But they did – a slithery, slurpy, chompy noise. They gave me the creeps but I couldn't tell Daniel. It is silly to be scared of earthworms just because they're:

slimy,

wriggly, and

really, really, really sinister.

I asked Daniel early on in our relationship how many worms were in there.

'There were two thousand to begin with, but they've been breeding so … Are you all right Edie?'

He must have noticed how pale I was. I'd been thinking ten or twenty tops. *Two thousand? And breeding? Earthworms were breeding in our lounge room?*

Daniel gazed lovingly at his worm farm. 'Annelids breed every seven to ten days and double their population every two or three months.'

'Annelids?'

'Segmented worms. What's interesting is that they're hermaphrodite.'

'Hermaphrodite?' I didn't like the sound of it.

'They have both male and female sex organs. They still mate though.'

'Oh.' *Every night while I was asleep thousands of bisexual worms were fucking nearby.*

'Pretty good, huh?'

I nodded. I was speechless.

Daniel went to a lot of trouble with the worms. He chopped up their food nice and small so they could eat it easily. Sometimes he tore up bits of paper and added that. He was like a farmer. It made him happy. He whistled while he tended to his earthworms.

Daniel is a practical person, but he became almost poetic when he talked about his worms. 'You should see them when they mate, Edie. They lie together and cover themselves in mucus and then pass sperm into each other's body. It's beautiful.'

I think if I could have excreted enough mucus to engulf us both when we made love we might still be together. 'What happens then; do they give birth?' I was still feigning an interest in earthworms at that stage.

'No, they get a ring of slime around their body with the eggs in it. The ring moves up their body and slips off. It looks like a pearl.'

I might not have liked earthworms, but I did like the proud and loving look on Daniel's face when he talked about them. It made me think that he'd make a good father one day. If he could get that excited about a worm's egg, imagine what he'd be like with a baby.

A dark brown and pungent liquid gathered in a tray below our worm farm. Worm wee. Daniel treated this like a magic elixir. He'd dilute it to the colour of weak tea, bottle it and give it to his friends. When we went to dinner parties he'd often take along a bottle of worm pee instead of wine.

I watched his friends' reactions when he gave it to them, waiting for the recoil. They were always overjoyed.

Fantastic. You got it from your own worms? I didn't like to ask what they did with it, but I always filled my own wine glass.

I figured out early on that I was in a 'love me, love my worms' relationship. And I did love Daniel, so I coped. I went to extraordinary lengths to avoid being the one to feed them. Doing the washing up every night at feeding time worked well. Sexual favours were my fallback position.

This all worked well until Daniel went away for a week; he had a court case down the south coast. I had never been left in charge of the worms before. When we went on holidays his friend always came around.

Daniel briefed me on worm care. I tried to pay attention but the words jumbled in my head. All I could think about was feeding a quivering mass of worms. *Fruit and vegetables, dairy, citrus, meat, onion, garlic ...* It sounded straightforward.

The first night Daniel was away I picked up Subway for dinner. I ate at the table, my eyes on the worm farm. Daniel always fed them after dinner, so they'd be circling their box, their wet pinky brown noses sniffing the air. I couldn't eat much.

Sweat broke out on my forehead as I approached them. Opening the box, I closed my eyes, tipped the best part of a foot-long roll in and slammed it shut, breathing hard. I ate fast food a lot while Daniel was away and I was diligent in feeding the worms. I did it for Daniel.

I did notice a strange smell coming from the box by day five. I hoped they weren't dying of starvation.

I ramped up my efforts, giving them the remains of breakfast and lunch as well.

It turns out that worms are quite fussy feeders. Maggots, however, just love fast food. By the time Daniel returned they had totally routed the worms. Daniel took it hard. He looked like a farmer facing a crop ruined by drought.

'It's taken me five years to build up that worm farm, Edie,' he said. 'I told you not to feed them meat or dairy.'

It was like an outback tragedy. If tumbleweed had blown through our lounge room at that moment I wouldn't have been surprised. I was tempted to say, 'We can start again in California, cain't we?' but Daniel hadn't read *The Grapes of Wrath*.

I now wonder if I subconsciously killed the worms on purpose. Freud would say that I chose not to listen to Daniel's instructions. And Freud could have a point. Freud might also say that my id was looking for a way to escape a relationship that was destroying my ego. Maybe Sally was right and it does, after all, come down to ze vorms.

The good part is that my vermiphobia hasn't been an issue since Daniel and I went our separate ways.

Now, as the garbage truck roars up our street, I am concerned that Daniel is going to get a poor impression of me by inspecting our rubbish. I am also very, very concerned about one piece of rubbish in particular.

Daniel steps closer to the bins as the truck nears our driveway.

'Daniel,' I squeal and run up to him. I fling my arms around him, pressing my sweaty body against his pressed shirt.

He puts his arms around me, but in a holding off sort of way, trying to keep some distance between us. He is still looking over my shoulder at the garbage truck, which is now lifting up the bin.

I grasp his chin in my hand and press my lips against his. This is successful in distracting him. His eyes meet mine, 'Edie, I —'

I stop him with another kiss.

He steps backwards.

I try to hold on to him, but my hands are too sweaty to get a good grip on his.

'I just called in to say —'

There is a rumble as the rubbish flows out of the bin. Daniel turns, just in time to see his bonsai vanishing into the maw of the rubbish van. It is pathetic, its tiny limbs naked of leaves; a brown and withered remnant of the glossy-leaved tree that once graced our coffee table. The only thing that connects it to the bonsai Daniel knew and loved is its red pot with Japanese writing. He pales visibly.

I feel like a murderer. 'I didn't do it,' I say. 'It killed itself.'

Daniel turns back to me. He blinks. For a moment I am afraid he is going to cry. He shakes his head. 'You didn't separate out the plastic properly either.'

We look at each other silently for some time. I feel like I know him so well and yet not at all. I wonder why he is here; whether he was missing me. Perhaps he thought I deserved another chance. Whatever he thought doesn't matter now. I have murdered his worms, killed his bonsai and failed to separate out the plastic properly. I don't know which of these crimes is the worst.

My legs are trembling from the run and the stress of seeing Daniel under such trying conditions. If there is a worse way to re-encounter a lost love I don't want to know about it. As the garbage truck departs I sink to the kerb and put my head in my hands. While I don't think I love Daniel anymore, we were, after all, together for twelve months and twenty days and the loss of love is sad.

I feel a hand on my back. Daniel sits down beside me on the damp, mouldy concrete.

'Your pants,' I say.

'They'll wash.'

I meet his eyes.

He smiles and I remember that we did have something nice together once. It wasn't all a total waste of time.

'What are you doing here?'

'I've got a meeting nearby. At the Environmental Defenders Office. I wanted to see ... how you are.'

I flap my Garfield T-shirt to dry it out. 'And so, how am I?'

His smile broadens. 'Just the same.' He blinks again.

'Have you got a new girlfriend?' The question pops out of my mouth before I can stop it, but Daniel had lived with me for too long to be surprised by my gaucheness.

'I'm seeing someone. It's still kind of casual.'

I wait, my head on one side.

'She's a lawyer.'

'A barrister?'

He nods.

The bonsai was right. I smile. 'That's nice. Nice for you. You can talk about law.'

'Yes.' He sounds doubtful.

'You like to talk about law.'

Daniel nods his head in a vague way.

'You used to like to talk about law.'

He shrugs. 'Law's all right. It's nice to talk about other things too.' He chews his lip. 'I did love you, Edie.'

Now I'm the one blinking. That 'l' word. Who knows what it means? 'I loved you too, Daniel. I'm sorry about your bonsai. I tried to look after it, but, I think it had a death wish.'

'It never would have worked.'

'No. Bonsais obviously need special care. And we didn't really get on. I think it meant well, but it didn't have a very good bedside manner.'

'I mean *we* never would have worked.' Daniel looks at me strangely. 'In the long term.'

'Oh. No. We wouldn't. You are from Mars and I am from …' I pause, not sure what comes next.

'A galaxy far, far away.' He reaches out and squeezes my hand. 'It's an interesting world you come from, but it's not my world.'

'No. I can see that now.'

Daniel lets go of my hand. He glances at his watch.

'I'd better go.' He stands up and brushes the dirt from his pants.

'Thanks for coming. It was nice to see you.' These tea party words are the best I can do. If I tried to express how I really feel we'd be here all day.

Daniel kisses me on the cheek before he gets in the car.

I lean over and look in his window. 'I'm sorry about everything.'

He gives a one-sided smile. 'I'm sorry too.'

'You're going to make a great father one day,' I say, but he is starting the car and he doesn't hear me.

I watch him go, waving and waving until his car vanishes around the corner. As soon as he is gone I want him to come back. I think of a million things I should have said. If only my life was scripted better; if only I was more competent. And even though I think that I no longer love Daniel, I find I am crying. But not in a way that hurts.

'You all right, Edz?' It is Tim. He is perched on a bike which has a carry basket full of rolled-up pamphlets.

I nod, wiping my cheeks.

'Did he dump ya?' He gives Daniel's departing car a narrow-eyed look.

'Yes. I think I'm over it now though.'

'That was quick.' He sounds admiring.

I smile. 'I suppose it was, wasn't it?'

'And you've got other guys, haven't you?'

I now remember that he saw me coming out of the motel room with Professor Brownlow. Tim thinks I am a sexually adventurous surf star. I don't want to disabuse him. It is flattering to have at least one person who thinks of me as a Sooty Beaumont type. 'Yeah, you know, I've got a few.'

'Way to go.' He gives me a thumbs-up and coasts down the street, flinging papers with frightening force. I hear a window shatter as he vanishes out of sight.

Chapter Thirty-one

What do women want?

SIGMUND FREUD

I climb the stairs; I now have lead weights strapped to my ankles as well as in my shoes. My cheeks are wet with tears, but I am not sad about Daniel. It is more of a Lassie-Come-Home moment, a happy sadness. Daniel and I could never have worked, but we did love each other once. I can move on now.

When I reach the middle level I see Rochelle trimming branches in her Japanese garden. She is naked and, as I suspected, has no tan lines. The naked gardening must be a frequent pastime. I'm surprised I haven't encountered it before.

She doesn't notice me at first and I am not sure if I should just keep going up to the house. But then if she sees me going past she'll feel snubbed and maybe embarrassed. She might take it as a judgment call on her nakedness.

'Hi,' I say.

Rochelle looks up. 'Oh, Edie, I wasn't expecting you, I ...' She holds her secateurs in front of her crotch.

'Don't mind me. It's cool, nothing wrong with a bit of nude gardening.' I concentrate on looking at Rochelle's face, at being relaxed. Nudity is cool. Nudity is very north coast.

Rochelle smiles. 'Oh good.' She starts to trim the bushes again. 'I feel so much freer without clothes, don't you?'

'Yeah.' *No.* I like wearing clothes, but it sounds uptight to say so. The more clothes the better as far as I'm concerned. 'I guess I've kind of cramped your style. Did you and Dad used to hang out in the nude a lot before I came home?' I have probably interrupted their honeymoon Shangri-La.

Rochelle shrugs. 'Yes, but it doesn't matter. I just got used to nudity in Hawaii.'

'Oh yes, Hawaii. How was that?'

Rochelle gets a dreamy look on her face. 'It was ... primal.'

Primal. And as she stands there, nude, in our garden, I can picture her working in the taro field. Rochelle is an earth goddess. If I had strong arms, brown skin and thick, gold, sun-bleached hair maybe I would like working naked too.

If I was to be naked outdoors I would model myself on that painting by Manet, *Le déjeuner sur l'herbe*. Reclining naked under a tree with a picnic would be fine. Working in a field in hot tropical sun is out of the question. I would fry in an instant.

'I felt so at one with the land,' says Rochelle. 'I think I was a Hawaiian in my past life.'

'I think I may have been an Inuit,' I murmur. I continue up the stairs, leaving Rochelle to bond with the garden.

On Friday morning I wake to find myself in a strange frame of mind. It may have something to do with my dream. For a change, it was not a nude hiking dream. It was a nice dream. I curl my toes, remembering it.

Jay and I are sitting in separate armchairs, writing in our notebooks. I am feeling happy to have all the time in the world just to be in his company.

Jay looks up from his book. 'Can you use purling in a sentence?' he says.

'A purling stream ran beside the house?'

Jay raises his eyebrows. 'Good work.'

'Kismet,' I say.

Jay pretends to ponder, then he stretches his bare feet towards me so our toes touch. 'We are each other's kismet.'

The dream has left me feeling full of possibilities. It has reminded me that Jay likes words, he likes my writing. It has given me an idea. I am not sure if it is a Good Idea or a Bad Idea. Should I, or shouldn't I? I lie in my warm bed like a mountain climber who has camped just below the summit of Everest on their way up. The blizzard is closing in, but this is a do-or-die day. Tomorrow I leave

307

for Japan. Tomorrow, I suddenly realise, is also my birthday. I don't want to leave for Japan on my birthday feeling that I could have done more.

If the bonsai was here it would probably tell me not to be ridiculous. But the bonsai has gone, and weren't its last words *Do what you want*? In any case, I am in no mood to be deterred. Did Hillary listen to naysayers? Did Tenzing? Did Murakami? No, no and no. I look at the papers on my desk and decide this is a Very Good Idea. It is time to get off that carousel duck and back onto the highway.

Jay's door is closed, as always, when I come downstairs. We have somehow managed to avoid each other all week. He has been out every night. It is like we have created a roster to ensure our paths do not cross. I imagine a time-lapse sequence of our house with Jay and I moving through it at a rapid pace, almost, but never quite intersecting.

I stand outside his room, holding my 'Creamy Tuna Pasta' piece in my hand. My eyes flicker over the words *salty and sticky* and *olive oil*. For a fraction of a second I wonder if this is, in fact, a Good Idea. I accelerate my motorbike, my heart beats faster. Before I can think too much about it, I push it under the door, leap out into space. Will I make it over the chasm? Who knows what effect it will have?

I walk into the kitchen and am opening the fridge door before I realise Jay is sitting on a stool drinking coffee. He was so quiet and so still, and so unexpected that I almost missed him. He gives me a faint nod. I stare at him. My fantasy motorbike runs smack into his brick wall and explodes with a bang. A queasy aftershock hits me.

He hates me.

I turn on my heels and retreat. What strange and warped side of me ever thought that sliding erotic literature under his door was a good idea? If that person was here now, I'd give her a good slap around the face.

I find myself outside his door again. My eyes look back towards the kitchen. All is quiet. Perhaps I could just open the door ...? That seems a little scary. Or perhaps ... I kneel down and push my fingers under the door. Yes, I think I can feel the edge of the paper.

I am stroking the paper towards me with my fingertips when I notice a pair of bare feet beside me. They are the feet from my dream. I freeze. I don't look up. A number of possible explanations for being on the floor outside his room run through my head. 'I —' *Dropped my pen? Fell over? Saw a snake go under your door?*

'Excuse me,' says Jay in his waiter voice. He opens the door and steps inside. The paper slides away from my fingertips as he picks it up.

I decide to skip breakfast and leave for work immediately. I turn the radio up loud as I drive and try to forget that I have humiliated myself in the worst way possible. I have exposed my fantasies for him to sneer at, or worse, ignore.

Professor Brownlow brings in a cake for my last day.

I smile as he opens the box at morning-tea time. 'Did you make this?'

He shakes his head. 'I have many talents, but cake decorating is not one of them.'

It is a crab larvae.

'I gave them one of your drawings to model it from.'

'That explains the missing maxilliped.' I point at the licorice strips poking from its legs. Picking one off, I eat it. 'Two missing maxillipeds now.'

We work companionably for the rest of the day. At five o'clock I get up. 'Well, *sayonara*, I guess.'

Professor Brownlow stands. 'I'd prefer to say *au revoir*.' He walks over and kisses me on the cheek.

Oh, how that would have made me weak at the knees not so long ago. Now, it is just pleasant.

'You've done a lot of good work here, Edie.' He waves his arm towards my pile of drawings. He has stacked them next to the scanner in preparation for his Japanese Brine Shrimp paper. It is for a conference in America next month.

'I hope your paper goes well.' I turn at the door of the lab for one last wave. 'I hope you're big in LA.'

Professor Brownlow is watching me. 'I hope you're big in Japan,' he says.

We look at each other, smiling. Our strange, shared history hangs between us but there is no way to put this into words. I break away first.

As I drive off I am nostalgic already for the fun times I have had drawing crab larvae with the beautiful and mysterious Professor Brownlow.

*

My working day has distracted me a little, but not enough. All day 'Creamy Tuna Pasta' has been rising to the surface of my mind. Each time, I have pushed it back down with a huge mental effort. What was I thinking? I may as well have lain naked on his bed with a bunch of parsley tucked between my legs. And it wasn't even meant in that way. I just wanted to remind him that I exist, that we had a connection once. Or did we?

I climb the stairs to my room and freeze when I get to the top. A folded square of paper is sticking out from under my door. I know immediately it is from Jay. I can hardly bear to look. I bend down, unfold it. Nausea grips my stomach. There aren't many words on the page.

Doing a gig at the pub tonight – 8 pm. Jay.

I read it about ten times. While scanty in words, it is big in meaning. The only trouble is I don't know what the meaning is. In what way is this note an appropriate response to a week of not-talking followed by an erotic missive? I give him a fantasy roll in olive oil and tuna and in return he gives me his gig guide. Why? My shot in the dark seems to have produced something, but I am not quite sure what. I begin to wonder if I really gave him the 'Creamy Tuna Pasta' story at all.

Writing can be good, but sometimes talking provides more clarity. I go downstairs in the hope that:

Jay will be there;
We can exchange words;
We will understand each other; and
We will make up.

That's a whole lot of hoping; way too much as it turns out. His door is closed. I knock but there is no reply.

I ring Sally. I decide not to tell her about the creamy tuna pasta. I feel this may cast me in a bad light.

'Well, duh,' she says. 'He wants to see you there.'

'You think?'

'Obviously.'

'Should I go?'

'You like him, right?'

Like. Has ever one word had to encompass such a range of meanings? I like apple pie. I like hot baths. I like puppies and kittens.

For Jay, I feel a mixture of:

Pain,
Longing,
Empathy,
Sadness,
Hate, and
Joy.

'Yeah, I like him.'

'How are you going to play it?'

It has never occurred to me to play it any way other than straight. I like you. You like me. Can we please hold hands and talk again, because that's about the only thing in my life that makes me feel sane, real and whole?

'How do you mean?'

'Edie,' says Sal, in that pitying way she has, 'you don't get it with guys, do you?'

'No, I guess I don't.'

'It's a game. You don't let them know how you feel or they'll run a mile. It's the caveman instinct. They have to chase you or they're not interested.'

I think it may be too late for that. Girls who know how to play hard to get probably don't share tuna fantasies with their love interest. But perhaps I can recover lost ground. 'How can I act like I'm not interested and still turn up?'

'Difficult.' She pauses. 'Not impossible though. Turn up late and act bored, like you just happened to wander in. Be cool.'

I try to visualise how this would work. Fail abysmally. My heart rate accelerates at the thought of it. 'I don't know how to be cool.'

'You've seen the movie with John Travolta, haven't you?'

'*Be Cool*? Yeah.'

'Well, there you go. Ask yourself what Chili Palmer would do.'

'But —'

'Sorry Ed, gotta go, I've got a client waiting. Remember the golden rule of dating: don't let him know you care. And dazzle him with your conversational skills; you've been practising, right?'

'But —'

'You could try the wink. That worked well last time.'

'But —'

'Byee.'

Chili Palmer. Don't let him know I care. Be cool.
It's a game. They have to chase you. None of this makes
any sense, but Sally is the expert on these matters and
my relationship history says I'm not. Maybe if I'd learnt
these rules earlier, things would have worked out better
in the past. Maybe if I'd learnt these rules earlier, I
wouldn't have given him the tuna fantasy. I try not to
think about that. *Cut my losses. Move on.*

Dazzle him with your conversational skills. Was
Sally being ironic? There is no way I can wing this.
Preparation is required. What I need is a script. I turn on
my computer.

Edie at the Pub: Draft One – Cool

Edie enters pub at 8.45, sees Jay, strolls languidly over.
She punches him lightly on the shoulder.

Jay: You're late.

Edie: If you're important, people will wait.

Jay: You're looking good.

Edie (gazing over his shoulder): Cheers dude.

Jay: Wow, Edie, you're so cool.

My powers of imagination break down at this point.
Cool doesn't seem to be within my repertoire. I decide to
see what happens if I try warm.

Edie at the Pub: Draft Two – Warm

Edie enters pub at 7.45, sees Jay, strides over. She punches
him lightly on the shoulder.

Edie: Yo.

Jay: Yo.

Edie: So, you're playing tonight, huh?

Jay: Yeah, I was really hoping you'd make it.

Edie: Of course I made it. Wouldn't miss it for the world.

Jay (gazes meaningfully into her eyes): I'm sorry about what I said the other day. (He steps closer, puts his arms around her.) You know you're very special, don't you?

I gaze at the computer screen. The scene is going well, but the only problem is that Jay is getting all the good lines, not me. This would be fine, except he won't have rehearsed, so it would be better if I controlled the action. I think I can manage the shoulder punching, just, but what will happen next?

Dazzle him. Ha. I glance at my watch: seven o'clock. I still have time to work on some dialogue. Witty repartee would be good. I think Jay would go for that. But witty repartee is not one of my stock in trades. If only I was one of those old-time romantic comedy queens like Katharine Hepburn. I must have been asleep when the sparkling-dialogue gene was handed out.

I tap my fingers on the keyboard, then in a sudden flash of inspiration or desperation, type *sparkling dialogue* into Google.

I take it all back. Google is terrific. Way better than a three-day horse trip to a library. One of the references is a software program that provides examples of dialogue for any situation. It only costs twenty dollars and offers 101 dialogue techniques.

315

One hundred and one dialogue techniques! I had no idea there were so many. Why hasn't Sally ever told me this? I bet she knows and she's holding out on me. She thinks I can't take it. Well she's wrong. I grasp my mouse and click on *Buy Now*.

Five minutes later I have downloaded *Have Fun with Dialogue*. I scan the list of techniques. The meaning of some is obvious from their titles – avoidance, backhanded compliment, blurt and retract – I think I might be pretty good at that one. Others are mysterious – antithesis, bait and switch, breaking the fourth wall.

I wonder if everyone else knows about these techniques. That would explain a lot. For most of my life I've had the feeling others are playing by conversational rules unknown to me. But now, mastery is within reach.

Half an hour later, I am deep in a morass of conversational possibilities.

Edie at the Pub: Draft Three – Blurt and retract
Edie: Jay, I've been feeling this thing about you. I can't keep it to myself anymore. I just sense somehow we're meant to be together, like it's fated. Don't you feel that too?
Jay: No, I don't actually.
Edie: Me neither. Not at all.

Edie at the Pub: Draft Four – Bait and switch
Jay: Edie, I've had this feeling ...
Edie: Yes, Jay?

316

Jay: It's becoming very strong.

Edie: I feel the same way.

Jay: What, you want to throw up too?

I am so involved that by the time I come up for air it is eight pm. I should be at the pub. But I still haven't cracked the right tone with my dialogue. Besides, like Sally said, I should be fashionably late rather than too-keenly early as is my usual practice.

A knock interrupts my thinking.

'Yeah?' I look up, sighing. I really need to get this dialogue sorted.

Dad peers through a gap in the door. 'Hi.'

'Hi.'

He coughs. 'You busy?'

'Mmm, kind of.' I gesture at the screen. 'Just, you know, writing.'

'I was wondering how your set-up is here. Do you need a new desk? I could build you one.'

'No, I'm fine. Thanks.' I eye my dialogue, a rising anxiety in my stomach.

His eyes flicker to the computer. 'Going well?'

'No, not really. And I've got a deadline.'

'Oh.' He backs out, the Dad-look on his face. 'Sorry.'

'No, it's —' It's too late. He's already shut the door.

I stare at it for a moment, wondering what he wanted, but there are more pressing matters at hand. Plunging back into my dialogue, I continue to search for the perfect note.

Edie at the Pub: Draft Five – Cry from the heart

Edie: Jay, Jay. You're tearing me apart.

Edie at the Pub: Draft Six – Hard-boiled dialogue

Edie: Okay, Jay, we need to get one thing straight.

Jay: You're not playing that old record again are you?

Edie: Show me the money or I'm getting out of here buddy.

I try my hand at curt, double-dutch and formal and then come to climactic speech.

Edie at the Pub: Draft Ten – Climactic speech

Edie: Jay, I love the way your fingers are rough at the ends but soft in the middle, I love how your hair looks when you've slept on it, I love how I never know what's going to happen next when I'm around you, I love how you look at me like I'm the funniest thing you've ever seen, but most of all I love the way you make me feel like it's okay to be the crazy, weird, shy, awkward geek I am.

I pause after I've written this one. I don't think it is going to get any better. There is a reason Sally has chosen not to induct me into the 101 dialogue techniques; she knew I'd be crap at all of them. There is only one thing to do: wing it.

I read back over my climactic speech. This says what I want to say. What I can never say. And certainly not in the Darling Head Pub. Because it is true. For a little while there Jay did make me feel it was okay to be the strange and crazy person that I am. That is a very scary thought. Daniel only rejected a sanitised and well-presented version of myself, but I think I might have let Jay see who I really am. Was it enough? Was *I* enough?

I glance at my watch. It is nine-thirty. I can't believe I am so late. I can't believe I have been wasting my time fiddling around with dialogue when Jay is playing at the pub. When I could be there listening to him. Why aren't I there now?

I pull on jeans and a T-shirt and rush for the door.

Chapter Thirty-two

The goal of all life is death.

SIGMUND FREUD

I have my car keys in my hand and am almost out the door when I hear the phone ring. I hesitate, thinking that Dad will get it, but then I hear the shower running. I pick it up.

'Yo.'

'Edie, is that you?'

'Yo.'

'It's Ralph.'

For a moment I am flummoxed, then I realise it is Professor Brownlow. 'Hi, Ralph.'

'Do you normally say yo?'

'Sorry, no, it's a new thing I'm trying out.'

'There's a bit of an emergency here, Edie.' His voice sounds strained.

I immediately think of Belinda. 'Belinda hasn't hit you with the tennis racquet, has she?'

'No, no, it's work ...'

'A crab larvae emergency?' An image of a rampant crab larva massacring its beaker-mates springs to mind. *That'll teach you to say my telson's fat.*

'Yes. My Japanese Brine Shrimp paper, it's due tonight. I had your drawings in a pile ready to scan in. They're very strict about submission deadlines ...' His voice trails off.

'You spilt coffee on them?'

'No.'

'Your dog ate them?'

'No.'

'What then?'

'They disappeared. Not all of them, just the *Pyromaia tuberculata* and the *Stimdromia lamellata*.'

'Oh, no, not the *Pyromaia tuberculata*, that was one of my favourites.'

'Yes, I was very fond of it too,' says Professor Brownlow, missing my irony. 'I think they were stolen.'

'But, who would do that?' I try to sound mystified, but my mind springs to the sleazy crab man. I wonder if he lives at home with his elderly mother and hides his crab larvae porn under the bed with the *Playboy*s.

'I have a rival; one of the other professors. He's out to stop me getting departmental head. I think it must have been him. If I don't get this paper in, he'll have had more publications than me this year and that will sway the balance his way.'

'I didn't realise academia was so cutthroat,' I say. I still think it was the sleazy crab man though.

'That's nothing. You should see the staff meetings; lucky to get out alive half the time.'

As I twirl the car keys in my hand, I already know what he is going to say next.

'Can you come in and re-do them?'

I think of Jay and I wish I had got there earlier, that I hadn't been so stupid spending time writing dialogue I can never use. A tug in my chest pulls me towards the pub.

'The paper has to be in by midnight but, of course, I'll understand if you have other things ...'

I think of Professor Brownlow and how kind he has been, the crab larvae cake, the allowances for my slackness. And part of me is relieved not to go to the pub – the social anxiety, facing Jay, the chance of rejection, the attempts to use my stupid dialogue.

I bite my lip. 'I'll be right there.'

It is a little strange meeting up with Professor Brownlow again so soon after our fond farewell. It could have been awkward, but he smiles when he sees me and puts on a fake German accent. 'So, ve meet again.'

This is sappy, but it breaks the ice. It is only then that I realise how this will look if Belinda turns up. *Alone. Together. In the lab. At night.* I hesitate at the door.

Professor Brownlow tilts his head.

'Is Belinda ...?'

'Gone to the movies.'

I sigh with relief and take my place at the bench. By the time I slide my first zoea under the microscope

I am already over my nostalgia for this job. What was I thinking? It is worse than watching *March of the Penguins*. Despite my boredom, we work together happily for a couple of hours, me drawing, him typing and then sending off the completed paper. The *Pyromaia tuberculata* and the *Stimdromia lamellata* are nowhere near as much fun the second time around.

'Okay.' I hand him the drawings. 'Guard them with your life.'

He is suitably grateful.

Our farewell is more stilted this time as we have already used our best lines. We end up just waving at each other in the car park, hesitating for a moment with the possibility of another kiss on the cheek hanging in the air, then jumping in our cars.

Professor Brownlow beeps as I drive off.

On the road I am, once again, nostalgic for the fun times we have had.

It is twelve-thirty by the time I reach the Darling Head Pub. It is closed. A few drunks loiter on the verandah like discarded wrappings. I get out of the car and peer in the window in case Jay is still there, ignoring their oh-so-tempting mumbled invitations to have a fuck. What would they say if I turned to them and said, yes please, I'd love a fuck, thanks for asking?

The stage is empty except for a microphone and drum set. Up until now this has been about me, but now I think about him. Perhaps he really wanted me there? I imagine Jay holding the microphone and I hope the crowd was friendly. If only I wasn't so incompetent with these personal interactions. Why didn't I at least pop in to say I couldn't make it? Why did I listen to Sally and turn this into some kind of adversarial game? Do I want Jay if I have to play games to keep him interested?

I already know what the answer is. I get back in my car.

I am surprised to see the lights still on when I get home. I imagine Jay is there, winding down. I'm not sure what I will say, but I run up the stairs. I will make it all right between us somehow. I will be honest. I won't play games.

Dad and Rochelle are sitting on the couch outside holding hands. There is no sign of Jay.

'What's up?' I ask.

Rochelle waves her hand in a manner meant to be dismissive, but due to its jerkiness, has the opposite effect. 'It's Jay.'

I slide onto the couch next to her. 'What happened?'

Her hand tightens around Dad's. 'It's my bloody father again. He waltzes in, waltzes out, talks big and forgets us once he's out the door.'

I wait.

'He was supposed to line up some record company guy to hear Jay play at the pub tonight. You'd think Jay would have learnt by now.'

'Did you go?' I ask.

'Yeah, I went,' says Rochelle. 'Jay was great. There weren't many people there, though. I think he might have been hoping you'd come.'

'I meant to.'

Rochelle looks at me as if I am not the person she thought I was.

I want to explain it's not like she thinks. I'd leap tall buildings for her brother, swim through shark-infested waters, wrestle a minotaur if necessary. If only I knew he wanted me to. 'Where is he?'

'He's gone out,' says Rochelle. 'I tried to stop him, but he said he needed a walk.' She is a bundle of repressed emotion.

I know she is thinking of the scars on his arms. I am thinking of them too, but I can't tell her as I am not supposed to know. 'Shall I go and have a look for him?'

Rochelle's smile is a vestige of her usual radiance. 'Oh, would you, Edie? He won't talk to me.'

'I'm not sure if he wants to talk to me either.'

'He likes you,' says Rochelle. 'I know he doesn't show it much, but I can tell.'

I think Rochelle may be kidding herself, but it's the least I can do. I get up. 'I'll look at the beach.' I don't think Rochelle notices the catch in my voice.

'I'll come with you.' Dad half-rises to his feet.

'No.' I put my hand out. 'I think it's better if I go by myself.'

Dad's forehead creases but he sinks back onto the couch. I walk down the stairs, ignoring the nervous quiver in my chest.

It is very dark at the park. A sea breeze blows back my hair and raises goose bumps on my arms. I rub them, trying to warm myself up inside and out. My heart is now beating so hard I can't ignore it. I know this is stupid. There is nothing to be scared of. But I haven't been on the beach at night for a long time. Not since the night I followed Mum. I almost turn back but the thought of Jay pulls me on. Leaving my shoes on the grass, I set off. And I can't help remembering.

Mum is ironing sheets when I come home from school. I haven't seen her do this before and I already know it is not a good sign. She has been doing a lot of housework in the months since she gave up her job at the newspaper – to have a rest, she said.

I watch her through the window. She irons slowly, purposefully. Every now and then she pauses, gazes into nothing as if she has forgotten what she is doing.

'Edie,' she cries when she sees me. She envelops me in a hug and for a moment I think it might be all right. But then she straightens and wipes at her eyes. 'I've had such a boring day. Look at me, ironing sheets.' She laughs, but her laugh is high-pitched. 'Why don't we go swimming?'

I reach behind her and lift the iron off the smouldering sheet.

It's a fifteen-minute walk to the boat channel and by the time I get there my eyes are growing accustomed to the dark. I can see him – an outline perched on the sand. He is holding his guitar, but not playing it.

He looks up as I approach. 'Roch sent out the huskies, did she?' His voice has only the smallest twinge of sarcasm.

I shrug and sit down.

He plucks a string on his guitar. 'It's all right, I'm not about to top myself. My big sister worries too much.'

I don't say anything, because I haven't been here in the dark for eleven years and the memories are too strong.

'Thanks for coming, though. 'Preciate it.' Jay says with an American drawl.

For some reason this sets me off. 'Why do you have to be so bloody ...' I search for a word, 'ironic all the time. Why can't we just ...' I trail off. I feel like crying. Damn, I wish I could untangle those tangled and unspoken thoughts between us. It shouldn't be this hard. It wasn't this hard on the couch.

Jay plays a few notes. Stops. 'So, where were you tonight?'

He says this neutrally and I can't see his face for clues on how to read him. 'Was that an invitation, was it?'

'What did it look like?'

'A program. An announcement. Not an invitation. It looked like maybe you wanted me to come, but you wanted to keep your options open too. Pub, eight pm. What am I, a dog?' I can hear the petulance in my voice and I want it to go away. I don't want to be like this. I want to be honest, true to the way I feel ... I take a deep breath. 'Anyway, I *was* coming, but something happened.'

'I can be a dickhead sometimes, can't I?'

I search the dark shadows of his face. I know there is something there I want to connect with, but I can't find it, can't find the words to bring it out. *I know you're in there*, is what I want to say. *You can't pretend you're not. I can feel you.*

'I'm sorry.' Jay's fingers brush my shoulder. His touch is light and brief, but it is like he has said what I wanted to say. 'Thanks for the tuna story.'

'Oh.' I twist my hands together. 'I don't know why I gave you that, I —'

'It reminded me ... of you. Of what a funny person you are.'

I look at him. 'Funny ha, ha? Funny peculiar?'

'Funny is the wrong word. Unusual. Different. Unique. It made me want to talk to you again.'

I smile in the darkness. 'Well, it worked then.'

'It was brave of you. Especially when I was being so ...'

'Mean.'

'Yes. Sorry.'

'I'm sorry too. I'm sorry I missed your gig. I wanted to come. I'm just not good with that stuff.'

'There weren't many people there. And those that were had better things to do than listen to me.'

'Do you take that personally?'

'How else could I take it?'

'So, how does it make you feel?'

'Like the worst kind of idiot. But, hey, I'm still getting paid. I'm playing music. I just try to finish as quickly as possible.'

We are silent for a while. The waves on the reef remind me of the last time I was here at night. 'I used to come here with Mum. With Jenny.' I can hardly believe I have said her name.

Jay strums a soft chord. 'Tell me about her.'

My heart quickens. I have never talked to anyone about this, but now I want to. It is scary, but I am heading for the precipice. I can't stop. 'We always went swimming in the boat channel.' While it is hard, at first, the more I talk, the easier it gets, like water rushing through a hole in a child's sand dam, breaking away the barriers as it goes.

'She wanted me to come swimming with her that afternoon. But *Ninja Turtles* was on. I was going through a phase. I was crazy about those guys. I thought she'd be back by the time the show was over. But she wasn't.'

'How old were you?'

'Twelve.'

'Yeah, I was into the turtles too. Who was your favourite?'

'Donatello.'

'Makes sense.' Jay smiles. 'Gentle, clever ... Guess who mine was?'

'Raphael.'

'Right. The sarcastic one.'

'But also funny and loyal.'

'You see the best in everyone, don't you, Edie? So tell me about your mum.' He plucks his guitar again, while I talk.

'When she didn't come back I came down here to look for her. Her towel was on the sand. I couldn't see her, but I waited and waited.' As I tell Jay, I feel like I am there.

Behind me the sun is dipping below the horizon and still she is not here. The beach is almost empty.

A hundred metres or so away, a fisherman is casting a line. I should talk to him; ask him for help. But I don't know him and the thought of the explanations I would have to give cramps my tongue. How can I explain that I think my mother is out there? Maybe it's all a mistake. Maybe she is swimming in somewhere else. Maybe that isn't her towel. The thought of starting a train of panic I can't control panics me. My heart pounds. I couldn't talk if I had to so I say nothing. I strain my eyes. I crouch on the sand.

If I don't look for her for five minutes she'll be there.
If I don't look for her for two minutes she'll be there.
If I don't look for her for one minute she'll be there.
I look. She isn't there. Maybe she's:
At home,
Gone for a walk,
Gone to the movies,
Gone to meet Dad at work.
Perhaps she's:
Cooking dinner,
Playing tennis,
Writing poetry,
Playing hide and seek.
And one hundred possibilities later, when it is dark, when the fisherman has gone, that is where Dad finds me.

*

'I haven't been swimming since then.'

Jay has been playing his guitar the whole time I've been talking. He stops now. 'What was she like? Your mother?'

'She was funny. She used to make me laugh and laugh. She was interested in big questions, not small ones. She operated on a different level to most people, connected things up in different ways. I see that now; I didn't at the time.'

'Like you then,' says Jay.

'You think so? Yes. I guess she was. Like me. Sometimes that scares me a bit.'

'Do you think she meant to go?'

'I don't know. There wasn't a note. She kept a notebook though.' *Wanting everything. Wanting nothing.* 'She said nothingness was all she wanted.'

'Why?'

'I don't think there was a reason. It wasn't that things had gone wrong. It was the way she was. I was just a kid, I didn't realise. She had pills, but she didn't like taking them. They made her feel stupid. I think Mum had a fascination with the edge of things.'

'The liminal.'

I look at him.

'You don't know that one? It means the border, the transition point.'

'Good word. Yes, the liminal. She liked to see how far she could go and still return. Whether she meant to come back that night, I don't know.'

'You wouldn't have saved her, Edie.'

'What if I'd spoken to the fisherman? What if he'd organised a search? What if I'd gone swimming with her? She wouldn't have done it then.'

'If she was determined to go, I mean. You couldn't have stopped her. She would have done it sometime.'

'I've been looking for that fisherman my whole life. I want to ask him how she looked when she went in. Then I'd know ...'

'Do you think it would make any difference?'

'I want to know if she was crying or if she looked happy.'

'Do you think you can tell how someone feels by looking at them?' Jay's eyes settle on mine.

I shake my head.

'No, so ...'

'But he's like my guilty conscience. I keep thinking I see that fisherman everywhere. I should have known she was so sad. Why didn't I know?'

'Edie.' Jay's voice has a sharp edge. 'You can't blame yourself. You were a kid. She made a choice; a bad choice, but it's not your fault. If someone wants to leave, they're checking out regardless.'

And I know I shouldn't say it, but I can't stop myself. I accelerate, fly out into midair, start to freefall. 'Did you? Want to leave? Really?' My voice is small and squeaky. It is an apology of a voice. A cry into the wind.

Jay's face is dark. He doesn't talk.

I have done it again. He will leave now. And this time we will never talk again. I feel like a damp weight has settled on my chest, but I am resigned to it. I know I couldn't have done anything else. I had to ask.

'Yes.' He plays a chord or two, 'And no. So, I guess that means no.'

I take a breath. The damp weight lightens. We are still talking. 'Why did you do it?'

'Artistic angst,' he drawls, plucking at his strings.

I bite my lip. 'You can't be ironic all the time.'

'Sorry. It's hard to stop. Bear with me, Edie.' He gives a rueful smile. 'I'm trying. Why did I do it? My music was shit, my life was shit. There was a girl ...'

'Tell me.'

Chapter Thirty-three

Being entirely honest with oneself is a good exercise.

SIGMUND FREUD

'Her name was Caroline.' Jay strums a chord or two and hums a tune I recognise as that old one, 'Sweet Caroline'. 'She auditioned to be the singer in our band. She got the gig.'

I wait. Wanting to hear. Wanting not to hear. My stomach doing strange things at the thought of what he might say next.

'You know how some people seem to have the knack of seeing into you straightaway? She was like that. She saw me. She wanted me. She made me feel I was like no one else she'd ever met before. When I was with her I was smarter, funnier, wittier.'

'I know what you mean. I was like that with Daniel at first. I became someone else.'

'I was obsessed with her. Could think of nothing

else.' He glances at me, stops plucking his guitar. 'You want to hear this?'

I nod. It's hard to listen to, but I want to know.

'Then I found out it wasn't just me. She was with … the drummer too. Same deal with him. He thought he'd found his soul mate.' Jay plays a few chords.

I listen, enjoying the melody, the sense that this is him talking too.

'When I think about her now, I think she was a chameleon. She changed her colour to reflect the person she was with. I thought I was getting *her*, but I was getting a reflection of myself. I don't know what it says about me that I fell in love with my own reflection.'

I think about that. 'Maybe that's what we all do. Look for someone who mirrors us, so we don't feel alone.'

'She was an unusual person,' says Jay. 'I think using her sexual power was what gave her life meaning.'

I bite my lip. 'She would have made a good lead singer then.' I hope Jay doesn't notice the twinge of jealous pique I am unable to keep out of my voice.

'The band broke up, but Caroline and I … I couldn't give her up, even though there was nothing positive left. It was sucking me up, but I was addicted to her. I felt like losing her would be losing myself, losing the person I was when I was with her. Seems strange now, but that's how it was.' His guitar stops. 'It hurt.'

'I know.' I wait. The sea roars louder in the silence.

Jay coughs. 'She was killed in a car crash. Six months ago.' His voice is so soft I have to strain to hear him. 'The drummer was driving. He survived. He's in a wheelchair now.'

There is something about the way he says *the drummer* that makes me ask. 'What's his name?'

'Ben.' His voice is flat.

'Ben who you met in Year Eleven?'

'Yeah. We don't see each other anymore.'

I want to ask more, but his voice warns me off.

'She was supposed to be with me that night; I'd been waiting for her. Everything kind of spiralled out of control. It was too intense – her ... Ben – I needed to escape.' He touches his wrist. 'It seemed like a good idea at the time.' He pauses. 'It was the only idea I had at the time.'

'Do you still feel like that?'

'I don't at the moment. Not while I'm talking to you.' And there is just enough light to see him smile.

'So, after, when you realised you weren't dead, did that feel like ...'

'A resurrection?'

I nod.

'No. I felt tired. I had to face all that hard work I thought I'd got out of. I was still down there in the underworld, trying to find a way out. I never decided to live; it was more that it was too much trouble to try again. It seemed easier to let myself be rescued.'

'So, you didn't care either way?'

'I thought I may as well go with the flow, for now.'

'And then?'

'I found someone who made me feel less alone.'

I wait.

'You were so kooky and yet, at the same time ... honest. I thought maybe, maybe you'd be someone I could talk to.'

'I thought that too.'

He meets my eyes and I am suddenly shy.

'Do you feel weird that you're going to be answering questions about those scars all your life?'

'I'm working on a bear mauling story.' Jay fingers his scars. 'In a way, I don't mind them. They're kind of like a souvenir.'

'From the edge.'

'Souvenir from the edge. Good name for a song.'

'Tangled web's a good name too. That song's about you and Caroline, isn't it?'

'Yeah. I guess the Caroline thing is why I acted like a dickhead with you, Edie, after that laboratory hoe-down. It's no excuse, but it's a reason. It brought back feelings I didn't want to feel. I'm sorry.'

'I was only helping Professor Brownlow with his typing.'

'I believe you. And even if I didn't, well, maybe it's none of my business.'

'No, it is your business. I want it to be your business.'

Jay is quiet after I say this. I wish I could see his face, get a clue of what he is thinking. Maybe I have said too much again, presumed too much. Turned holding hands on the couch into something it was not and never will be.

The silence goes on, but it doesn't feel like a strained silence. I know this from the way the air is calm between us. I sense it in my bones. Not all words are spoken. So

337

when I do speak, it is not from awkwardness, but to extend the conversation already running between us.

'Do you ever feel like you're a child failure?'

'Because my father is a big success and I'm not?'

'Yes.'

'Why? Is that the way you feel?'

'Mmm, always have.'

'Because your father's a surfing legend and you don't like swimming?'

I nod.

'Yeah, I feel like that. Doesn't everyone? Look at the Lion King. I'll never be able to fill the paw prints of my father.' He puts on a corny voice. 'The spirit of Gary Jaworski lives on in me, but I'm not half the guitar legend he was.'

I laugh. This time I am grateful for the irony. It cuts through the seriousness like a puff of warm wind.

He smiles back at me. 'I like it when I make you laugh.'

'I like it when I make you laugh too.'

'You know someone's on the same wavelength as you if you can make them laugh.'

'It's funny, isn't it, how we use humour,' I say.

'When we get too close to something sensitive, you mean?'

'Yes.'

'The comic mask,' says Jay. 'I do it too much, don't I?'

'Mmm, maybe. I do it too. It can be good, but sometimes you need to let people know how you feel. Otherwise they're never going to know.'

Jay plucks at his guitar.

'Have you ever heard of John Bradman?' I ask.

'No. Should I have?'

'Son of Donald.'

'Oh, The Greatest Australian Ever, right?'

'Yes. He's like you and me.'

'You've been giving this some thought, haven't you, Edie?'

'What about Jesus's daughter?'

'I didn't know Jesus had a daughter.'

'Exactly.'

Jay laughs. 'Go on. You've got more, haven't you?'

A mischievous impulse seizes me. 'Geena Khan?'

'Let me guess. Daughter of Genghis?'

'Great-, great-, great-granddaughter. She's a timid, virgin, forty-year-old hairdresser in Ulaanbaatar.'

Jay laughs. 'You made that one up.'

'Yes, but I didn't make up Blanket Jackson or Lisa-Marie Presley.' I pause. 'Or Peter Pan.' As soon as I say this, I wish I hadn't.

'Peter Pan?'

There's no going back now. 'He threw himself under a train. The real life-Peter Pan, that is.'

The sea is black, but the moon casts a path across it to the horizon. The guitar stops.

'Yeah. Well, I guess I can relate to that too. That "Jaybird" song. I had to fight my way through primary school because of it. They still introduce me that way half the time when I perform. I almost gave up playing again, I got so sick of it.'

'What stopped you?'

'Seems like I don't have a choice. The thing is, with the music … it's when I feel most like myself. That's why I do it.'

'That's how writing poetry is for me.'

'It's the only way I can let people see what's inside.'

'Do you think everyone has something inside that they're trying to get out?' I ask.

'Probably, but some of them don't know it.'

'So it never comes out?'

'Or maybe it isn't there in the first place.'

'It's scary letting your inside out.'

'But exciting,' says Jay.

'But what if people don't like it? What if you hadn't liked my tuna story?'

'Does it matter?'

'Sometimes. If you care for someone.' I think of Daniel and the rain in Glenorchy. 'It can make you feel like …'

'You've been sucked into a black hole.'

Our eyes meet and I want to kick my legs in the air with delight. *He completes my sentences. He gets me.*

Jay smiles. 'We've got something, haven't we?'

This is now so obvious I don't bother to reply. I let my breath out in a big sigh as I fling myself back on the sand. I run my arms up and down to make a sand angel. Gaze up at the stars.

Jay does the same. Our hands brush at the top of our wings.

'Do you want to go swimming?' Jay asks this as if he doesn't care either way.

'Now?' My voice comes out in a half squeak.

'Don't you think you've waited long enough?'

'What about ...' My mind searches for excuses. 'Sharks?'

'Well ...' Jay squeezes the top of my fingers. 'We'll have to fight them off, won't we?'

'Jellyfish?'

Jay links his fingers through mine. 'I'll eat any jellyfish that dares to touch you.'

'Aggressive sea hares?'

Jay laughs. 'You're running out of excuses.'

I roll my head sideways. His eyes are sparkling with mischief. And I don't feel safe with him, not safe at all. I think he could break my heart in a million ways, but I don't have time to worry about endings.

I only want it to begin.

Chapter Thirty-four

We are never so defenceless against suffering as when we love.

SIGMUND FREUD

Jay and Edie swam. They swam naked, their bodies floating ghost-like beneath the water. They swam side by side, not touching. Edie had forgotten how it felt to be:

> *Buoyed up,*
> *Immersed,*
> *Surrounded,*
> *Enclosed.*

It was a homecoming, a welcome. She was astonished she had stayed away so long. She was grateful. She floated on her back, tears running down her face. If Jay noticed he didn't say anything.

They came to rest in the shallows. Their hands brushed against each other like seaweed, fingertips touching lightly, shyly, eyes skating away from their nakedness. Edie had never felt like this with a man before. Never felt so alive, so intensely aware of another person.

She thought she was probably in love.

Jay and I sneak up to the house. There is a charge, an energy, a bubble around us. We are holding hands but we still haven't kissed, haven't hugged. We are co-conspirators in a journey towards a mystery. I wonder if he is planning to make love to me. Personally, I don't have plans. I am in the moment, poised within a perfect pearl of possibility.

I feel powerful after my swim – an Antarctic explorer, an astronaut, a lion-tamer. I can do anything now. It hardly matters what happens next. I know I will handle it perfectly. I am invincible.

Well, almost … 'You're not into earthworms, are you?' I ask as we go up the stairs.

Jay stops and considers this question. 'No. I have an open mind about most things though.' He gives me a mischievous look. 'Earthworms have possibilities. What did you have in mind?'

My face goes hot. 'Nothing. Forget I ever mentioned them.'

Jay smiles. 'Whatever you say.'

I am hoping Dad and Rochelle have gone to bed; that they have given up their verandah vigil. But we do not have such luck.

Jay drops my hand as he sees them, but not quickly enough.

Dad takes in my wet hair. His eyes flicker from me to Jay and back again.

I can feel the energy blazing in an aura around us and wonder if Dad can sense it.

He probably can because now he looks like a duck whose swan baby has taken up high-board diving – surprised, alarmed and cautiously impressed. 'Have you been swimming, Eddie?' he asks.

I want to laugh because his voice is so casual, but that question is so loaded it could explode on impact.

I respond in kind. 'Yes. Jay and I had a dip.' This is a bit like saying the *Titanic* had a minor mishap.

Dad and Rochelle look from Jay to me, from me to Jay. They have the same smile. They look like people whose plans have come to fruition but are now wondering if they were such good plans after all. I think maybe they wanted Jay and me to be friends but now something else has happened.

Rochelle scans Jay's face.

I follow her eyes. His hair is plastered back from his face and he looks younger, less world-weary than before. His sleeves hang over his wrists and his feet are bare.

'Don't worry so much, Roch,' he says.

She smiles and frowns at the same time, but doesn't say anything.

The energy between Jay and me is fizzling out. I can hardly bear it.

'Do you want a cup of tea?' asks Rochelle.

No, no, a thousand times no.

344

Jay reaches out, takes my hand. As he squeezes my fingers the glow reignites and spreads through my whole body.

'No thanks,' he says.

Jay and I sit on his bed, side by side, not touching. The possibilities between us make me shy. I feel as if I have never done this before. In a way I never have. I have always let desire paper over the awkwardness, the strangeness of these close encounters.

But I don't want it to be like that with Jay. I want to approach this with caution. I want to be mindful, conscious of every moment. This is not from lack of desire, far from it. It is from respect, closeness and another word I hardly dare to say in my head, let alone out loud. But it enters anyway.

I have been thinking a lot, lately, about love. It's a funny thing the 'l' word. It can sound like a claim, a demand. *I love you*, said out loud rings bells of alarm. That isn't how I mean it. I mean I want the best for him. I want him to take what he needs; for us to connect unconditionally. I want to land with a light touch, not to grasp, hold, cling like a vine. There are so many different types of love. You can be smitten, fall and lose control. You can be selfish or selfless, choose what is best for someone else or think only of yourself. Even murderers can justify their actions with the word *love*.

Sometimes it's best not to talk when words are so inadequate.

'I feel quite dreamlike, here with you,' says Jay.

It is the perfect thing to say. 'I feel the same, like I've made you up inside my head.'

We are holding hands again; I am not sure how this happened. I wonder if this is as far as we will ever go. If so, that seems fine, because holding hands with Jay is much, much better than anything else with anyone else.

Our heads are close. We gaze into each other's eyes, lean forward, touch cheeks. I rest my head on his shoulder, feel his heartbeat through my chest.

He moves his head away, wraps his free hand around the back of my head, touches his lips to mine. His breath is warm on my face.

I am no longer sure which body is his and which is mine.

Being with Jay has a lightness to it; a playfulness I haven't felt for a long, long time. Bubbles of joy float up through my body; explode in tiny bursts.

I undo the buttons on his shirt and slip it from his shoulders. His chest is pale, sinewy, beautiful. I can't resist touching the scars on his wrist.

Jay watches me as I run my finger along them. 'Do you find them ugly?'

'No, the opposite. I find them ... part of you.'

He smiles. 'I'm going to have to work on that cover story.'

'Crocodile attack?'

'That should do it.'

I touch my cheek to his shoulder.

He sighs, holds me tight, then slips his hands under my T-shirt, running them up my back. 'You're very soft,' he says.

I lift my arms and he pulls my T-shirt over my head.

He looks into my eyes; smiles. 'This feels different with you, Edie.'

'Different how?'

'Like coming home.'

At first I like the analogy, but then I'm worried. 'Is home a sleeping-in-a-comfy-armchair kind of place?'

Jay laughs, runs his hand down my arm. 'No, home is a very, very sexy place indeed.' He pushes me with a gentle touch and I fall backwards onto the pillow.

Sex with Jay is much different to sex with Daniel. For a start, he comes first.

'Oh, God, I'm sorry, Edie,' he moans, pressing his face into my shoulder.

A giggle rises in my chest and although I know it is inappropriate, I can't stop it exploding out my nose.

Jay raises his head and searches my face. He looks wary.

'I'm not laughing at you.'

Jay glances over his shoulder. 'Is there anyone else here?'

'No, it's just you coming first.'

'I'm sorry, it was just so …'

I stroke his face. 'I know. I appreciate it that you felt that way. I love how you're so … uncontrolled.'

I can see he still thinks I'm having a go at him.

'I'm not saying I want it that way all the time. But I don't mind. It's a compliment.'

Jay presses his face into my shoulder again. It is cool and wet.

I tilt my head and look at him. Run my finger under his eyes.

He smiles. 'I'm all right. I'm more than all right. I don't know what that's about. Sorry.'

'It's okay, I feel the same way.'

'What does it feel like to you?'

'Like my heart is too close to my skin.'

He nods, then presses his nose to mine. 'Can we try again? Maybe in a few minutes?'

348

Chapter Thirty-five

Like the physical, the psychical is not necessarily in reality what it appears to us to be.

SIGMUND FREUD

I am nude hiking in New Zealand. The sun is shining. The usual man approaches.

'I made you a possum skin coat.' Strangely, he doesn't have a New Zealand accent anymore. He slips the coat over my shoulders. It is soft and warm.

I notice his face for the first time. He is Jay.

In the morning I wake with a start. I am in Jay's bed. Alone.

The clock on the bedside table tells me it is nine o'clock. My flight to Tokyo leaves at one and I have to get to the airport two hours before. Sally is coming around at ten to drive me.

I sit up. It seems crazy, but I haven't told Jay about Tokyo. I can't believe I haven't told him about Tokyo.

First we weren't talking, then I thought there was time. And now I am leaving.

A note is propped up on the table next to the bed.

Edie, my father just texted me to say the guy from the record company wants to hear me play this morning. His flight was delayed so he didn't make it last night. I'll be back about ten.

There is a gap and I can imagine him thinking about what to say next.

My brain's kind of shot and anything I say is going to sound all wrong in writing so I won't even try. See you soon,
    Jay

I read this last part several times, but it is unyielding. My paranoid side reads it as *that was nice, check you later* even though I know rationally it is nothing like that. I sit up in the bed, clutching the note, a lead weight settling on my chest. What am I going to do? Stay here and wait for Jay? Miss my flight? Try and find him?

There is a knock on the door. I clutch the sheets to my chest, sit up, hoping it is Jay, although, of course, he wouldn't knock.

Rochelle peers around the door. 'Oh, Edie.' She looks taken aback.

I blush. 'Jay's gone out. To see a record guy.'

She gives a tentative smile. 'Great. Dad was just on

the phone, checking he made it. Amazing, first time in his life he's come through.' She looks at the clock. 'Aren't you going soon?' Something about my face must show the state I'm in. 'Are you still going?' Rochelle comes over to the bed, sits down and gives me a big hug. 'So, you and Jay, huh?' she says over my shoulder. It's hard to read what she thinks about this.

'He doesn't know I'm going.'

'What?' Rochelle backs off and looks me in the eye.

'We haven't been talking. I didn't get around to telling him.'

'Oh, Edie.' Rochelle gives me a long look. 'You can't make plans around Jay. He's just not ready.'

I shrug her hands off my shoulders. She is probably right, but something about the way she says it makes me angry. How can she know what it is like with us? Hadn't he said it was different with me? 'I never said I was. I need to pack.'

'Hey.' Rochelle gives another tentative smile.

I wait.

'Happy birthday.'

'Oh. I forgot.' It doesn't feel all that much like a happy birthday.

'Konichiwa,' yodels Sally up the stairs at ten o'clock.

I have been in my room alternately packing and crying for half an hour and have now reached a kind of washed-out acceptance.

Mum's notebook has been sitting on my pillow while I pack. It is only a small notebook and there is room for it in my bag. I pick it up, hold it for a moment, then open it at the last page. I read the end one last time and return it to my bedside chest. It will still be there when I come back.

Lifting up my backpack, I trudge down the stairs. I don't know if I want to see Jay coming in the door or not. What would I say?

'Hey, babe,' says Sal.

'Yo.' I look her up and down. 'Hey, new hair.' Her blonde tips have been replaced by streaks of red and copper. 'Let me guess. New guy?'

'You remember the sexting guy from the supermarket?' I nod.

'He's been upgraded from the virtual to the real world.'

'He must have been a good sexter.'

'He was, but he's even better in the flesh.' Sally gives a lewd wink.

She makes it all seem so easy.

Sally pulls something out from behind her back. '*Ta da.*' She hands me a parcel and gives me a hug. 'Happy birthday.'

'Gee, thanks.' I unwrap it. It is a paperback edition of *Wuthering Heights*.

'I figured it was time you re-read it, seeing as you've forgotten all the good bits.'

'Thanks, Sal. I'll read it on the plane. Too much Heathcliff is never enough.'

Sally looks me up and down. 'You look like shit, Ed. Burning the candle at both ends?'

'Crab larvae emergency.'

'Bullshit.'

'Think what you like. Crab larvae drawing is a fast-paced field where rapid response is sometimes necessary.' Jay is a secret I want to keep to myself for now.

'You make it sound like a commando-type thing.'

'It's exactly like that. I am a crack crab larvae drawer, called in for surgical strikes in the laboratory.'

'Is there abseiling involved?'

'I can be inserted by land, sea or air, pencil in hand. In this case, I drove.'

'What's Ralph going to do without you?'

'He says he's keeping my job open for me. Maybe he'll get a five-year-old in to hold the fort. Hope they don't show me up too much.'

'ANT.' Sally smacks me on the shoulder. 'You've got to stop that. You are an expert and highly valued staff member.' She nods at me.

'I am an expert and highly valued staff member,' I repeat.

'It's a pity you're going,' says Sal. 'I think you're getting the hang of this. Hey, I wonder what your dad's got you for your birthday.'

My father's inappropriate birthday presents are a running joke between Sal and me. On my fifth birthday my father gave me my first surfboard. It was pink and soft. It made a nice shelf for my picture books. Undeterred, he followed up over the years with:

A body board and flippers;
A wetsuit;

A book called *The Girls' Guide to Surfing*;
A short fibreglass surfboard;
A longer fibreglass surfboard; and
A surf mat.

After that, he got creative.

'Remember that pink lycra bodysuit?' asks Sal.

Possibly deciding that the reason I wouldn't surf was that I didn't want to get sunburnt, on my twelfth birthday Dad gave me a full-length bodysuit and a hat with straps to hold it on in the surf.

'There was no way I was ever going to be seen in public in that get-up, with or without a surfboard.'

'You would have looked like a cheerio,' says Sal.

Despite the fact that I avoided the water from then on, the gifts continued: framed surf photos, a paperweight in the shape of a surfboard, Roxy Girl T-shirts, Hawaiian-print board shorts ...

'I can't wait,' I say.

Dad and Rochelle are waiting on the verandah to say goodbye. A parcel sits on the table next to them. It is about the size of a coffee-table guide to surfing locations around Australia.

Rochelle gives Dad a surreptitious nudge as we approach. She mutters something out of the side of her mouth. It sounds like *Tell her*.

'Sally,' says Rochelle, 'let me show you the Japanese garden.'

'I've already seen —' Sally catches Rochelle's look. 'Oh, okay. Great.' They wander off along the balcony.

Dad's moustache is drooping, as it does when he is worried. He gives me a hug then lets go. His hands hang by his side looking like they don't know what to do with themselves.

Dad has the awkward hand gene too. I have never noticed before. At least that is something we share. If I inherited that from him, who knows ...

'Maybe we'll go for a surf when you get back? Now that you're ...' He trails off.

'Swimming?'

He nods.

'Sure. It's a date. You and me, six am, out the Point.'

He smiles.

I smile.

'You mean it?' His moustache is looking perkier already.

'Hey, why wouldn't I?'

He coughs. His face goes a bit red. He opens and shuts his mouth, then speaks quickly. 'I'm so proud of you, Eddie.'

'You are? Why? Since when?'

'I always have been. I know I haven't shown it, but I've always felt you were something special.' He thrusts his hands in his pockets and rocks back on his heels.

'You have?' This is so unlike Dad, to talk about feelings.

'You're the only one on my side of the family who's ever gone to university. And now, look at you, off to Japan. All by yourself.' He blinks and for a moment I'm afraid he might cry.

Tears aren't that far from my eyes either. I step forward and hug him again.

He wraps his long, muscular arms around me. 'You look just like your mother. She was beautiful too. And clever. I couldn't believe it when she chose me. I'm just a dumb surfer. She was amazing, your mother. And you're amazing too.'

I feel a lump in my chest. I step back so I can look at him. 'I always thought ... you would have liked a boy. One who surfed.'

'That never mattered, Eddie. All that mattered was —'

'Spit it out, Dave,' says Sal. She and Rochelle have come back. 'We've got a plane to catch here.' She winks at him.

Rochelle nods in an encouraging way.

'All that matters is that you're happy,' says Dad. 'You *are* happy, aren't you?'

It's a big question and a difficult one for a girl who's been crying all morning to answer properly. 'Yes,' I say. And it's almost true.

Rochelle steps in for an embrace. She feels solid in my arms, strong and warm.

'Say bye to Jay for me?' I say this lightly, keeping its meaning between the two of us.

She nods. 'He'll be sorry he missed you.'

'Let's rock, Ed,' says Sal.

Rochelle nudges Dad again.

'Oh. I almost forgot. Happy birthday.' He picks up the parcel and hands it to me.

It is fairly heavy. *Definitely a hardback book on surfing.* I unwrap it. It is a small laptop computer.

'Because you only have a desktop. And you'll be travelling ...' Dad looks at me anxiously.

I hug him. 'It's perfect. It's just what I need.' I run my hand over its shiny surface. 'I love it. I love it to bits.'

Dad beams.

'He thought of it himself,' says Rochelle. 'I didn't know what to get you.'

'Thanks, Dad.'

I turn halfway down the stairs and wave to Dad and Rochelle. I feel the way I always do at partings: as if I want to run back, start again, do it all so much better. Do my whole life so much better. I wonder if everyone feels like that.

Then I'm in the car with Sal, driving through Darling Head. In twelve hours I'll be in Tokyo, but for now I'm still here in this place I know so well. I wind down the window, smell the salt air and try not to look for Jay.

It is Saturday morning and the streets are busy with surfers: getting out of cars, strolling across the road, walking languidly back from the water with an ease and calm that reeks of satisfaction.

I know I'll be back, and perhaps next time I'll be one of them. Next time I'll do it so much better. I smile, thinking of what Dad said. *You're amazing.* Am I? Damn it, maybe I am.

'Look at that old dude.' Sal slows the car to avoid hitting an old man on a bike who wobbles across in front of us. He is wearing a yellow raincoat and gumboots despite the warm morning. His leathery face is etched in a criss-cross of wrinkles. Grubby canvas bags hang off the back of his bike. He looks like an Indian sadhu with a fishing rod.

It is him; the man on the beach from that night. It is definitely him.

I lean forward, open my mouth and am on the verge of calling out. Then I stop. I no longer know why I wanted to talk to him. Jay was right. What difference would it make? Was she happy? Was she sad? *Can you ever know how someone feels by looking at them?* I watch him wobble away.

The last words from Mum's notebook are still in my head.

I push off and swim, as if that is a way to leave this behind, like a cloak swept away in the current. And sometimes it seems that it might be. As my arms move through the water I can feel the darkness leaving me. If I go hard enough and fast enough it can't catch me. But I have to stop eventually. I can't swim forever.

'You know him?' asks Sal.

'Kind of.' For all these years I have been searching for absolution, for explanation; to be told that there was nothing I could have done. To be told she was smiling. To be told she was crying. I am surprised to find it doesn't matter anymore. His yellow raincoat vanishes around the corner, taking all those questions with it. *I can't swim forever.*

It could be that I have forgiven her. It could be that I have forgiven myself.

'I'm expecting some Japanese-influenced erotica from you,' says Sal, as we hit the highway. 'They're pretty wild over there, I hear.'

'I can't do that anymore.'

She looks at me over the top of her sunglasses. 'Why not? Chance of a lifetime – hot tubs, kimonos, those kinky little fans – think of the possibilities.'

'But sex isn't like that.'

'Like what?'

'Trashy and cheap.'

Sally meets my eyes. I'm expecting her to try to talk me around, to say something sarcastic to lighten things up, but she doesn't.

'No, not when it's good.' She reaches out and squeezes my hand.

We are silent for a while and I am beginning to think she has found a previously unexplored vein of sensitivity until she speaks. 'You were so good at it, you know. I think it's your forte. If it's a matter of money, I could probably —'

'It's not about money. I don't think I want to keep writing about lust, Sally.'

Sally looks as if I have just admitted a sexual interest in cockroaches. 'What *do* you want to write about then?'

'I don't know. Something deeper.'

'Damn, Ed.' She slaps the wheel. 'Where am I going to find another writer?'

'Do it yourself. You've had sex, right? You know what it's like. It should be easy enough.' I can't resist the little dig.

'I've tried.' Sally gives me a sheepish smile. 'It's not as easy as I thought it would be. I can see where you were coming from with the manly sea cucumber now. It's hard finding good metaphors.'

I raise my eyebrows at her. 'You're telling me, babe.'

'Fuck. Send me back some of those sexy Manga comics then, will you? I might be able to do something with them.'

'You're still doing it then? The sex counsellor thing?'

'Shit, yeah. This stuff is big. I'm going to be setting up franchises in Sydney and Melbourne soon I reckon. There's a job for you here any time you want, Ed.'

'Advertise,' I say.

'Huh?'

'For an erotic writer. You'll find someone for sure.'

Sally nods. 'Yeah. Right on. I'll do that tomorrow.'

I get Sally to drop me off at Departures. I've already told her I don't want her to wait. I can't stand long farewells, hanging around making small talk.

She pulls over in the drop-off zone and gives me a hug. 'I'm still your life coach, you know; if you need anything – dating advice, hot-tub etiquette, inter-cultural flirting ... Can't wait to see what bad habits you come back with.'

'Thanks, babe. You're the best life coach I've ever had.'

'You keep up those conversational skills, won't you? Remember start shallow, move deep.'

'I'm not sure that I've mastered that one yet. I always hit my head in the shallow end because I try to go deep too fast. I'm not one of your success stories, am I?'

Sally laughs. 'Yes you are. Totally. Look at you. Here you go, off to Tokyo. How cool is that? You're taking control of your life, mate. You're walking the walk. Talking the talk. High five.' She holds up her hand.

I slap it. As I open the car door I almost take out a harassed-looking woman with a loaded trolley. 'Sorry.' She glares at me as she goes past.

'Hey, Edz.'

I look up.

Surf-boy Tim is standing on the footpath beside the car. He has a padded board bag over his shoulder. 'I'm going down to Bells.' He pats his board bag. 'I got a longer board, like you said.'

I eye his board. 'Six one, is it? That's the shot. Good luck.'

'Where are you going?' he asks.

'Japan.'

'You going to that big comp in Shikoku?'

I nod in a noncommittal way. 'Hey,' I pull my purse out of my bag. 'Here's your autograph.'

Tim's face lights up. He takes the greasy paper bag and looks at Dad's signature. *Hey Tim, carve one up for me*, it says. He folds it carefully and slides it into his pocket. 'Now I'll have good luck for sure. Do you mind if I tell the Rip Curl people I'm a friend of yours?'

'Better not. I've jumped to Billabong and they're a bit shitty. Tell them you know Dad. You've got the autograph.'

'Yeah, cool.' He waves and heads towards the check-in, where a broad-shouldered man is waiting for him.

'Edz?' says Sally.

I shrug.

'Rip Curl?'

'It's a long story.'

'You're a dark horse, Edie McElroy. Well, go get 'em,' says Sal. 'Be all that you can be. Play hard or go home. No guts, no glory. Live the dream.'

'You'd better save up some of that motivational pep talk for when I get back, Sal.'

Sally leans over and plants a kiss on my cheek. 'And look after your heart while you're at it, Ed.'

Sally and me. Me and Sally. I wave as she goes and wish we could do it all again, only better this time.

Chapter Thirty-six

When inspiration does not come to me, I go halfway to meet it.
SIGMUND FREUD

T-shirts and thongs are the travelling uniform of choice in Coolangatta Airport. The business suit has no place in this departure lounge. If the mood was any more laid-back it would be comatose. It is hard to believe you can get on a plane here and arrive in Tokyo nine hours later. The idea seems ridiculously far-fetched. Coolangatta to Tokyo should be at least a ten-day journey.

I should fly by light aircraft to Darwin, or maybe ride a camel. On arrival in Darwin I'd locate a sturdy boat in need of crew and sail north into the mysterious East. On the way I might sight whales, fight off a giant squid or repel pirates off the coast of Taiwan. As I sail into Tokyo harbour the sight of the snow-capped Mount Fuji would fill me with elation ...

But here I am on the Gold Coast, standing in the queue for the Jetstar check-in.

Sunburnt surfies are catching jets back to Sydney or Melbourne. Soon I will join my fellow cut-price flight passengers. I will watch formulaic Hollywood movies and eat salty chips as Australia slips away beneath me. The blinds of the plane will be pulled down against the sun. It will be dark when we get to Japan. Maybe I will see the lights of Tokyo as we land.

Tomorrow I will eat ramen in a Tokyo noodle bar or battle with the crowds on the subway. I will practise saying *O genki desu ka?* and *Konichiwa*. I will use chopsticks and try to fit in, but I will always be a foreigner, a *Gaijin*. It is hard to process a world that moves so fast.

'Tokyo?' says the girl behind the counter.

I nod, hardly believing it myself.

I am early for my flight, so after I've checked in my bags I don't go through customs. A sign on the wall says 'Free Wi-Fi' so I sit down on a plastic seat and open up my new computer. Dad has set it up for me; all I need to do is connect. All around me people are saying goodbyes and hellos. A big Maori man embraces an embarrassed-looking boy who must be his son. There is an emotional charge about airports, even this one. They are a no man's land, a place to voice feelings you might not admit to at other times. If you don't say it now, you'll never get the chance.

The computer gives a soft ting. I have two emails. I am intrigued by the second one, but my mouse slides over it to the first.

Dear Sooty,

    I too was deserted by my father on the streets
of Paris. I remember —

I delete this one. Philip is not quite as much fun as I
hoped he would be. He seems reluctant to drop his
cover story. The second email is titled Japanese Crab
Drawings? It is from Djennifer and is very long. My eyes
flicker through it.

Hey Edie,

    You must be the hardest person in the world to
track down ... staying at the Sands Resort ... boring
as bat-shit conference on crabs ... rather sexy
man in short shorts ... put up these drawings ...
Poirot ... superhero. Erotic crab writing ...
connection ... inner muse.
    God ... so good, Edie ... so whimsical, so
funny-sad, so deeply philosophical. It spoke
to me ... divine feminine ... dragged away ...
emergency design issue ... on your trail. I didn't
know it was actually you!
    I just rang your father again ... Japan. Amazing!
Serendipity! Kismet!

I slow down as I reach what seems to be the crux of the
email.

I have a new idea for a Japanese-influenced
crab-themed Hotpunk range. I'm sure you're in

365

big demand, but I'd love you to create a suite of original illustrations to go on the merchandise. Think crabs in kimonos, samurai crabs, crabs doing tea ceremony. Please say yes! It's a big job, but I'll pay you what you're worth.

Hugs and kisses, Djennifer

Pressing Reply, I type Yes and send. I smile as I close my emails. Whimsical, funny-sad, philosophical. I'll take it as encouragement; maybe I am in big demand. This day, which seemed doomed, is now picking up – first Dad, then this.

I still have a few minutes left until I need to go through security. Maybe it is time ... Yes, I think it is. I open Google. The story I have been avoiding can't be sidestepped any longer.

The tale of Sylvia Plath's suicide is well known. Struggling to write as a single mother after her separation from Ted Hughes she succumbed to depression. She carefully sealed the kitchen to ensure the gas would not escape and harm her sleeping children. She left food in their room in case they got hungry.

Frieda and Nick Hughes were the children sleeping in the bedroom at the moment their mother decided wanting everything was the same as wanting nothing. What happened to those two sleeping children?

Sadly, Nick's story is one that I already know. Despite being a successful marine biologist in Alaska, a few years back he took the same path as his mother. He could not escape her legacy. That is why I have been so scared.

But what happened to Frieda? I haven't dared to find out. I identify with her too strongly, as if my life is on a parallel track to hers. Is her life warped and twisted? Will mine be too? I breathe in and out to calm myself. I know I need to follow this path to its logical conclusion. I think I am ready.

My fingers pause on the keyboard, hesitate and type in the words *Sylvia Plath's daughter*. I hardly dare to see what I will find. As I peer through lowered eyelids, a wave of relief washes over me. I open my notebook at the front. Only a tattered page edge is there to remind me of my pain diary. Otherwise the slate is clean.

Frieda is a highly regarded artist who has published two books of poetry. There is indeed a certain symmetry here. But it is a beautiful symmetry, not an ugly one. Perhaps she dabbles in erotic writing too? There doesn't seem much else to find out about her, but there is enough for me to imagine what her life might be like.

I wonder, now, why I was so scared. Does it matter that Frieda is a *highly regarded artist*? I don't think it does. It is the rest of her life that counts. I imagine that she might enjoy baking. Sylvia was a great one for making cakes. On the day she wrote 'Medusa', she made banana bread. Lemon pudding cake was the accompaniment to 'Lady Lazarus'. Perhaps Frieda makes the best cakes in town. Perhaps not. In any case, it is the pleasure she takes in it that matters. Maybe she and her girlfriends like to drink cask wine in the afternoons and recite poetry? I don't know. I'd like to think they do.

And maybe that is what success is about, finding simple pleasures that make life worthwhile. Coming to terms with the past and moving on.

It seems strange now that I have worried about Frieda for so long. I am not her and she is not me and just maybe I am not a failure at all. I might be a work in progress, but I have potential.

When I look up I see a figure at the far end of the terminal. He is wearing a black hoodie and his dark hair falls over his face. He is staring at the departure board. For a moment I am suspicious. I am familiar with the apparition of the lover syndrome, where you see the yearned-for face in every crowd.

But it is not an apparition, it is him. Slinging my bag over my shoulder, I walk towards him. I punch him on the arm. Just like that. This is how far I have come.

He turns and his face lights up like a hundred million suns have caught on fire.

Mine does the same. We stand there smiling at each other. I don't know what to say.

'I can't believe you were about to go to Tokyo without saying goodbye,' says Jay.

He's right. It is totally unbelievable. 'I don't know, when you weren't there. I thought ...'

'Well, you thought wrong.'

They are calling my flight now. Jay puts his hands on my shoulders. He leans forward, presses his forehead against mine. We back apart, touch our hands palm to palm, pressing them together. I want to store this moment in my brain forever.

'I'll be here when you get back,' says Jay.

'So will I.'

Jay smiles. 'Well, if you're here and I'm here, I guess we'll see each other then.'

'I guess so.' There is so much more I want to say but I know I'll never find the words. I wonder if leaving now is the worst mistake of my life. But if that's the case, I'll have to live with it, because right now I'm practising letting go.

'I think you're good for me, Edie.'

He's jumped in with just the right words again. I smile. 'And you for me.' This is true. I feel lighter than I have for years.

'So, bye,' he says.

'Bye.'

My flight is called again. 'I have to go.' I start to back away. Then I remember something. 'Hey, I saw my fisherman.'

'Did you talk to him?'

I shake my head. 'I threw him back.'

Jay smiles. 'Well done.'

I blurt it out before I can change my mind. 'You should see Ben again. You don't need to lose a friend as well as a girlfriend.'

Jay clenches his jaw. 'You don't —'

'No, listen. When Mum died, I didn't cry. I was angry. I've held onto that anger for years. I didn't know how incredible it would feel to let it go.'

Jay looks into my eyes.

'You did that for me,' I say. 'You listened.'

Flight 529 ...

Jay half smiles. 'Maybe I will.'

I take another step backwards, but Jay reaches out, grasps my wrist.

'I hear there's a pretty good rock scene in Tokyo.'

I stare into his face, my heart skipping a few beats. 'I guess there is.'

'I wouldn't mind checking it out.' He squeezes my hand. 'If I wouldn't be cramping your style too much.'

A laugh bubbles out of me. 'Do I look like someone with style?'

Jay looks me up and down. 'You have a certain writerly finesse about you. At a quick inspection I would say it seems fairly robust and not easily cramped.'

'In that case, okay. Let's do Tokyo.'

'Harajuku nightclubs, baby. You and me.' He twines his fingers through mine.

Behind Jay's back I am surprised to see Tim still lurking in the departures area – his flight must be delayed. He gives me a thumbs-up and a wink. I am fulfilling his expectations.

Can all passengers on flight 529 to Tokyo proceed through customs as your flight is about to commence boarding.

'That's you,' says Jay. 'Go.' He releases my hand with a flourish.

I shuffle towards customs, then stop. Look back at him. He is still watching me. 'I forgot to ask. How did you go? With the record guy.'

He holds out his hand, thumb up.

'No way.' I run back and punch his shoulder again. Hard this time.

He winces.

'I can't believe you didn't tell me. You got a record deal?'

He nods, smiles, shrugs, rubs his shoulder.

'You're a rockstar.'

'Maybe one day.'

'No. You are. You really are. Why didn't you tell me?'

He laughs. 'You know how we rockstars are. Mysterious.'

'I am so going to start stalking you now.'

'I'm counting on it, Edie.' He flicks his hair out of his eyes, gives me an impish look. 'Wouldn't miss it for the world.'

'But you won't want someone like me hanging around. Not now you're a rockstar. I'll bring down your cool.'

Jay laughs. 'Cool? I am the opposite of cool. That's why I wear black. I don't need to think about colour coordination. You should have seen me before I figured that out.'

'What about the eyebrow ring?'

Jay shrugs. 'I got it done when I was sixteen. I'd probably get rid of it, but ...'

'It's rockstar, right?'

'Hey, you've got to make some effort. It's like being an air hostess and keeping your hair nice.'

'Or being a newsreader and getting botox.'

'Yep; my public expects it.'

Flight 529. Your flight is boarding.

'So, bye.'

'Bye.' We stand there, looking at each other, saying nothing, but it is not the Bermuda Triangle. It is the Sea of Tranquillity and I am finding it hard to leave its balmy waters.

There is a miaow and we both look down.

'Hey, it's Kafka,' I say.

Jay bends down, picks up the cat and tucks it inside his jumper. 'No cats allowed in here, mate. He seems to have taken a liking to me. He jumped in the car.'

'You know what this means, don't you?'

Jay smiles. 'Rockstar?'

'You've got the seal of endorsement.'

Jay hugs me awkwardly, the cat between us, then pushes me towards the barrier. 'Don't miss your flight.'

I join the queue, holding on to my boarding pass, letting go of everything else, lost in a crowd of Japanese and Australians.

Then I am out in the sun, on the tarmac. I turn as I reach the stairs to the plane. I can see Jay inside the terminal, leaning on the glass. He presses his hand to the window, fingers spread. I hold mine up in a matching sign. Then I climb the stairs.

Epilogue

Somewhere in Tokyo

Edaline adjusts the sash on her cotton kimono, admiring her black-painted toenails in the Japanese clogs. Her long, red hair is twisted up on top of her head and secured with two chopsticks. Her pale face is even paler with the white powder she has delicately applied to her cheekbones, her neck, her chest. Tonight she is meeting Jason.

Her heart flutters like a fan in the hand of a geisha. They have only been lovers once but the memory glows like the eyes of a ninja behind his mask.

It is cold outside. Snow is falling on the mountains two hours' drive away. Maybe she will take him to the Emperor's Palace.

They will buy hot coffee in a can from the vending machine, find a hiding place among

the ruins to roll the cans along each other's
stomachs, press cold noses together, blow steam
in each other's faces, kick dried leaves in the air
as they run along the cobbled paths.

Maybe they will catch the subway to Shibuya,
the busiest intersection in the world, join the
throngs under flashing lights, feed each other
hot noodles with their chopsticks.

Maybe the talk will dart between them like
fireflies as they down sake in a Tokyo keyhole
bar. They will hold hands as white gloves push
them on a peak-hour train, press against each
other as they go through a tunnel, get high on
the chemistry arcing between them.

Maybe they will go to the mountains, lie
naked in a hot spring while snowflakes settle on
their flushed skin. He will hold a parasol over
her head, kiss her hot, wet lips and slide his
hand along her burning thigh.

She will meet him at the airport.

He will come back to her room.

He will pull the chopsticks from her hair, let
it fall over her shoulders.

He will unwind the sash from her waist, slide
the slippers from her feet …

This much she thinks she knows, the rest she can
imagine.

Acknowledgements

I would like to give a very big thank you to my
writing group – Helen Burns, Jane Meredith,
Jessie Cole and Jane Camens. You keep me
going back to the keyboard.

Thank you to Peter Bishop, formerly of the
Varuna Writers Centre, who provided valuable
feedback on this book. The Northern Rivers
Writers Centre has also helped in many ways.
Particular thanks to Siboney Duff and Sarah Ma.

A special thank you to Anna Valdinger at
HarperCollins for steering Sex, Lies and Bonsai
through to publication, for coming up with the
title and for giving me such a beautiful cover –
it was love at first sight. Jane Finemore, Anne
Reilly and Mel Maxwell at HarperCollins, Jody
Lee, Cathie Tasker and my agent, Sophie Hamley,
have also been a great support and help.

To all the readers who sent me messages
about Liar Bird – thank you so much. It was such
an unexpected pleasure to get your feedback.
A big thank you to my family – Simon, Tim and

375

John – I couldn't do it without your continuing support and love.

And if there is anyone I have omitted to mention – thank you too. I hope you already know how much I value you.

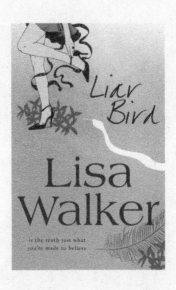

Liar Bird

LISA WALKER

Can a cityslicker fall for a wildlife ranger?
PR whizz Cassandra Daley isn't afraid of using all the dirty tricks of the trade to spin a story her way. A glamorous city-slicker, she has never given much thought to wildlife until she humiliatingly loses a PR war with a potoroo.

Sacked and disgraced, she flees the city for an anonymous bolt-hole. But small-town Beechville has other plans for her.

Feral pigs, a snake in the dunny, a philosopher frog and a town with a secret – could things get worse? Add one man who has the sexiest way with maps she's ever seen and they soon do. Her best friend Jessica thinks she's been brainwashed by some kind of rural cult, and Jessica could be right. Can Cassandra reinvent herself or will she always be a liar bird?